TRACKING BACK

TRACKING BACK

BILL HODSON

The Book Guild Ltd

First published in Great Britain in 2023 by
The Book Guild Ltd
Unit E2 Airfield Business Park,
Harrison Road, Market Harborough,
Leicestershire. LE16 7UL
Tel: 0116 2792299
www.bookguild.co.uk
Email: info@bookguild.co.uk
Twitter: @bookguild

Typeset in 11pt Minion Pro

Printed and bound in Great Britain by 4edge Limited

ISBN 978 1915603 968

British Library Cataloguing in Publication Data.
A catalogue record for this book is available from the British Library.

To Angela

ONE

Don has been fretting about the standard roses on the patio. If it had been left to him, he would have gone for a simpler, more Italianate look for the garden. Bay and laurel in ceramic pots set against old stone paving and offset by a wooden trellis, with a citrus tree or an apricot trained against the wall. He has never tried to create an espalier effect but has seen it in many stately homes and fancies it would look good in the expansive grounds of their new house. It might take a while to bear fruit in a garden in Lancashire, but it is sheltered and south facing – he and Jackie can feel the day's heat still radiating from the bricks as evening sets in – and it would be a thing of beauty in any case.

He hasn't got anything against roses but why not a pergola with a variety of climbers, stretching away from the patio towards the boundary, drawing people's eyes to the horizon and views of the moorland beyond that can only be appreciated as the visitor ventures further from the house? A garden that would give you sensory pleasures from the outset – sharp scents of herbs – basil, rosemary, dill, thyme and sage interspersed with sweeter notes of lavender and honeysuckle – but which does not reveal itself all at once. A garden that entices you to explore further and deepen your pleasure. A garden that emphasises how far he has come in life and the new levels of sophistication he aspires to.

But Jackie is an old English garden traditionalist and wanted to create something that she'd always craved as a child. She'd been brought up in a small, terraced house with a tiny backyard mostly taken up by a redundant coal shed and an outside toilet. The only greenery on offer was at the local park and as a little girl she would spend hours in the rose garden there, drinking in the heady perfumes, closing her eyes and dreaming of a better life as the bees buzzed hungrily about her.

When they bought this house, she wanted to bring all those memories back to life and Don didn't have the heart to deny her. So, it is deep borders of hollyhock, foxglove, lupin and delphinium with flowering annuals spilling onto the edges of a striped, rolling lawn. Every colour under the sun. A real cottage garden, Jackie declared. Only, they hadn't moved to a cottage, Don thought. This is a mid-Victorian gentleman's residence, and it ought to have a garden to match. Still, what did it really matter? So long as Jackie is happy. It's all been for her anyway.

But the roses are not prospering. He'd staked them as well as he could the previous autumn, but the prevailing wind has gradually pushed them all eastwards. Each standard is now leaning away from the wind, bowing its head to find shelter, reminding him of those lonely hawthorns you see on the moors, bent double like old farmers tending the soil. The angle is so acute that some of the roots are beginning to be exposed. They're not going to flower much like this, he thinks.

He is looking out from the conservatory window – technically it is an orangery, but Jackie thought that sounded pretentious. "What's the difference?" she asked him. About £30,000 he told her. Sipping his morning coffee he thinks he can also see signs of canker or rust on the barks. Something needs to be done. Jackie insisted that the garden should be organic – otherwise how would the bees and butterflies survive, and they would propagate the flowers and fruits for them so it would save work in the end, wouldn't it? But she is out seeing one of her cronies and won't be back for a couple of hours at least so this is his chance. He'd smuggled a few handy chemicals into the shed and there is plenty of time to do a bit of furtive spraying. The roses would be saved and Jackie need never be any the wiser.

He could also clean out the greenhouse while he has his gardening gear on. Chuck out the remnants of last year's tomatoes and cucumbers and get ahead of the game before the weather turns warmer. He takes another sip of coffee and slips his leather gloves into his pocket. It will be good to do something physical, out of doors, after being cooped up for most of the winter.

He is patting his jacket and looking round for his phone when the first bullet shatters the patio glass door and smashes his collarbone to pieces. Don has no idea what is happening, but it feels as if someone has taken a hammer to his neck and beaten the bone to bits. The impact slams him backwards against the dining table. He shudders as his head cracks against the edge and he slumps to the floor. He can feel the blood seeping down his chest like a warm poultice.

He wants to be sick with the pain but somehow, he can't shift into a position where he can throw up. His vision is blurred and he can't move his arm to get his glasses from his jacket pocket. He hears broken glass being crunched underfoot and feels something cold being pressed against his forehead.

And then the pain goes away.

Two

'It's what your father would have wanted.'

Jim Glassbrook has been eating raw spinach again. Sarah is transfixed by the tufts caught between his front teeth, like weeds sprouting between paving slabs. He believes that a daily intake of raw, leafy vegetables – he also favours kale, cabbage, spring greens and, when he is in holiday mood, cavolo nero – is a recipe for health and long life. To maximise the effect he may occasionally chew on a raw onion and top it all off with a pinch of yeast.

No one knows quite why he does this or what gave him the idea it would do him any good. Sarah has known him all her life and the gamey, slightly rancid air that wafts out every time he opens his mouth is… well, that is Mr Glassbrook. To be fair, he is well into his seventies, still taking the stairs two at a time and has scarcely a grey hair. Having said that, his face looks like it is melting, a candle that has been left burning too long. Even so, there might be something to this diet of his.

All this is familiar enough even after so many years away, but Sarah has forgotten how distracting the spinach can be. They are sitting in her father's old office. Mr Glassbrook has motioned her to take the chair behind his desk but that didn't seem right to her, so they are opposite each other at the small conference table. This is the first time they have sat down to go over the books since her father died and she is finding it hard to focus.

'Sarah?'

'Oh… sorry… yes. Well, Mr Glassbrook… it's a bit hard for me to say what Dad wanted as he never actually told me.'

'How old are you now?'

This throws her a bit but no point in being coy.

'Thirty-three. Why?'

'I think you're old enough to call me Jim. Don't you?'

On the desk between them is a set of buff folders, neatly arranged and labelled. All the papers needed to sum up the current state of Curtis and Curtis, Solicitors. Mr Glassbrook believes in the printed word. It is only when you can hold a legal document, riffle through it with your fingers and scribble on its margins that you really come to grips with it. Virtual documents are just that. Not real. Jim, as he now prefers to be known, pushes a pile of folders towards Sarah and flips open the top one.

'He changed the name last year. Added a Curtis. That's you.'

Sarah glances at the top paper and then closes the folder. Ostentatiously, she pushes the pile back across the desk.

'Dad and I hadn't really spoken much since the divorce. He never consulted me about this.'

'How is your mother?'

Sarah gets up from the desk, goes over to the window and looks down Churchgate. When her father opened this office in the early seventies, he'd said it was still humming and bristling with activity but gradually, little by little, the local businesses have closed or moved away. Now the boarded-up shops are like missing teeth in an old man's head. What is left is in decay.

She sighs heavily.

Jim is watching her carefully. You've always loved drama, he thinks, but don't overplay your hand.

'She's been managing OK. It's taken her years to come to terms with it. Dad's death… set her back, you know.'

5

She turns and leans on the desk, pushing her face close to Jim's, getting a good blast of onion in return.

'That's why I want to get this wrapped up as quickly as possible. The uncertainty will only cause her more distress.'

She raps the top of the folders.

'When can you put this place and Dad's house on the market?'

'There are other people's futures at stake besides your mother.'

Sarah relaxes and sits back down again.

'With all due respect... Jim... you could have retired years ago.'

Jim is disappointed in her. She can see that. He has that reproachful look on his face, like you would have if a child said a rude word in public. He takes his time to reply, judging her silently.

'I wasn't thinking of myself. There's Kelly – she'll find it hard to get another job in her fifties. And her husband can't work, you know. Scottie's never worked anywhere but here. It's all he knows. Asif's still doing his articles and then there's...'

'Yes. Yes. I know who works here.'

'They'll all be out of work if you don't take it over.'

'Someone might buy the business. Keep them on.'

Back come the folders across the table. This time, Jim raps them.

'You need to read the accounts. It's not a going concern as things stand.'

Sarah lifts the palms of her hand in response, as if to say "There you are then". Jim keeps at it.

'But you could build it up. The name still counts for something locally.'

'Come on. If Dad couldn't make it pay...'

'He was tired.'

Jim takes off his glasses and rubs the bridge of his nose.

'He was hanging on. Hoping you might...'

His voice peters out. Sarah feels herself getting more and more frustrated. If it meant that much to Dad, why didn't he tell me? I'm not a mind reader.

'Look, Jim, I don't…'

A loud knock. A woman's head juts round the door.

'Not now, Kelly.'

'Sorry, Mr Glassbrook, but she insists. I can't get her to leave.'

'Who?'

'Eileen Bradshaw. Gerry's wife.'

'Tell her to come back this afternoon. I'll see her then.'

Kelly squeezes some more of her body into the room.

'It's not you she wants to see. It's Sarah. Sorry. Ms Curtis.'

'I've never heard of her. Why is she asking for me?'

'Gerry and your father were old friends. Weren't they, Mr Glassbrook?'

Jim sighs. He doesn't have time for this.

'Gerry Bradshaw played for the Wanderers for years. A one-club man. You know what your father was like about football.'

Sarah nods. She'd been dragged to matches as a little girl. In her memory it is always raining; always toe-numbingly cold; always one-nil to the other team. She'd never been able to see any sense in the game. A load of sweaty men heaving through mud to get to one end of the pitch and then the other lot slogging back in the opposite direction. But that wasn't how her dad saw it. Blue and white scarf knotted round his neck, screaming at the top of his voice, he was totally absorbed. Everything else in his life was blotted out for ninety minutes, all the tensions and frustrations given full vent. A football ground, he would tell her, is one of the few public places left where you can yell out insults and obscenities without being arrested or sectioned.

He'd hoped she'd catch the bug. She didn't. He'd hoped she'd be a boy. She wasn't. The day came, around the time puberty kicked in, when she simply refused to go. Sat on the couch in her pyjamas and would not budge. Something broke between them that day.

Jim is still filling in the back story.

'When Gerry finished playing, he stayed on at the club, doing this and that, helping behind the scenes. Things got desperate on the pitch. Relegation, financial crises, talk of selling the ground. Anyway, the board thought that bringing back an old player might turn things round so they made him the manager. Didn't work. Went from bad to worse and after a few months they sacked him. Broke his heart, your father said. He always had a soft spot for Gerry.'

Sarah swivels to face Kelly who is still half in and half out of the room.

'Did she say what she wants?'

'She's very upset. Keeps bursting into tears.'

'Yes, but did she say why?'

'She says it's something she can only talk to your father about, but as he's errm…'

'Dead?'

'… she wants to see you.'

Jim sighs heavily again and his eyes flick above the rim of his glasses.

'It'll be something and nothing. Give her a hankie and get her to come back. We've more important things to sort out here.'

Sarah pushes back her chair and stands up.

'On the other hand, like you said…Jim… it's probably what Dad would have wanted.'

She can see Eileen through the small panel in the door to the interview room and watches her for a few moments, trying to weigh her up.

If you wanted one word to describe Eileen Bradshaw, it would be… neat. She would be happy to hear it. Trim. Tidy. These would also be acceptable words. She's looked after herself; hasn't let herself go like some women she could mention. Kept her weight down by careful dieting and regular exercise and is proud of her figure. She isn't saying that she could still get into her wedding dress but there aren't many women of her age who are still a comfortable size 12. That is not something to be sneezed at.

But as Sarah sits down opposite her she notices that Eileen has been chewing what had been carefully manicured and polished nails. She is twisting an embroidered handkerchief round her fingers. Not crying at the moment but the slight swelling round her eyes says she has been.

'You probably won't remember me, love. We used to come round your house a lot when you were little, me and Gerry.'

'Mrs Bradshaw...'

'Eileen.'

'... Kelly said you were asking to see me.'

'Your dad... I was very sorry to hear... your father, he used to handle Gerry's affairs personally. So, as he... you know... must have been a shock... I'm so sorry... he can't... I mean, as he isn't here now. Oh God!'

'Just take your time, Eileen. What's wrong?'

More twisting of the handkerchief.

'Gerry told me. If anything ever happens to me, go and see Matthew. He's got instructions on what to do.'

'Something's happened to your husband?'

'Been gone three nights now. Took off without a word.'

'Have you been to the police?'

Even more twisting of the handkerchief.

'Gerry told me. If anything ever happens to me...'

'Yes, I see.'

'And I'm still getting the phone calls.'

'What phone calls?'

'They started a few weeks ago after we heard about...'

Eileen starts to wipe an imaginary spot off the sleeve of her coat. She begins to address the surface of the table, not catching Sarah's eye.

'Gerry was very quiet after the last one. Next morning, he went out to get some milk and I haven't seen him since.'

'Look, I really think you should go to the police if you think something's happened to him.'

'They told me not to.'

'Who did?'

'I just said. The ones who keep phoning.'

'What did they actually say?'

Eileen lifts her head and looks Sarah full in the face.

'Oh, they were quite clear about that. If he doesn't contact them in the next couple of days then they're going to burn down our house.'

Sarah sits back and takes this in.

'I wonder, Eileen... would you mind if I asked Jim Glassbrook to join us?'

THREE

1956

I'd never been away from home on my own, so I was worried.

'How will I know when I get there?'

I'd just had a stand-up wash in the kitchen sink and Mam was rubbing me down with a towel as soft as a Brillo pad. It felt like she'd decided to remove the top layer of skin in the hope that the next level down would be cleaner.

'Don't be silly. The coach stops there. It dun't go any further. Where's yer vest?'

Mam had laid out my clothes wherever she could find a space. I pointed at the kitchen table.

'See, get this on before you catch cold.'

She pulled the vest over my head. I was growing fast and it were a tight fit. I felt my hair go flat against my scalp as she forced the neck over my ears and then it sprang up again as the vest scraped into place. Mam tried to smooth my hair down with the towel but soon gave it up as a bad job. There was no mirror, but I was sure I looked like a startled hedgehog.

'I don't want to be left on t'coach looking for my stuff while everybody else gets off. What if he drives away with me still on?'

She threw my socks over to me. They'd been resting on the oven, so they were nice and warm. It was still a bit wet between my legs but I didn't let on. I didn't want Mam having a second go with that towel.

'There's a windmill just outside Blackpool. When you see that, start getting your coat on and ask someone to help you get your case down from the luggage rack.'

'Yeah, but what if…'

She threw my underpants at my head.

'Put these on before t'neighbours see you.'

I shuffled into them and tucked myself up as comfortably as my soggy crotch allowed.

'Why can't you come with me?'

'Now don't start. You know I have to work.'

She put her hands on my cheeks and leaned close into me.

'You'll enjoy it once you're there. Your Uncle Bill will look after you.'

It was crowded by the time we got to Moor Lane bus station. All I could see were queues of families lining up alongside a row of coaches. It seemed totally chaotic to me. Which one was ours?

You could tell it was holiday time even though it was drizzling and there was a nip in the air. The men were wearing ties, but they had sports jackets and flannel trousers on rather than the dark suits that only came out at weddings and funerals. Most of the women had scarves or hats in bright colours or floral patterns, trying to look excited but already getting fed up with entertaining kids who couldn't wait any longer for the fun to start.

I could see that there were a lot of boys about my age and most had on their holiday gear – short-sleeved shirts or T-shirts, light-coloured shorts and sandals over white socks. A few lads had fishing rods or crab nets which they clutched close to their chest; a lot more had what looked like a new football dangling against their leg from a string bag. The girls had their summer frocks on and were keeping a tight hold on their favourite dolls. The younger kids were in charge of the buckets and spades. I felt self-conscious in my school coat and only my little suitcase to carry.

Mam almost wrenched my arm out of its socket as she hauled me past the first two or three lines.

'Hargreaves. That's what we're looking for. Don't get mixed up with this lot or you'll end up in Rhyll.'

We pushed through the crowds until we saw a sleek, snub-nosed coach, done out in blue and grey; shiny chrome window frames and bumpers and with a sticker saying BLACKPOOL on the inside of the windscreen. Just the job. It sparkled in the thin sunshine. But the queue for this one was enormous. I couldn't see the end of it. Mam could tell I was getting anxious again.

'I've paid for your ticket. It'll be alright.'

'We can't all get on this coach.'

'Follow me.'

She thrust her chest out and strode to the front of the queue. I shuffled behind, trying not to catch anyone's eye but I could hear the chuntering and grumbling as we passed people.

'Now then, Missus.'

A huge man in a blue uniform and a peaked cap was blocking our way. He had a silver badge on his chest with the single word – Driver.

'These folk are before you.'

A self-righteous murmur of approval rippled through the queue.

'I've got an advance ticket. Bought it last week.'

A chorus of objections swelled around us.

'So has everyone else.'

He held his arms out wide and started to move towards us like a farmer shooing cows that'd wandered onto the road back into their field.

'If you'll just go to the back of the queue, please…'

Mam tried to hold her ground, but the driver just kept coming.

'We're not all going to get on.'

He was swinging his arms in our direction, and we had to start backing away.

'Don't worry about that. Company's put on another coach. She'll get you there.'

Everyone stared at us with satisfaction as we backpedaled to the end of the queue. There was a spluttering, grinding, rattling, banging commotion over to one side as the reserve coach shuddered into view. It must have been borrowed from another firm as it was done out in a dusty crimson and cream livery and looked as if it had been kept in a stable since the war. I looked up at Mam. She said nothing, but we both knew. I'd be going on that one.

I got put next to a man who were that fat he really needed two seats to himself but had only paid for one. I was nearly crushed against the window but at least I had a good view. As the coach pulled out, I watched as Mam faded into the crowd and gradually disappeared from view. I think she waved but I couldn't be sure.

It wasn't difficult to see how the man next to me got that big as he never stopped eating for the whole of the trip. Sandwiches, pork pies, crisps, biscuits – he seemed to have a never-ending supply in his holdall. He was sweating cobs and I tried not to look as he rubbed his fingers over his face and forehead and then licked them dry again. I was hungry but it weren't any hardship to turn down his offers of food as we chugged along.

The towns gave way to fields and then open country, flat moorland stretching far into the distance. I'd never seen a sky that big. The view seemed endless, no houses or factories standing in the way. Finally, I spotted the windmill on the horizon poking above the ribbons of houses that now started to line the road again. I strained my eyes to look for the streak of blue that would be the sea.

'There!'

The man next to me put down his egg sandwich and stuck a huge forearm across me. At first, I couldn't make it out but then I realised that the dull, grey smear which looked like the bottom layer of cloud, was actually the sea. A ripple of excitement ran through the coach as families started to get down their cases ready for a quick getaway. I tightened the belt of my coat.

In the end, I needn't have worried. Uncle Bill was waiting at the coach station and helped me get my case down. We were all newcomers, pale and hesitant, looking round and trying to get our bearings. But he was at ease, the wide collar of his cream shirt pulled over the lapels of his blazer, his skin a nutty shade of brown and a big smile on his face, joking with the driver as if they were old friends.

'Now then, Gerry. You've shot up since I've seen yer.'

He grinned and put his hand on my shoulders, nodding to himself as if appreciating the distance between them. Uncle Bill wasn't really my uncle. He'd been Dad's best friend in the war. Both had felt lucky when they'd been recruited into the Royal Engineers because of their experience as mechanics. That meant they wouldn't be on the front line, but Dad had fallen under the tracks of a tank during manoeuvres on Salisbury Plain, so he never even made it overseas. Uncle Bill had looked Mam up after the war and always kept in touch. He and Auntie Ina lived over the bike shop they ran, hiring out to tourists and day trippers. We set off down some back streets and I could catch glimpses of the promenade, crammed with visitors.

I was desperate to get onto the sands, but I had to wait until the shop closed for the day. It was quiet on the beach by then. Auntie Ina explained that the guest houses all served tea early so it was the best time to find a bit of peace and quiet. I was disappointed but didn't like to show it. I was hoping to find some other boys my age and have a kick-around.

The tide was well in so there was only a narrow strip of sand to play on. We ended up sitting near the sea wall. Uncle Bill tossed me a tennis ball.

'Try kicking it against the wall and seeing if you can get the rebound.'

The wall was made up of large uneven stones that jutted out at irregular angles so it was impossible to know which way the ball would bounce back. At first it was hopeless. The ball would shoot off sideways and I'd have no chance of getting to it. But then I found that if I aimed at the mortar between the stones there was less chance of getting a crazy rebound. Bit by bit I started to get to the ball as it shot back at me, mostly with another kick but occasionally getting in a header.

Uncle Bill had been watching me all this time while Auntie Ina read a magazine. When I finally sat down to get a drink, he was still looking at me with his head a little to one side.

'You've got something there, Gerry. You wanna go for a trial at t'Wanderers. They could do with you.'

FOUR

As Taylor steps out into the street, a swirl of wind and rain slaps him hard and forces him back into the doorway. He pulls his thin raincoat tighter round his chest, bends his head into the squall and pushes on in search of a café.

Within a few yards his hair is soaked and rain is starting to slither down the back of his neck. At times like these he finds it comforting to imagine he is starring in a movie rather than slogging through real life – which has lately been no fun at all. He decides it is a French film. This means that although he is still an unemployed private investigator struggling to find his next case, buffeted by stinking weather, stony broke and homeless, he nevertheless retains a certain sense of style. Élan, perhaps. Even a shabby French flatfoot has a run-down charm about him – think Alain Delon or Jean-Paul Belmondo. Designer stubble, threadbare suit and greasy hair can all be turned to advantage with a cool jazz soundtrack and a Parisian vibe. Shame he is in Bolton.

This cheers Taylor up a bit as he slips into a snack bar he'd noticed last night. If this was a British film then his seediness would have been more profound, bordering on the insanitary. Rather than having a sexy undertone to his hard-luck story he would have come across as weaselly, underfed, bitter and a bit smelly. Any chance of pulling a femme fatale in the line of duty would have been right out of the window.

An American adaptation wouldn't have been much better. He could have fallen back on the Sam Spade tough-guy persona, but he didn't really have the physique for it. More likely he'd have been cast as some kind of Columbo clone picking his way through discarded syringes and fighting off an unquenchable drinking habit.

No, French is best. He thinks he should go for a café au lait or espresso with a croissant topped off with a crafty Gauloise afterwards. After examining the menu he discovers that this place is more greasy spoon than coffee shop, so he opts for a pot of tea and a fried-egg sandwich. Films are all very well, he concludes, but you have to live in the real world. Unfortunately.

The windows in the café are nicely steamed up and Taylor feels sensation coming back into his fingers and toes as the warm fug embraces him. There is a pervasive smell of hot fat in the air, and he can feel an oily film settling on his hair and clothes. But he isn't exactly in pristine condition, and this is a small price to pay for being out of the driving rain.

He also needs some quiet time to bend his mind to getting somewhere to sleep tonight. Carrie has made it very clear that she wants her sofa back and, in retrospect, his decision to bring home a late-night takeaway wasn't one of his best. He'd tried to mop the tandoori sauce off the chair arm, but he'd only succeeded in spreading an orange-yellow slick over a wider area. He'd slung his raincoat over it and Carrie didn't have time to notice as she bundled him out of the flat that morning. But when she comes home from work…

It is safe to assume that he'll need a new nest tonight. He sucks his tea slowly. No rush to move on. He takes stock of the cash position, opening his wallet surreptitiously under the table. Don't want to spook the café owner. Twenty-five in notes and about five or six pounds in coins. Was that all that's left of the fifty quid he'd touched Carrie for? Another reason not to have bought that takeaway. Being poor is really expensive. He might have to try the back entrance to the supermarket again. The staff usually leave out a few expired food containers.

Hole in the wall is no good any more. One more attempt and it would eat up his card. Mind you, as there isn't any money left in the account and no prospect of any coming in, it doesn't really matter much.

Just as he thought, then. Shit creek. No paddle. No boat.

He imagines himself as the CEO of a large corporation addressing the shareholders. It's been a tough year, he tells them. Income opportunities have been very limited. Clients have faced a squeeze on their resources resulting in a downsizing of contractor liabilities. The consequential impact on cash flow has necessitated painful decisions to move out of office accommodation, a downward pressure on salaries and regrettable redundancies. Not to put too fine a point on it… we're skint.

'Do you want another cup of tea or were you thinking of bed and breakfast?'

The café owner is a big unit, blocking out what little light there is from the window. He's carefully placed himself between Taylor and the entrance. He's been done that way before.

'Tea. Great. Yeah.'

'Anything more to eat?'

'No, tea's fine.'

The owner is still standing there, giving Taylor a close inspection. Grubby raincoat. Greasy hair. Malnourished pallor. Shifty behaviour.

'Four pounds eighty.'

Taylor affects a quizzical look.

'For what you've had so far.'

'Oh right.'

Taylor pours the coins from his wallet onto the table and laboriously counts out the exact amount. He scoops up what little is left back into his pocket. The owner looks disgusted.

'Service isn't included.'

Taylor retrieves a twenty-pence coin and adds it to the pile. The owner gives a grunt, shovels the money into his bucket of a hand, sizes it up, tuts and goes back to the kitchen. Should be alright for another half hour, thinks Taylor, but better not push it.

He glances out at the street. The rain is showing no sign of easing off. Could he try Stuart again? His wife hadn't exactly taken a shine to Taylor but that was about three weeks ago. She might have mellowed since then. Mags is out of the question after the incident with the blocked toilet but what about Eddie? Haven't seen him for a while. Might be his best bet.

'I need to get some money, and quick.'

A few of the other customers look up in his direction. Jesus, he thinks, I said that out loud. He hunches low over the table and turns back to watch the rain pummelling the pavement.

FIVE

Kelly is keeping an eye on Eileen, making sure that she is topped up with tea while Sarah disembowels the safe in her father's office. They found Gerry Bradshaw's papers easily enough in the filing cabinet, but these are mainly the deeds to his house and correspondence on the conveyancing. His will is also there. Perfectly straightforward; everything to go to Eileen. But no instructions in the event of his unexpected death. No sealed envelope headed "To Whom It May Concern".

Sarah has insisted on going through the safe. Jim stands aloof, watching her ferret away, kneeling down, surrounded by discarded documents.

'It won't be in there. We've been through it.'

Waste of time, he thinks, and anyway, I can't be crouching down like that at my age.

'You might have missed something.'

Sarah's head is lost behind the safe door, but he has a clear view of her backside, wiggling about as she reaches inside. This is disconcerting and, he is certain, inappropriate so Jim inclines his face towards the window.

'I don't miss things. The only items of any interest were your father's will and the papers on the business. They're all in the files we made up for you.'

Sarah raises herself with a sigh, goes back to the folders on the table and begins flicking them open at random.

'Anything about Gerry in these?'

You'd know if you could be bothered to read them, thinks Jim.

'I wouldn't have let you waste your time pulling the safe apart if there was.'

'Any other place where Dad might have kept stuff he didn't want you to see?'

'Your father trusted me. We worked together for over forty years.'

'Don't get precious, Jim. Eileen thinks there will be a letter with instructions and we've got to find it.'

'Have we?'

Sarah looks up from the table.

'Alright. Come on then.'

Jim sits down and places his elbows on the table, angling his arms upwards so that they form a little pyramid with his forefingers at the peak, lightly touching his lips. Here we go, thinks Sarah. Lecture time.

'Firstly, if Eileen is right and Gerry has disappeared because he's hiding from some desperate villains, then this is clearly a matter for the police. We can't deal with it. The only criminal work we get involved with are speeding offences and council tax fines. We can't protect her. Leave it to the professionals. That's what we pay taxes for. Secondly, how do we know there is a letter? Gerry is a retired footballer on a fixed income, not an international man of mystery. Why would he lodge a letter with your father? Thirdly, what if Eileen is making all this up? I've known her for a long time and she's what I'd call a romancer.'

'What?'

'Likes to invent a tale. Make herself seem more interesting. No, my bet is that Gerry's buggered off somewhere with another woman because he's fed up with sharing a house with Eileen where the only excitement is a slice of Battenburg at four o'clock, and she's come up with this story to cover her embarrassment.'

'She's lying, you mean.'

'I didn't say that, but I'm surprised you're so convinced. Lapped it up like Mother's milk. I thought you couldn't wait to get back to your boyfriend in London. Suddenly you're Miss Marple.'

That's it for Sarah. Light the touch paper and stand well back.

'You know what... Jim... I'm getting pretty pissed off with your attitude. If I want to help Eileen, then that's up to me. OK? I'm not a kid any more so don't try and patronise me. This is my business now and I decide what goes. And if you don't like it, you know what you can do about it.'

Jim calmly taps his fingers together, purses his lips and nods.

'Hmm. I see.'

He gets up slowly and leaves the room.

Sarah stands looking at the closed door. Well done. Only been back two days and you've already alienated Dad's right hand man and taken on a hopeless case for no fee. Brilliant. She begins to pace round the office.

Come on, Sarah. Think it through. You're a good lawyer. You can work this out.

Yeah, but Jim's right. I've never dealt with criminal work. We say that business mergers can be brutal, but no one burns your house down.

Eileen needs you. She's got no one else to help her.

Err... excuse me... but isn't that what the police are for?

If they find out she's gone to the police, they might kill her.

On the other hand, if they find out she's come to you they might kill you.

Oh – I see what you're saying...

The door swings open and Jim bustles in with Kelly and Eileen trailing in his slipstream. He is in full flow.

'Firstly, Eileen can't go home so we've got to get her to a place of safety. Kelly's come up trumps. They haven't sold her grandma's place in Moses Gate yet. Her furniture is still there, and the services are on, so it'll do until this blows over. I've told Asif to book a cab

23

and we'll get them down there after lunch. We're going to have to buy some spare clothes and whatnot for Eileen. Kelly can see to that. I don't think anyone should go near her house. They're probably watching it. Meantime, I suggest you go back to your father's place and start looking for that letter. We can't do much until we know what instructions Gerry left. That doesn't buy us any more time though so we're going to need to bring help in. Like I said, this isn't normally our cup of tea. There'll be costs involved so I'm going to need your authorisation. Is that alright with you, Sarah?'

She realises that her mouth has been open all the while Jim has been speaking but nothing comes out so she just nods.

Eileen has placed herself at the head of the conference table and is twisting her handkerchief again.

'What about Treacle?'

Confused looks from Sarah and Jim. Kelly chips in.

'Their dog.'

Jim sniffs.

'You can't go back to the house, Eileen. It's too dangerous.'

'He'll starve.'

'They may be waiting there for you.'

'What if they set fire to the house and he's inside?'

'You've got to be...'

Eileen bangs the table. Her wedding ring leaves a dent where she brings her fist down.

'I'm not leaving him there to be turned into a kebab.'

Sarah pats Eileen's arm.

'Don't worry. I'll go round and fetch him.'

'And don't forget to bring his basket. Gerry bought it for him not long ago. Now he can't sleep without it.'

'I won't.'

Jim isn't happy but Sarah raises her hand before he can protest.

'It'll be fine. Now, is there some place round here where we can order in sandwiches?'

After Eileen and Kelly have left for what they have decided to call the "safe house", Sarah and Jim tidy up the office and he places the documents about the practice back in the safe.

'We can sort out the arrangements about the business when this is over.'

'You think I'm being stupid, don't you?'

'Like you said, you're in charge now. You decide.'

Sarah brushes some breadcrumbs off her blouse.

'When you walked out, you know, after... I didn't expect you to come back.'

Jim fiddles with a bit of vegetation caught between his front teeth.

'That wouldn't have been very helpful, would it?'

He begins to bang a few, disorderly papers on the table to get them into line. Sarah wills him to say more but he avoids her eye.

'I know, but... you didn't have to...'

Jim clips the documents together and slides them into a folder.

'I worked for your father for over forty years. Now I work for you. That's all there is to it. Now, what's next?'

'Alright. You said we're going to need some help. What did you have in mind?'

'To be honest, this is all new to me. Eileen claims she doesn't know what this is all about but if someone really is threatening to kill her... for what, I don't know, a gambling debt?... then we need someone who can root around and find out what Gerry's been up to. I was thinking of a private investigator.'

'How do we find one? Does *Which?* do Best Buys on detective agencies?'

Jim sucks a morsel of food off his fingernail.

'There is someone your father used occasionally. They seemed to get on, but I never really took to him. Scruffy bugger as I recall. But cheap.'

Six

Taylor hasn't been for a job interview for quite a while. Sarah and Jim have been giving him the once-over. She is not what he expected. Businesslike and brisk on the outside but he can feel an energy within, perhaps even some wayward recklessness that he finds quite sexy. The fires burning beneath the cool exterior. This is not helpful at the present time, so he pushes those feelings down. It's an interview not a date, and he hasn't had one of those for an even longer time.

The old feller is also difficult to work out. He's wearing a heavy woollen three-piece, charcoal-grey suit with a discreet pinstripe, but there are bits of food scattered here and there as though he'd been picnicking off his clothes and forgotten to shake himself down afterwards. He looks pretty trim of a man his age – whatever that is – but his face! The flesh seemed to be slipping away, sliding down his neck. Not quite the Elephant Man but he was getting there.

Don't get nervous, he thinks. I know I don't look the part, but I must be confident.

His belongings are spread around various friends' houses, so he's had to make do with what he had with him. Eddie has lent him a clean shirt and he'd taken an iron to his trousers. Now that he's showered and shaved he looks reasonably presentable. Apart from his shoes. They are falling apart. Mr Naylor, his first editor, always said that you can tell a man's worth by his shoes. Polished, good quality, well heeled – these are signs that you could trust a man. Taylor angles his legs back under his chair so that his feet are out of sight.

'Very sorry to hear about your father. He was a good man.'

Sarah looks up briefly from her notes to acknowledge this and then goes back to studying Taylor's resumé. She brushes her blonde hair back behind her ears.

'Jim says he hired you from time to time. What for?'

'I think he liked me. We always got on well. Liked a chat about football.'

Sarah rubs her fingers in circles round her temples. Give me strength.

'No. What did he hire you to do?'

'Oh, sorry. Yes… errm. Delivering papers to people who didn't really want to receive them. Doing background checks on people that clients are thinking of doing business with. That sort of thing.'

'Any missing persons work?'

'Err… yeah, I had to find a distant relative who was the sole beneficiary of quite a substantial legacy.'

'And did you?'

Jim butts in.

'No. I did.'

Taylor can feel the redness rising up from his neck and into his cheeks.

'It was quite a complicated family relationship.'

Sarah is looking at him straight in the eye. Must be confident, he reminds himself. Don't panic.

'I was making good progress. Would have found her quite soon but then she just turned up.'

Jim snorts.

'She didn't just turn up. She responded to the advertisement I placed. Something you should have thought of.'

Keep calm.

27

'I like working as part of a team. As long as we get a good result what does it matter how we do it?'

'It matters when we're paying a daily rate for no bloody benefit.'

Sarah places her hand gently on Jim's arm.

'I understand you were with the police.'

Good. Firmer ground. Just don't say what you did there.

'Yes. I was with them nearly three years. Learnt a lot. Still got contacts there. Very useful in my line of work.'

'So, why did you leave?'

'Errm... it's not for everyone. I prefer to work for myself. More autonomy. Freedom to operate. You know.'

Sarah and Jim turn to each other and exchange a glance. Taylor thinks he can see Sarah raise her eyebrow slightly and Jim seems to shrug in response. I think I might be in here, he thinks.

Sarah picks up Taylor's CV, looks him up and down again, puts the papers back on the desk, takes a deep breath and lets it out slowly.

'Time is of the essence in this case. We need someone who can start right away.'

Easy. Don't come across as desperate.

'OK. I understand. Errm... like I said, I was very fond of your father so... err... yeah, I'll put aside this other job I'm on. I'm all yours.'

Sarah gives him a frosty look that suggests she is not too thrilled at the prospect.

'We need to find Gerry before someone else does. See if one of your old mates in the police can do a check on Gerry's car, CCTV footage, that sort of thing. My guess is that he won't have gone too far.'

Taylor tries not to look nonplussed by this and nods in what he hopes is a knowing manner. Sarah stands up and turns to Jim.

'I'd better go and pick up that damned dog. Kelly's agreed to look after it. You fill Taylor in on the details and sort out a contract.'

Nodding curtly she leaves the office. Taylor watches her go.

Good-looking woman. Nice behind. He turns back to find Jim glaring at him.

'Keep your mind on the job.'

Jim takes him through what they know so far. Taylor makes notes. His old shorthand skills still come in handy sometimes.

'Gerry's either been mixing with the wrong crowd and got in over his head or he's done a runner and is shacked up in a seaside chalet with a nice widow. You need to find out which.'

'You don't believe his wife about the phone calls?'

'Let's say I'm sceptical. Here's a list of some of his pals. The ones I know about. Start with them. See if they've heard anything.'

Taylor casts his eye over the names.

'I recognise some of these.'

'Used to be footballers. Now, I want daily reports. In writing. In person. Here. Understood?'

Jim picks up his papers and begins to leave.

'Err – hang on. We haven't discussed my terms. Thirty pounds an hour plus expenses or I can offer you an all-in day rate of 200 pounds, although that doesn't cover anti-social hours or weekends. Three days in advance would be acceptable.'

Jim sucks his teeth and leans down close to Taylor's face. A terrible reek seems to be coming from his mouth that turns Taylor's stomach over.

'Now you listen to me. Her dad might have reckoned you, but I wouldn't pay you in washers. But it's not up to me. I'm going to give you a hundred pounds in cash, and you'll get another 150 pounds when you finish the job. If you've not found him in three days then you're on your bike. How does that suit you?'

Taylor is breathing through his mouth to avoid the rank odour Jim is giving off, but he manages to get his protest out.

'No way. That's not even minimum wage.'

'Not if you find him quickly.'

'I could report you to the regulation authority for this. It's illegal.'

29

'You do that. You can tell them about the last time you paid taxes while you're at it.'

Taylor wrinkles his nose.

'Cash, you say?'

Jim nods.

'Well, like I said, I was very fond of Matthew...'

Seven

Treacle is not much of a guard dog. Sarah opens the front door tentatively, half expecting to find him baring his teeth and ready to fly at her if she dares to cross the threshold. In fact, nothing happens. She stands in the hallway, wondering which door he might be lurking behind, until, after a while, a tiny, grizzled Yorkshire Terrier, sporting a droopy grey moustache, waddles into view.

God, thought Sarah, you look worse than Jim. She crouches down on her haunches and adopts a sing-song tone, like you would with a baby.

'Hello, sweetie. Your mummy's sent me to fetch you. Would you like to go and see her? Would you?'

Treacle, realising that this intruder isn't offering any treats or titbits and, quite possibly, objecting to being infantilised by a complete stranger, turns his back and limps into the kitchen. By the time she catches up with him he is fast asleep in his basket, tucked up on what looks like the remains of an old eiderdown. Sarah decides to follow the standard advice about sleeping dogs. She holds out her arm towards him in warning.

'Stay, boy!'

Treacle snuffles and his back legs twitch. She wishes him sweet dreams and sets off on a tour of the house, looking for some clue to Gerry's whereabouts. In detective stories there would usually be a pad in the hallway with a scribbled address, a deserted warehouse for instance, or the impression of a name or telephone number that could be revealed by lightly shading a pencil over the surface. But a quick nosey round the ground floor reveals no such luck. Eileen's house is like Eileen. All very tidy. Everything just so.

It feels like a show house minus the sales brochures. Brand new furnishings and fittings that hardly looked used. No personal items left lying around except for a few framed wedding and holiday photographs of a younger Eileen and, presumably, Gerry. Sarah prises what looks like the latest from its frame and stashes it in her bag. Other than that, there is very little outward sign that anyone has ever lived there. No books or magazines left lying around to be picked up later; no cups or glasses unwashed from the night before; no clothes tossed over the backs of chairs; no biscuit crumbs on the carpet; no takeaway cartons or half empty wine bottles in the kitchen. The only sign of life is Treacle, and that is stretching a point.

And another thing. Eileen's house is not what Sarah expected. Jim had said that she and Gerry had suffered a series of disappointments since his football career ended and she thought they would be eking out a modest retirement in a non-descript suburban semi, struggling to make ends meet on their state pensions. She isn't prepared for a four-bedroom detached with a double garage and a sweeping drive, at the poshest end of the Ladybridge estate overlooking Deane Golf Club. She isn't up to date with Bolton prices, but this would have to be well north of half a million. And it doesn't look like much expense has been spared on kitting the place out. The slightly chintzy three-piece suite and complementary floral curtains set off against a deep-pile cream carpet and focused towards a monstrously big television mounted on the wall are not to Sarah's own taste, but she can see that everything is top quality. She also finds a late registration Mercedes 'E' class saloon safely tucked inside the garage. The Bradshaws are doing very nicely, thank you.

The upstairs confirms the picture. Fitted wardrobes, king-sized beds covered in scatter cushions, en-suite bathrooms and carpets as thick as an unmown lawn. Just like you'd see in a feature in Ideal Homes and just as soulless. And nothing to indicate why Gerry has never returned from his errands. There is what looks to Sarah like a full outfit of men's clothes, including several pairs of shoes, in one set of wardrobes so if Gerry had planned his disappearance, it doesn't look like he'd packed much of a bag.

Nothing to see here. Move along.

Eileen had been quite insistent that Treacle would have to have his basket ('Gerry would never forgive me if we lost that') so Sarah decides it is easier to just pick it up with the dog in it. He doesn't miss a beat in his snoring as she lifts him from the floor. If this was an Agatha Christie story she thinks, the dog could be a vital witness to what has really happened if only we could get it to tell us what it saw. However, it looks as if Treacle's natural state is a coma, so he isn't likely to be much help. She has found a few tins of dog food in one of the kitchen cupboards, so she pops them in the basket with Treacle and heads back to her car.

As she leaves the house there is a sudden rustling in the laurel hedge by the side of the driveway.

'Keep an eye out' Jim had warned her, 'Someone may be watching the house.'

She thought Jim was being melodramatic but as she gets nearer the hedge she can feel her heart thumping. Without warning two magpies fly out and nearly knock her over as they whizz by. She shrieks and drops the basket. Treacle is thrown clear and lies absolutely still on the paving, his little legs splayed out and motionless. There is a clanging sound as the dog meat tins clatter down the drive. Oh my god, she thinks, I've killed the dog. She stoops to pick up the limp body, his head lolling lifelessly to one side. What am I going to say to Eileen? She strokes his ears and rubs his tiny belly, the flesh still warm beneath his coat. At her touch, Treacle breaks wind with enormous force and sleepily opens his eyes. Seeing it is only Sarah he drifts off for another doze.

Sarah slides the basket on the back seat and sets off to Kelly's house. They'd decided that Eileen wasn't really up to looking after anyone but herself at the moment. Jim also pointed out that it was not sensible to draw attention to the fact that the grandma's little terraced house is occupied again. They, whoever they are, would be putting out feelers for Gerry and Eileen.

'A howling dog will only attract speculation.'

As Sarah pulls up outside Kelly's house in Harwood, all that seems a bit belt and braces. Treacle's speciality appears to be heavy breathing rather than barking. Still, it means he'll be no trouble for his hosts. She carries him into the living room and deposits him by the radiator. He licks his lips, appreciative of the heat, and settles down for some serious snoozing. Kelly closes the door gently and tiptoes into the kitchen. Sarah shuffles after her.

'I don't think you need worry about waking him up. There's a strong possibility he's stone deaf. How was Eileen when you left her?'

'Pretty quiet. Bit bothered about the dog.'

'Well, you can tell her that's sorted now. Can she manage on her own?'

'I got some ready-made meals from M&S on the way over so she should be fine...'

'But...?'

'She's terrified. Whatever they've said to her, she thinks Gerry's life is in danger.'

'Jim thinks she's making it up.'

'Mr Glassbrook has very limited experience of women.'

'You amaze me.'

'He was married once. Marion, she were called. He never talks about it but her death knocked him for six.'

Sarah tries to look sympathetic, but she has other things on her mind.

'Do you think Eileen's lying?'

'No, I think she's telling the truth. But not all of it.'

'I agree. See if you can get her to open up a bit more. She trusts you.'

'Alright, Ms Curtis.'

'Sarah.'

'Are you sure? I never called your father by his first name. Nor Mr Glassbrook.'

'I don't think he'll faint if you call him Jim. But I'd steer clear of Jimmy if I were you. Right, I'm off.'

It is dark by now. Kelly's house is in a quiet, dimly-lit cul-de-sac of identical mid-century semis. All the curtains are drawn, all the doors closed, everyone safe inside. God, I'd go mad if I lived here, thinks Sarah. As she walks back to the turning circle to pick up her car, she thinks she sees a cabin-light go out in one of the other cars there but as she gets closer it seems to be empty. I need a drink, she thinks, as she switches on the ignition and sets off for her father's house.

EIGHT

1959

Archie Wilcox was a hard bastard and he let all us lads know it.

'You don't know you're born these days. None of yer would've lasted five minutes when I were playing.'

Archie was what they call well travelled. He'd played for the Wanderers after he came back from the trenches in 1918. Sometimes we asked him about what the war was like, but he'd always say:

'Don't bloody ask.'

According to Archie he was the best left back Bolton had ever had but they moved him on after a few years, so he missed out on the FA Cup wins in the twenties. That was something he did like to talk about because he'd never got over it.

'Twisted me knee, didn't I? Home match against West Brom. Can still hear that tearing sound it made. I knew it were serious then.'

They patched him up, but his pace had gone. He had a couple of seasons at Bury but then started sliding down the league – Rochdale, Stockport, New Brighton, Barrow – and ended up a part-timer at Chorley.

Anyway, he reckoned we were all too soft and it was his job to toughen us up. He was supposed to be a trainer but all we ever seemed to do as apprentices was run round the streets near the ground – we weren't allowed on the pitch – or we'd get taken out to the moors round Belmont and told to run back. The rest of the time we were just used as skivvies. I spent more time sweeping the terraces, painting seats and crash barriers and sometimes repairing concrete than I ever did playing football.

Looking back, I suppose the idea was that if you got through that you'd be hard enough to make it as a professional. And if you couldn't stick it then you weren't going to make it as a pro so it was no loss either way. But after a year of feeling more like an odd-job man than a footballer I was getting fed up. In them days Bolton ran loads of teams – the Colts, the "A" and "B" teams and the Reserves – so you had to work your way through all that lot to get into the first team. It just seemed impossible – there were too many lads ahead of me. I was about to turn seventeen and already thinking my career at Bolton was over.

'Hey, Gerry, come here. I want a word with you.'

I was washing down some seats in the Manchester Road stand and Archie was stood on the touchline, watching me.

'Come on, I haven't got all day.'

As I made my way down to the pitch I was thinking – what have I done? Nothing came to mind, but he made me nervous just by the stern expression on his face. I couldn't ever remember seeing him laugh. But when I came and stood in front of him, he put his arm on my shoulder and started walking round the pitch with me.

'You're seeing Mr Bartram on Thursday, aren't yer?'

I nodded. Mr Bartram was the club secretary in them days and would decide whether Bolton would sign me as a professional or not.

'You know what he'll offer you, don't yer?'

This was news to me. I didn't know he was going to offer me anything, but I knew the minimum wage then was ten pounds a week. As I was only on five pounds as an apprentice, I would be very happy to shake Mr Bartram's hand and double my wages.

'Ten quid a week and another tenner for signing on.'

Archie grabbed my arm and pulled me back.

'And will you take it?'

So that's it, I thought. Mr Bartram's asked Archie to have a word and make sure I know what's good for me.

'Oh yes, Mr Wilcox. 'Course I will.'

Archie spat on the turf.

'Then you're a bloody fool.'

He walked away in disgust and I stood there for a moment, not knowing what to do, and then ran to catch him up.

'I don't understand. Don't you want me to sign?'

He stopped in his tracks, turned and prodded me in the chest.

'Look at me. Is this how you want to end up?'

I didn't know what to say. I was embarrassed. I'd never seen this side of him before.

'If you've got any sense you'll go in there and ask for thirteen pounds a week.'

'They'll never give me that.'

I saw his features soften for the first time.

'You don't know, do you?'

'Know what?'

'How good you are.'

He put his arms on both my shoulders and held me in his gaze.

'They want you. You make sure you get as much as you can because, believe you me, this doesn't last long.'

And he left me standing there on the touchline.

Mam came with me to the office a couple of days later. I'd only seen Mr Bartram occasionally although I'd washed his car a few times. He didn't mix much with the players, left all that to the trainers, but I knew he had the final say on anything that involved spending money. When we got shown in, I was proper nervous. It were like going into a bank or summat – all lovely polished wood, pictures on the walls and him sat behind this huge desk like some kind of tycoon.

He stood up and motioned us to sit the other side of the desk. I felt like I was back at school and I could feel my face going red. I'd been thinking about what Archie said but I wasn't sure I'd have the nerve to look Mr Bartram in the face and ask him for more money.

'Now then, Gerald. I've heard good reports from the staff so I'm very pleased to tell you that the club is willing to offer you a professional contract. You'll get ten pounds per week and I'll also give you ten pounds now to take away as a signing-on fee.'

He peeled two fresh fivers from his wallet with a flourish, like a magician completing a trick, and placed them in front of me on the desk. Then he stood up and held out his hand. As soon as I saw his outstretched hand in front of me, I realised I couldn't turn this down. I started to get up from my chair to shake on the deal when I felt Mam pull on my shoulder, stopping me from getting up.

'Not so fast.'

Mr Bartram looked puzzled.

'What's to do, Mrs Bradshaw? It's a great honour for your lad, you know. There's not many apprentices get put on staff.'

Mam sniffed.

'He's worth more than ten pounds a week.'

I looked at her astonished. She hadn't said anything to me about wanting more money. Mr Bartram was fuming, and his face went beetroot red. It was like Mam had slapped him across the cheek.

'And what do you know about it?'

Mam wasn't fazed. She sat quite calmly there with her handbag on her knee.

'Gerry could earn thirteen pounds a week on a building site. You're not telling me he's worth less than a brickie.'

Mr Bartram was stunned for a moment. I don't suppose he was used to people contradicting him, especially a woman, but he took a deep breath and slowly picked up the two five-pound notes and put them back in his wallet.

'If that's what you want for your lad that's up to you. But that's the best I can do.'

I was devastated. I'd been that close to my dream and my own mother had ruined it for me.

'Mam!'

Mr Bartram was looking calm and in control again. He could see I was panicking.

'You won't get a better offer than this. If I were his dad, I'd tell him to take it.'

He shouldn't have said that.

'Well, his dad's dead, as you well know, so I decide what's best for him.'

'It's a pity. Gerald's got potential. We start 'em all off at ten pounds but if he gets into the first team, we could look at it again. All the clubs do the same. You won't get a better offer.'

Mam sat back in her chair and the corners of her mouth twitched. She was smiling.

'I wun't be so sure of that, Mr Bartram. There's been some interest from a couple of other clubs. They've seen him play and liked what they saw.'

That flummoxed him. I'd been picked a few times for the mid-Lancashire schoolboys' team and done well. There were always scouts at the games but no one had ever come to me about asking me to play for them. Mam gave me a look that said "Keep your trap shut".

'What other clubs?'

'That's our business.'

He was quiet for a few moments, a distracted look on his face.

'Excuse me, will you?'

Mr Bartram slammed the office door behind him and we could hear voices being raised in the other room. After about five minutes he came back in looking flustered.

'What are you looking for then?'

'Thirteen pounds.'

He rocked uneasily in his chair.

'I can't do that. If word gets out they'll all want it for signing on.

No, no. Be reasonable.'

Mam stood up and signalled to me to do the same.

'Thank you for your time, Mr Bartram. I'm sorry we couldn't see eye to eye.'

We walked back across the office, and she had her hand on the doorknob before he spoke.

'Twelve pounds then.'

Mam gave me a little smile and we went back and collected them two fivers.

On the way home I asked why she hadn't told me what she was going to do and how she knew she could get more money.

'That Mr Wilcox came to see me. Told me to ask for thirteen pounds and they'd offer me twelve pounds. He said you were too scared to do it yourself.'

I hung my head when she said that. I fancied myself as the man of the house, but Mam still wore the trousers.

'What about these other clubs that are after me? Why didn't you tell me about them?'

'Now, don't be daft, Gerry. I made that up. Mr Wilcox said that if they thought somebody else might pinch you they'd be sure to snap you up.'

I took the five-pound notes out of my pocket.

'Here. You'd better look after these for me.'

NINE

Matthew Curtis had been a bit old school.

As Sarah returns to his house with a takeaway she feels she is stepping into one of those National Trust places where they have tried to recreate how people lived in the past. Over the years her father decorated his homes as if he was moving backwards through the decades to find the era he should have been born in. His final home, after the divorce, is Edwardian and furnished accordingly. Like a film set, everything is consistent with the period as if there had been a checklist to root out any anachronisms. Heavy wooden furniture dominated the rooms, complemented by dark velvet fabrics and drapes. Even the television set was imprisoned inside a mock-Victorian cabinet to maintain the illusion. Most people move with the times, but Matthew had ambled back in history, found it to his taste and stayed there.

He'd been the first person in his family to go to university, his father and mother both having left school at fourteen, and consequently acquiring a reverence for education and its potential for breaking down barriers. Passing his exams became a rite of passage for them all and Matthew felt an increasing weight of obligation as he went on to study law and embark on a profession rather than just a job. His success was a vindication of the sacrifices his parents has made and a kind of redemption for the opportunities they had been denied.

But, as many of his generation discovered, the more he fulfilled their dreams the further he moved from their world. Matthew was never ashamed of his parents, but he was conscious of their shortcomings and reluctant to introduce them to his new friends. He also began to have a slight resentment that they could not prepare him better for the life they wanted him to have. As he moved into increasingly middle-class circles, he found he had no reference points for how to behave and this triggered a troublesome set of anxieties. For instance, how should he dress? Other men seemed to move seamlessly from three-piece lounge suits in the office to jeans and polo shirts at the weekend, but what if he misjudged the mood and turned up for a social event either too casually dressed or out of place in shirt and tie? In the end he found that inoffensive neutrality offered the best peace of mind. Outside of work he would wear a thin V-neck sweater – fawn or mid-brown – underneath a tweed jacket. And have a tie in his pocket just in case.

And so it was with his home. When he bought his first house in his mid-twenties – semi-detached, so a step up from the terrace he'd grown up in – he knew he was past the point of no return. Every step now would be upwards; every move would place a little more distance between him and his parents. But he felt hesitant to define his own taste in case his friends and colleagues ridiculed it. He knew from magazines and television that the fashion at that time was for clean lines, unfussy Danish-style wooden furniture, stripped floors with rugs and, above all, the employment of every shade of brown in wallpaper and fabrics. But he had no sense of how these elements fitted together and whether they were too trendy for an aspiring solicitor with a reputation to build.

So he had opted for safe choices; the middle way; neither one thing nor the other. He chose items that he was confident had always been popular with men of his position. Leather armchairs, deep-pile carpets of a single colour, reproduction wooden furniture that suggested the cosiness of Empire, an oak dining table with ladderback chairs. Bit by bit he built up a defence against any suggestion that he was not at ease in his new position in life.

Of course, all this made him seem rather dull. In one sense, that was no bad thing. Not many clients want their solicitor to be exciting. Dogged attention to detail and avoidance of risk are the assets they prize, and Matthew excelled in both. As he became more comfortable in his conventional pose, so he grew in confidence. The doubts about whether he was an impostor who would be exposed as unworthy were driven down deep inside until they ceased to trouble him much at all. But by that time the habits and trappings of a stolid man of business and a respectable member of the community had set hard on his skin and it was impossible for him to scrape them off and behave in any other way.

And so, while several of his contemporaries dipped their beaks in the overflowing cups of the sexual revolution and coped admirably with the hypocrisy of public virtues and private vices – a quality the wealthier ones had learned from their fathers – Matthew slipped quietly through the swinging sixties and on into the seventies, barely causing a ripple.

Sarah throws herself onto the sofa and rips the cardboard top off what is supposed to be chicken chow mein but turns out to be a pungent chemical cocktail with noodles and random chunks of something white, tasteless but very chewy. Not that she cares much. She is hungry, she needs to eat, and this is food. Sort of. What more do you want, she wonders? The answer came back to her quickly. A drink. A big drink.

She had discovered the cocktail cabinet on her first night. At first glance it looked like a wardrobe that had been misplaced in the living room. A heavy-looking piece of lumber – walnut probably – with large twin doors above that opened to reveal shelves of glassware and a spacious cupboard below that housed the booze. Sarah never thought of her father as a heavy drinker, but he clearly liked to be sure he was short of nothing in case he had visitors. The previous night she'd made some serious inroads into the gin so she thought vodka would be a nice change. Some lime cordial is tucked away at the back of the cupboard so she mixes that in a jug with ice and a reckless slug of vodka and settles down to enjoy a gimlet or three.

Time to check her phone. Five messages now from Marcus.

Thinking of you. Don't work too hard. Marcus xx

Ring when you have a chance. Missing you. Marcus xx

Are you OK? M xx

I'm around this evening. Call me. M x

HELLO???

She drains her glass, tops it up, has another swig and takes stock.

Nearly ten o'clock. Bound to be a long call as he's clearly decided to be the injured party. As if I haven't got enough on my plate. All this lot to sort out. Sarah waves her hand at the furniture. According to Jim, the business is in a mess and now I've got to babysit an old lady who's lost her husband. Not to mention her narcoleptic dog. I can't do relationship stuff on top of that. Not tonight.

Sorry. Just got back. Exhausted. Speak tomorrow. Love. S xx

One message from Mum. Sarah could imagine her tapping out each letter with painstaking care, scrolling back to check the punctuation. Once a teacher always a teacher. She'd never accepted that texts are not letters and so they have to be carefully crafted as if they are part of a Jane Austen novel. This meant they took a long time to complete. A really long time. On the plus side it meant she is unlikely to get five messages from her mum on the same day. Her reproaches come in irregular fits and starts. She starts to work her way through this one in her head.

Darling. It's now two days since I've heard from you.

Yes – I know that Mum

I had thought that you would call round today to see how I'm managing.

Sorry. Meant to.

As you know, your father and I had not spoken for some time but his death has, nevertheless, come as a great shock. However, life goes on.

This is also known to me. Get to the point, Mum.

I need to talk to you about his estate.

Of course you do.

I don't trust Jim Glassbrook. He was Matthew's faithful guard dog, growling if you ever came too near his master. I wouldn't put it past him to have squirrelled some money away as a little long-term service award. Be sure you check the accounts thoroughly.

Shit. I'm going to have to read them all now.

And I'd like you to handle the sale of the house yourself. Jim's likely to suggest one of his cronies who'll undervalue it and sell it on to another of their confederates.

Ooh. You've really got it in for Jim, haven't you?

I leave the sale of the business to you. You know more about that side of things than I do.

Thank you for noticing.

I thought this would be an opportunity for us to spend some time together.

Don't start.

To share our grief and bond as a mother and daughter should. I can't understand why you don't come and stay with me until this is all sorted out.

Can't you?

Please reconsider. I can cook you a meal each evening and we could go over the day together. I know you have a lot of things on your mind but two heads are better than one.

I love you Mum, but No.

Anyway, think it over and pop round to see me. I'm always in, as you know.

Your loving mother,

Helen.

46

Sarah switches off the phone. No point in replying now; she'll probably be getting ready for bed. Call her tomorrow. Actually, better call round tomorrow.

It is strange to be in the house alone. She'd never lived there but everything seems familiar from her childhood. Her mum had opted to make a completely new start ('He can keep all that mock-Victorian tat') so her father had simply moved all the furniture from the family home to this place. There is the sofa they used to watch telly on; the kitchen table she'd done her homework at; the coat stand where she'd hung her coat after school; the same dark and dreary paintings of rustic life that peppered the walls. Everything she remembered seemed to be there except him.

I didn't visit enough, she thought. She remembered one of their last conversations on the phone.

'You blame me, but it isn't my fault.'

'I don't.'

'Then why don't you come to see me?'

'It's difficult to get away. Things are crazy at work, and I only get a chance to spend some time with Marcus at the weekends.'

'You came up to see your mother last month. You didn't have time to see me?'

'It's complicated. You know what Mum's like.'

'I haven't done anything wrong. I wasn't carrying on with another woman. I wasn't violent or controlling. I didn't keep her short of money. Your mum got bored, that's all. After you left home – well… there didn't seem to be much point any more. We'd done what we had to do – bring you up – and that seemed to be that. We were just a habit we'd gotten into.'

'Mum says you stopped talking to her.'

'I ran out of things to say. That's different.'

Round and round and round the same old stuff, she thought. When is it going to end?

There is a bit of lime cordial left so she mixes up another round of gimlets. By now she is on that delicate cusp between chilled enlightenment and crashing out. No point in getting maudlin. Might as well begin searching for that letter Eileen is counting on.

She stumbles into her father's study as a starting point. Most of the room is taken up by a huge desk that would have suited the Fat Controller of that railway with the talking engines. She can't remember their names. Gordon. That's one of them, isn't it? The rest of the room seemed to be floor to ceiling bookcases, a lifetime's accumulation of novels, text books, periodicals and football programmes.

As good a place as any, she thinks, knocking back a final gimlet and starting on the box files. They are neatly labelled on the outside – House, Car, Utilities, Finance, Receipts – but it is possible her dad had chosen to hide a letter from Gerry in with his bank statements – so she begins to pick through them one by one. The last thing she remembers is examining a sheaf of MOT certificates for cars sold long ago.

When she comes to a few hours later she has a painful crick in her neck and a sore cheek where her head is lying on her notebook. The wired spine has dug into her skin and created an angry-looking spiral pattern, as if she'd had a tornado tattooed along one side of her face. She has drooled extensively over the pages so that whatever notes she had made resemble a watercolour that has been left out in the rain.

She plods upstairs, thinks about cleaning her teeth, decides that is a bridge too far, lays down on top of the bed in her clothes and closes her eyes.

*

When Sarah was a little girl, they had a blue budgerigar called Joey. From time to time he had to be lured out of his cage so it could be cleaned up. This was her job. She remembered that the bottom of the cage was covered with a sheet of very rough sandpaper which would be splattered with budgie poo, feathers and uneaten seeds.

This is how her mouth feels when she wakes up next morning.

She looks into the bathroom mirror and tries to pull her face back into shape. There are a series of parallel indentations on one cheek. God knows how I did that, she thinks. She makes a mental note that, whatever everyone else says, you can get a stinking hangover from vodka. Everyone else is wrong. And not for the first time.

She remembers that she had planned to buy some provisions on the way home last night – orange juice, tea, milk, bread, cereal – so perhaps a bit of breakfast might help. By the time she reaches the kitchen her mind has cleared sufficiently to recall that she'd abandoned the idea of shopping after she left the Chinese takeaway and had opted to come home and get off her face instead.

There is an old jar of instant coffee in one of the cupboards. What few granules are left have become stuck to the glass so there is nothing else for it but to pour the boiling water into the jar, shake it like a cocktail and swill the contents into a cup. Not ideal but it helps a bit. But as she leans against the worktop, waiting for life to trickle back in, Sarah feels her father's eyes watching her and shaking his head in disapproval so she goes upstairs and stays under the shower for as long as she can bear it.

By the time she's towelled her hair and put on some clothes she is beginning to feel human again and a little bit peckish. She knows a place where she would be guaranteed to get a good breakfast but there are some strings attached.

TEN

Taylor doesn't really follow football. He'd never been good at games in school and heading a mud-soaked ball with the lace flicking into your eyes was not his idea of a fun afternoon. However, even he recognises some of the names on the list Jim has given him.

It isn't exactly a Who's Who from the Golden Age – Gerry hadn't been a drinking pal of Geoff Hurst or Bobby Charlton – but they would have made a pretty decent team back in the day. But what are they doing now? Might Gerry be holing out with one of them? Are any still living in the area, given that Sarah thought Gerry wouldn't completely abandon Eileen? Are they all still alive?

Taylor is not sure what a real detective would do to answer these questions, but it is raining again and pounding the streets doesn't appeal. Perhaps he would be better off in a different film genre – the political thriller. Immediately he begins thinking of *All the President's Men* and the investigative journalists who had blown the Watergate scandal. Yes, that might work. He can't carry off the Robert Redford role – too tall and too blonde – but he might get away with Dustin Hoffman – small but perfectly formed. They hadn't gone round kicking in doors or spending nights in their cars staking out suspects. As far as he could remember they did all their detective work by phoning people up or interviewing them in their homes.

I might have my limitations, he thinks, but I can definitely manage that. And I have something at my disposal that Woodward and Bernstein never had – the good old Internet.

He is sitting in the Central Library and has logged on for an hour. The other customers have an average age of about twelve and are pretending to do their homework in between swapping tall tales from the net. This is distracting but nothing compared to some of the press offices he'd worked in. He begins to work through the list and quickly gets absorbed in the chase.

After some time he becomes aware of a small girl in a hijab who is invading his personal space. He gives her a quick look and goes back to the screen, but the girl does not move and continues to hover by his shoulder. He tries to carry on but is finding it difficult to concentrate. What if other people look up and see a dodgy-looking middle-aged white guy apparently sharing images with an innocent Muslim girl? He turns back and gives her his best stony stare.

'This is private. Do you mind?'

The little girl doesn't respond except to gesture at the pc.

'I'm working. If you want to book a screen you need to see the librarian.'

He points over her head.

'Back there.'

The girl is unmoved. She meets his stare and counters with a look of contempt.

'I have done. You're in my seat.'

'What?'

'Time's up, Grandad. Better get off home before it goes dark.'

Taylor is about to give her a crash course in good manners when the librarian comes into view.

'Problem, Yasmin?'

'No. This gentleman's just going.'

He picks up his notes, smiles weakly and shuffles off to a seat near the bookshelves next to a man who is fast asleep. Interesting kid, he thinks. Probably end up as a lawyer. Or a bouncer.

He reviews the notes he's made. There had been nine names on Jim's list, and he'd managed to find something on all of them.

Tommy Goodwin – goalkeeper – like Gerry, a one-club man. Played on well into his mid-thirties and had a nice send off from a Testimonial Match. A recent newspaper article said that he'd moved to live with his daughter in Australia.

Ernie Fletcher – right back – well respected in the game and was taken on the staff at Liverpool when his career ended there. Ended up coaching the youth team. Now an occasional talent scout for the club.

Denis Green – centre half – solid performer who set up in business as a builder's merchant in Bolton. No recent references but likely to be in the area.

Frank Goodall – left back – transferred to Tottenham for a big fee and was part of the England squad for a while. Finished his career at Burnley and is now one of their match-day ambassadors.

Harry Lomax – right half – played alongside Gerry in midfield and was the core of the team that almost won promotion in the mid-sixties. Saw his career out at Bolton and ran a pub in Heaton for several years. No recent mentions.

Stan Roberts – left wing – snapped up by Everton when it became obvious that Bolton were not going to get back to the First Division any time soon. Career ended prematurely after a broken leg at a match in Newcastle that was called off soon after. Ended up as a kit man for the Toffees.

Gordon Clifford – inside right – promising early career but never fulfilled his potential. Transferred to Bury and then on to

Workington. Ended up in non-league with Radcliffe Borough. Current whereabouts unknown.

Bill Chadwick – inside left – England youth international whose chance of big-time football seemed to have gone until Manchester City picked him up for a song in the early seventies. Had a glorious Indian summer to his career and won a League Cup medal. Stayed on at City as an assistant coach.

Ronnie Shepherd – right wing – touted as Bolton's answer to Stanley Matthews, he soon became a target for all the top clubs. Secured a big-money transfer to Chelsea, but ended up more famous for his drinking bouts than his football achievements. Released by Chelsea he had another failed career as a salesman and ended up in a sheltered housing scheme in Westhoughton.

The man next to Taylor stirs in his sleep and murmurs something about what he'd do to Tucker (sounds like Tucker anyway) if he ever catches up with him. The library seems to be a daytime refuge for those who can't get their head down anywhere else. All you need is an open book on your lap – in his neighbour's case it is a pictorial history of England's stately homes – and the librarian seems to turn a blind eye. Taylor goes back to studying his list.

If I don't get a result on this job I'm going to be spending a lot more time here myself, he thinks. What would Dustin Hoffman do? Eliminate the unlikely leads and track down the ones who are most likely to come up with the information. And all those he could easily get to see by bus.

One is now out of the country. One is off the radar. One in Burnley and two in Liverpool. One is probably in Manchester so could be held in reserve. That left three who are in the Bolton area – Denis Green, Harry Lomax and Ronnie Shepherd. Could be a win-win situation. Knock all these three off without delay and he might get news of Gerry in time to make that bonus worthwhile.

And if he were really on a roll, he might find the man himself in the spare bedroom.

With any luck Denis would have his registered office for the business as his home address so a quick check on Companies House could turn him up. Harry had kept a pub so the obvious thing would be to pay a visit and see if one of the locals knows where he's got to. And he now has enough cash to buy a drink. As for Ronnie – well, there couldn't be that many sheltered blocks in Westhoughton, could there?

Another quick session on the computer would be handy. Yasmin is tapping away intently but the boy next to her is being escorted outside for throwing marker pens at a nerdy-looking lad in the next row. You never know. There might be a bit of unexpired time on his session, and it would give him a chance to get his own back by peering at whatever Yasmin is checking out.

ELEVEN

Helen Curtis has never settled into living on her own. Sometimes, as she goes over things, it isn't clear whether she had asked for a divorce or whether Matthew had manoeuvred her into one. It is true that she was the one who brought matters to a head. He seemed to be content to let their marriage drift into sexless apathy and indifference. He was either at work during the day or going over papers in his study when he came home. The evenings were the worst. She was left to read, or binge watch American box sets on her own. Mealtimes were perfunctory, functional and frequently silent. A ritual that continued but had lost its meaning. It was Helen who had issued the ultimatum.

'Either we see a counsellor and sort this out or I want a divorce. I'm not going to sit here every night being ignored.'

But lately she'd been wondering whether that is what Matthew had planned for her to do. That would have been typical of him, she thinks. Hadn't the courage to come out with it himself so he forced the issue by giving me the silent treatment and made me be the one to end it.

Since his death, Helen felt bad about thinking this, although that was also typical of Matthew. Whenever he was in the wrong, he found all sorts of ways to avoid responsibility and shift it on to her. Death didn't put someone beyond reproach (she could still feel angry with him when she remembered how unfeeling he had become) but it did put them out of reach. Nothing more could be resolved but although she knows that the lingering bitterness is corrosive and does her more harm than good she finds she isn't ready to let it go just yet. Even so, she admits to herself that Matthew wasn't really a bad man and she had loved him once. And, after all, it is only a few weeks since his remains had been placed in a sanctum vault at Overdale Crematorium.

'Room for two sets of ashes,' the undertaker had told her confidentially.

Presumably he intended this to be a comfort. You may be separated now in life, but you can be reunited in death. But Helen is in no rush to make the move, and in any case, she is not sure that she wants to spend eternity crammed into a granite urn with Matthew.

Divorcing a lawyer is a tricky business. Matthew himself didn't display any rancour but she suspected he had egged Jim Glassbrook on to give her a hard time, probably giving him a sob story about how badly she had repaid him for his years of hard work building their prosperity. Fortunately, she had persuaded one of Matthew's professional rivals to take her on and feels, overall, after a big battle over stocks and shares and a few skirmishes over pensions, that she has gotten a fair deal. They sold the family house, pooled the savings and investments and split the proceeds, and their lives, two ways. Matthew retired into some sort of museum of late Imperial chic in Smithills and she opted for a converted schoolhouse in Entwistle with a state-of-the-art kitchen.

On paper she has everything she needs. A secure income, a lovely home and the freedom to please herself. She tells herself that time is short (Matthew had died within twelve hours of the first, catastrophic stroke) and that you have to make the most of every minute. But what is she supposed to do and, to be frank, what is the point?

It isn't that she wishes she was still a teacher. More than thirty years of staffroom backbiting, endless pupil assessments and OFSTED inspections had squeezed all the fun out of a job she used to love. It isn't that she wishes she had never divorced Matthew. The marriage had become like an old pack of plasticine – the brilliant colours had mingled together until what was left was a featureless, dull brown lump. All you could do was throw it in the bin.

But she misses actually being a teacher, being a wife and, more than anything, being a mother. Because, even though all of these roles have driven her up the wall on many occasions, left her frustrated and sometimes unfulfilled, they provided an answer to what the purpose of being alive is. Or, she concluded, if that is being too romantic, they kept her busy enough not to have time to worry about it too often.

And so, when Sarah turns up out of the blue this morning, she feels a tingle of contentment as she plugs herself back into motherhood.

'You look terrible.'

'Thanks, Mum. You're such a comfort.'

'Go into the kitchen – I'll make some tea.'

'Coffee would be better.'

'You should have rung.'

'Have you got any eggs?'

She does have eggs. And toast. Orange juice. And lots of coffee. After that Sarah wanders into the garden for a smoke.

'I thought you'd given up?'

'I have but I've run out of vape fluid.'

Helen has a tendency to disbelieve most things Sarah says about herself but decides not to rise to this one. It isn't that she is a liar, but she likes to create a narrative about her life that makes it easier to cope, and bending the truth is a necessary part of that. Helen accepts this even though it annoys her. She has learned that you cannot pick your children up on every single thing they do wrong. She has tried the other way and would not recommend it unless you have an insatiable appetite for stand-up screaming matches.

She wants to ask about the house sale but the intensity with which Sarah is drawing on her cigarette makes her think this is not the ideal time, so she decides to approach the subject more obliquely.

'I suppose the house feels odd without your father in it. Must be sad to see it standing empty and neglected.'

Sarah blows a stream of smoke over a large potted marguerite by the back door that had been minding its own business and not annoying anyone. Helen takes the point. Best not to mention the house at the moment.

'How's Marcus?'

Sarah takes another powerful drag, grinds the remainder of the cigarette into the patio and turns to face her.

'Why are you suddenly interested in him?'

'I was just wondering how he is managing... you know... with you being here for a while. And I'm not suddenly interested.'

'Oh come on, Mum. You've never been that keen on us as a couple.'

'That's not true. I like Marcus.'

'Maybe, but you don't like him being with me.'

'I don't know why you talk to me like I was some sort of...oh, I don't know...'

'Racist?'

Helen is stunned for a few moments, her head droops and she slowly walks back into the kitchen.

'Mum!'

Sarah curses and follows her. Helen is sitting at the breakfast bar staring at an empty cup.

'I shouldn't have said that. I'm sorry. I didn't sleep that well last night.'

'Found your father's drink cabinet, I suppose.'

Sarah slides onto the stool next to her.

'I didn't mean it.'

'One of these days you're going to say something you can never take back.'

Yes, thinks Sarah, one of these days I will.

Silence hangs between them. Helen will not look Sarah in the face.

'Look... I should probably be going. Lot of things to sort out at the office.'

She begins looking for her phone and her car keys.

'I'll call you this evening... after work.'

She kisses her mother lightly on the forehead and heads for the front door.

'Why did you come?'

'To see you... and to get some breakfast. Thanks. I needed that.'

'You can ask me anything, you know.'

'About what?'

'Whatever you want to know. About me and your father?'

Sarah hesitates. No, not now.

'I really do have to go, Mum. I'll see you soon.'

She is almost out the door when she remembers.

'Oh, there is something I wanted to ask. Did you ever meet Gerry Bradshaw? Friend of Dad's?'

Helen is still staring at the coffee cup.

'Gerry?'

She sniffs dismissively.

'Your father invited him and his wife over a couple of times. She was an odd little woman. Like a bird. Twittered on but made no sense.'

'So you didn't know him very well.'

'Mathew got a vicarious thrill from mixing with footballers. It didn't do anything for me.'

After Sarah has left, Helen sits for a while. What do you do when you know your child is unhappy? When they are little it's straightforward enough. Comfort, support, love and the odd treat usually do the trick. But what about when they are fully grown and have stopped looking to you for advice? You can't kiss and make it better any more. You have to wait and see if they can find a way for themselves and hope it works out.

Meantime there isn't anything to do but get on with your own life. She picks up the empty cup and begins tidying the kitchen.

Twelve

1961

In the "A" team it were nearly all young lads like myself. You might get one of the older pros playing the odd game if they were coming back from an injury but mostly it was boys your own age. So when I got the nod to join the Reserves, I was nervous as well as excited because it meant I'd be training with seasoned players who'd been hardened up by years of league football.

Mam could see I was worried.

'What's up with yer? This is what you've always wanted, in't it?'

'I know, but what if I'm not good enough?'

She put down the Evening News she'd been reading, took off her glasses and shook her head.

'I could say "Just do your best, you can't do any more than that" but that'd be letting you off too easy. You're nineteen now. Your dad wasn't much older than you when he got called up. Now he had something to be frightened of but all you've got to do is kick a ball. So stop moaning.'

I was thinking about that when I went to training next day. National Service had just ended so I hadn't got caught up in that like some of the older lads. Mam was right. I was lucky, and I needed to make the most of it.

I knew a couple of the lads in the Reserves from when they'd been in the "A" team. Ernie Fletcher and Frank Goodall were well established as the full backs and Ernie had played in a cup match for the first team. But the rest were a lot older and I was only on nodding terms with them.

Joe Turner was the trainer in them days. We'd heard stories from lads at other clubs about new training methods being introduced, working with weights, gymnastics, developing tactics, working on your skills with the ball. But none of that had found its way to Bolton by then. Joe didn't see it as his job to improve you as a footballer. If you'd got that far you should know how to play and if you wanted to improve the best thing to do was to copy the ones who were better than you.

No, his job was to get you fit. That meant lots of running. And when you'd finished that, more running. Sprints, jogs, cross country – we did it all. The one thing we didn't do much of was play football, except in the matches. Joe had a theory – it was still very popular at that time – that you had to be "hungry" for the ball. So, he deliberately starved players of contact with a football to whet our appetites.

As it happens, that first session I joined we were actually practising with the ball because there was a game the next day. I knew the others would be looking at me, sizing me up, so when Joe told me to join the lads who were taking shots at goal I thought, this is it. There was a queue of us on the edge of the penalty box lining up on one side while Joe passed the ball into the penalty area. We had to run in, take the pass in our stride and crash the ball into the net. The only problem was that Tommy Goodwin was in goal and he'd got a couple of England Under-23 caps and was saving more than he let in.

When it came to my turn, Joe didn't pass the ball into the penalty area. He kicked it to the edge of the box so that when I collected the ball it was going to be a lot further out than for the other lads. I could see he was smiling. Bastard, I thought.

'First time now, Brads,' he bellowed.

I had no chance to think. I ran onto the ball and swung my right boot at it. The balls were heavy in them days and soaked up water and I could feel the laces slapping against my instep as I made contact. I must have caught it just right because it went like an arrow into the top corner. Tommy Goodwin barely moved. As I turned and jogged back to the line there was silence from the other players but I got a few nods as I passed them and I knew I was in.

Denis Green was only a few years older than me but had already notched up more than twenty games in the first team. Well over six-foot and nearly as wide he wasn't someone to mess with. Joe loved him. One time I saw him walking round Denis, looking at him up and down.

'No one's getting past you, son. No one.'

After training Denis told me that Joe had asked him to show me the ropes.

'You get new boots now you're in't Reserves. I'll take you down to Albert Ward's later on and get you sorted out.'

This sounded great. The boots I was using were the old, heavy sort, more like rugby than football, and I'd seen some of the new, slimmer brands from Germany and reckoned I'd look good in those and play better as well. Albert Ward's shop in town supplied sports gear for all the local teams and the club had an account there. Denis was chatting to the man behind the counter while I picked through the boots until I found a pair by Adidas.

'Have you got a size nine in these?' I asked the man behind the counter. 'The whole Spurs team wear 'em,' I said to Denis, expecting him to be impressed, but he started laughing along with the shop assistant.

'You can put them back. Who do you think you are? Jimmy Greaves? Club won't run to that. You'd best show him, Eric.'

I was taken to a small shelf of bargain boots in a plain, more old-fashioned style.

'Any one of these. If you want something else, you'll have to pay the difference yourself.'

I knew the club normally wouldn't spend twopence if a penny would do but I felt I'd been put back in my place. Denis could see I was disappointed so he took me for a cup of tea in the café a few doors down.

'We're all in the same boat, Gerry. Don't worry about Joe or the manager. You're one of us now. That's what matters. And we look after our own.'

Thirteen

It takes Taylor less than a minute to realise he shouldn't be there.

Mrs Green is wary at first when she answers the door.

'You're not a reporter, are you?'

'No, no. I'm working for Gerry Bradshaw's wife.'

'Nothing wrong is there?'

'Who is it?'

A thin, hesitant voice from inside the house. Mrs Green turns her head, uncertain whether to go back or keep Taylor at the door.

'Maggie!'

More strident now. Taylor can hear the panic in the voice. That decides it for Mrs Green.

'You'd better come in.'

He follows her into the living room. Denis is half out of his chair, trying to raise himself by pushing down on the arms, and is beginning to topple over. Mrs Green rushes forward and steadies him by grabbing his elbows.

'Come on, let's get you sat down.'

'Where've you been?'

'I've just been answering the door.'

'I didn't know where you were.'

'Here. I'm always here, aren't I?'

Taylor stands by awkwardly as Denis becomes less agitated and his wife lowers him gently back into the armchair and rearranges the cushions. She carefully replaces a tray on his knee with a plastic, lidded drinking mug and a few biscuits and then briefly cups his face in her hands and holds him in her gaze until he is calm. This is private. He shouldn't be watching. He shuffles behind the settee, thinking this might make him less obvious.

Denis sees him now.

'Who's he?'

'Says he's a friend of Gerry Bradshaw.'

Taylor starts to correct her but thinks better of it. Mrs Green motions him to sit down.

'We don't get many visitors these days, do we, love?'

'Gerry, you say?'

Denis is looking intently at Taylor who gives him an encouraging smile in return.

'You used to play together. For Bolton?'

'I was the best centre half Wanderers ever had, wasn't I, Maggie?'

Mrs Green nods as she sits down on the settee next to Taylor.

'We haven't seen Eileen and Gerry for a while now. They used to call round when Denis first got... but then we lost touch.'

Taylor is already desperately thinking how he could get out without causing offence but tries to put on his most sympathetic face.

'Has he come about the insurance?'

'No – that's tomorrow.'

She turns to Taylor.

''Course, they don't want to pay up. Everybody knows it's heading the ball what caused it, but they say there's no proof.'

'I'm disturbing you. I'll come back another time.'

'You know Gerry, do you?'

Taylor has been bracing himself to stand up and head for the door but sinks back down again.

'Not personally, no.'

'I thought you said you are working for him.'

'For his wife, actually.'

'Why, what's to do?'

There is a loud clatter as Denis pushes his tray off his knee sending the cup and most of its contents onto the floor.

'Gerry's dead.'

Maggie wearily gets up from the settee and starts to wipe up the mess. Judging by the state of the carpet this is a regular occurrence.

'Now. What are yer getting excited about?'

Taylor is paying attention now and leaning forward in his seat.

'What makes you say that, Mr Green?'

'They cremated him, didn't they? You don't do that if they're alive.'

Denis sits back triumphantly.

'There's only me left now.'

'When was this?'

Mrs Green has finished clearing up and is back on the settee.

'He dun't mean Gerry.'

'Don't start that again, Maggie. I'm not bloody daft. I know when someone's dead.'

'It were Les Collins.'

She turns to Taylor.

'Cancer. Everybody smoked in them days. Never thought 'owt about it.'

Denis is looking less certain now.

'Who did you say?'

'That funeral we went to last month. It were Les Collins. You remember.'

Turning again to Taylor.

''E were a goalkeeper in't same team.'

Denis seems to shrink back into the armchair as he takes this in. He begins muttering to himself, but Taylor can't catch what he is saying. Mrs Green continues.

'Has something happened to Gerry then?'

'I'm just trying to trace his whereabouts.'

'Gone missing, 'as he?'

'Well… we don't know. That's what Mrs Bradshaw wants us to find out.'

Mrs Green is watching as Denis drains what is left of the tea in his cup and then leans his head back and stares at the ceiling.

'I 'ave to be careful with Denis. If he gets out on his own he'd 'ave no idea where he was. Mebbe Gerry's the same.'

'Possibly. Look – I'll leave you in peace. Should Gerry contact you then you can reach me at this number.'

He hands her a business card – *Taylor Investigations* – *we find out what you want to know.* Mrs Green considers it carefully.

'There's something I want to know. Why did you come to us?'

'Teammates. Thought he might be looking up old friends.'

Mrs Green gives him a sour smile.

'If you find any of his old friends, send 'em round. They seem to have forgotten our address.'

Taylor rises and shakes hands with Denis.

'Very nice to meet you.'

Denis holds onto his hand and draws him closer.

'You won't find him, you know. He's gone. They're all gone now.'

*

Even by his standards, this has been a disappointing start to the investigation, but Taylor feels his spirits lifting as he sits on the top deck of the number seven bus. It is pretty much empty, so he's been able to bag one of the seats at the front, giving him a panoramic view of the Wigan Road as they approach Hunger Hill. It's a chance to enjoy the raggedy bit of countryside in the gap between towns and also to keep an eye out for Gerry's car along the roadside. But his mind soon drifts away as he remembers what a treat it was to get this seat as a kid so that you were able to pretend to drive the bus home as well as collecting the tickets. For a few minutes he is that boy again and his adult cares disperse like clouds being burnt off by the sun.

But as the bus crosses over the motorway and dips down towards Westhoughton his thoughts return to the job in hand.

He tries to tell himself that the visit to the Greens was not a complete waste but all he'd learnt was that they hadn't seen Gerry or Eileen for a long time. Not, it seemed, for any sinister reason but simply because they couldn't bear to visit Denis in his current state. Taylor understands that. If he had a close friend with dementia he is not sure he'd have the courage to keep on visiting him. If he had a close friend that is.

This has not left him feeling optimistic about interviewing Ronnie Shepherd. He'd tracked him down to a sheltered bungalow on an estate for older people, overlooking the cemetery, giving the residents the opportunity to while away their few remaining days by contemplating what lies ahead of them, handily just across the road. Contrary to popular belief, it seems that the borough planning officers do have a sense of humour after all.

It is early afternoon so, if Ronnie is still hitting the bottle, he shouldn't be too far gone to get some sense out of him. However, as he approaches the bungalow, he notes the ramp up to the front door and his spirits begin to sag. He presses the button on the intercom but before he can say who he is the door buzzes and the lock clicks open. The entrance hall is dingy and a powerful smell of urine and stale cooking hits Taylor as he steps inside. It isn't clear which room to head for until a voice shouts out from directly ahead.

'What time do you call this? I'm soaked through.'

Pushing open the living room door he finds Ronnie sitting by the window overlooking a piece of overgrown scrubland that used to be a garden. He swivels his wheelchair round and the empty trouser where his left leg had once been flaps to one side.

'Who the bloody hell are you?'

'Errm. I'm Taylor.'

'Different fucking person every time. Where's Chrissy?'

69

'I'm sorry, I don't know…'

'Well, come on then. I need changing. I've been sat here an hour waiting.'

Taylor looks back blankly and then Ronnie knows.

'Oh fucking 'ell.'

His head drops and Taylor sees his chest heave. For a few moments they endure the silence together until Ronnie recovers himself enough to speak.

'They said someone's on the way. But they didn't say when. Thought it was you.'

Taylor shakes his head.

'Sorry. Is there something I can do?'

'You can tell me who the fuck you are.'

'I'm making some enquiries about Gerry Bradshaw. You used to play together at Bolton.'

'Listen, mate. If you want an autograph you've come at a bad time, so fuck off.'

'I'm working for Gerry's wife, Eileen. Do you know her?'

Ronnie is gathering himself to give Taylor both barrels in reply but a voice from the hallway interrupts him.

'Mr Shepherd?'

A tiny Filipino woman in a pale-blue nylon uniform, carrying a large bag like the ones bike riders use for delivering food, marches briskly into the room. Ronnie closes his eyes in gratitude.

'Thank Christ.'

'No blasphemy, please, Mr Shepherd. My name is Gloria and I'm here to help you today.'

'What's happened to Chrissy?'

'I couldn't say. Who is this gentleman?'

'No idea.'

This stumps Gloria for a moment but she has no time to seek any further clarification.

'Out you go, sir. Mr Shepherd needs his dignity. You can wait outside.'

Taylor does as he is told. He wanders across the street and peers over the low wall surrounding the cemetery. Headstones are scattered across an open field leading to a small church. There had been divisions once to mark the separate graves but these have been removed, presumably to make it easier to mow the grass. And so they stand at rest, like a random crowd who wandered into a field but never found their way out. Few headstones seem to have any flowers by them or signs of recent attendance. Mildew and rain damage have obscured the inscriptions. Gone and seemingly forgotten.

Not the most cheerful outlook, he thinks, but at least the neighbours are quiet. He strolls back and hangs around by the front door. After about twenty minutes Gloria bustles out of the bungalow, waves briefly in acknowledgement, stuffs a large waste bag into the boot of her hatchback and speeds off to her next client. Taylor slips by her as she leaves, catching the door before it closes.

Ronnie has moved into the kitchen and is munching on a sandwich. He doesn't look surprised to see Taylor return.

'OK now?'

'Too many like me and not enough like them. Put the kettle on, will yer?'

Finding a clean cup without a chip isn't easy but he drops in the teabags and sloshes the boiling water into the two with the fewest stains. Ronnie pushes aside his plate.

'Rubbish. They use that processed cheese shit. No taste to it. What did you say yer name is?'

'Taylor.'

'Sorry about before. It's not easy to concentrate when you've been sitting in your own piss since breakfast.'

'That's alright.'

He pushes a cup of tea towards Ronnie and sits down opposite him at the small wooden table.

'How long since you err...'

He nods in the general direction of Ronnie's waist.

71

'Nearly two years now. Diabetes. Cuts off the blood flow. Turns out that getting pissed every night and smoking forty a day can be bad for your health.'

He sips his tea.

'Off the fags now. Still got a drink problem, though. Can't afford it.'

He waits for the laugh from Taylor, settles for a rueful smile, and has another sip of tea.

'What's all this about Gerry?'

'His wife has asked me to locate him. You haven't seen him recently, have you?'

'Left 'er, has he? Not surprised. Never knew what he saw in 'er. Wasn't even that good-looking. Not like some of the birds I used to know. When I was at Chelsea? Once they knew you were a footballer they couldn't wait to get their knickers off. I never went short.'

'No, I'm sure you didn't.'

'Great while it lasted...'

'... but getting back to Gerry...'

'I was good you know. I could play. You should have seen me then.'

'Yes, I know...'

'Pissed it all away though. Didn't I?'

'But you and Gerry kept in touch?'

'I never really knew how much I loved the game until I got chucked out. I thought it was all the other things – you know – women, cars, nightclubs. But that's not what I miss most. I was right-footed, useless on my left. Didn't matter though, I could do it all on one side. My left leg was just for standing on. Can't even fucking do that now.'

Ronnie stares into his teacup.

'Yeah. Gerry. I ended up back here a few years ago. I was in a right state. He put me in touch with some solicitor friend of his. Helped me get this place. Called round from time to time. Don't know why. We were never that close.'

'But you haven't seen him recently?'

Ronnie shakes his head.

'Not many of us left now, are there?'

'More than you think. Saw Denis Green earlier.'

'You're 'aving a great day, aren't yer? Which do you reckon is worst then? Being a fucking cripple or not knowing what day it is?'

'Eileen thinks Gerry might be in trouble.'

'Aren't we all, mate? Listen… do you think you could lend me a few quid? I could do with a drink.'

Taylor fishes a tenner from his pocket. He looks at it longingly as he shoves it across the table.

'Cheers. Don't worry about Gerry. Probably off for a dirty weekend. Lucky bastard.'

Taylor is almost at the front door when Ronnie calls out to him.

'Hey! Would you like my autograph? I played in front of 50,000 people in an FA Cup semi-final once.'

Taylor pulls the door closed behind him, turns up his coat collar, and heads for the bus stop. It is time to go to the pub.

Fourteen

1962

Sometimes it's a case of dead men's shoes.

Bob Ashworth had been playing at right half for as long as I could remember. He was a kind of fixture in the team. But somehow, he hadn't been quite the same that season. I was in the stands for the game against Blackpool and I could hear groans round me whenever he got the ball.

'Don't give it to 'im!'

'Get rid!'

'Course, when you hear that as a player it just makes you more nervous and likely to make a mistake. Even so, it was a big surprise when Joe Turner took me to one side at training the following Thursday.

'Don't say 'owt to the others but Bob's not feeling that well. If he's not fit, the boss wants you to tek 'is place.'

I couldn't sleep that night thinking about the match. We were playing Everton at Goodison Park. They were going well that year and I knew there'd be a good crowd – more than 35,000 – twice what we normally got at home. It was my big chance. I've never been the sort for praying but I remember wishing with all my heart that Bob Ashworth wouldn't get better.

Next day I got the nod. I was in the team for Saturday. When

I realised I was going to play I stopped feeling so nervous. I just wanted the next day to come and the game to start.

Preparation for matches was all very basic, more about making sure you got to the bus on time and had all your kit, and there was no real discussion of tactics in those days.

'Keep it simple,' Joe told me. 'When you get the ball pass it to someone who can play.'

I could have done with a bit more guidance than that, but Denis was playing centre half and that reassured me.

'I can see it all in front of me, Gerry. I'll give you a shout. Tell you who's on for a pass.'

Everton had a couple of Scottish lads playing in midfield who fancied themselves as hard nuts. One of them was only a few years older than me but a lot bigger. I wasn't so worried about him but the other one, Andy Murdoch, was in his thirties and had a reputation for leaving his foot in. Sure enough, about ten minutes into the game, I tackled him and won the ball. I looked up for who to pass to but the next moment I felt his studs rake down the back of my leg as he sliced into me from behind.

He grinned as he jogged back to the centre circle.

'Stay out of ma way, son, or I'll break your fucking leg.'

Denis ran over to me. I thought he was going to give me a hand, but he leaned down and screamed at me.

'Get your bloody self up. Don't show him you're hurt.'

I hobbled around for a bit, the game passing me by while I ran off the pain. Murdoch was bossing things in midfield, calling for the ball, moving it out quickly to the wingers or surging forward himself. I knew I had to get stuck into him again but I couldn't seem to get near enough.

I felt a sharp push in my back. It was Denis.

'Next time that bastard runs at you let him go past but shift him to my side.'

Murdoch was confident now that I wasn't going to take him on. He pushed the ball past me, and I could have blocked him off, but I just kept alongside him and stopped him going wide, moving him back into the middle where Denis was waiting for him. He smashed into him like a steam train and Murdoch was thrown into the air and started rolling on the ground, clutching his knee.

There were no substitutes in them days and the only remedy the trainers had was the "magic sponge" – the magic being that it was soaked in ice cold water. Murdoch got to his feet, but his knee was already swelling up and he limped through the rest of the game. He could still pass it alright but there was no way he could run with the ball.

After that, it was me running past him and ten minutes from the end I put Brian Hapgood through on goal for the winner.

Joe Turner slapped me on the back when we came off and I thought I'd made it. But it was Denis who got me through the game, and I never forgot that.

As it happens, I was dropped for the next match, but Bob Ashworth didn't play many more games that season and by the end I felt I'd made the position mine and it was him that would have to win it back off me.

It didn't come to that though. Over the summer Bob was diagnosed with lung cancer and he were dead by Christmas. Must have been growing for some time before they found it.

You need a bit of luck in this game.

FIFTEEN

It is that blessed time in a pub before the evening really starts. The bar has a feeling of lightness and an air of expectancy. Later, there will be more people, more noise, spilled drinks, urgent chatter, voices raised to combat the background music and raucous laughter that is a little too forced. But not yet. Not yet. This is the serene interlude for early, solitary drinkers before the compulsive socialisers and the loudmouths make their entrance. They don't exactly spoil a pub but they change it, drowning out and obscuring what can only be enjoyed now. The hissing of the beer taps as glasses are topped up; the way the late sunshine radiates through the windows, hanging like drifting dust, spawning pools of light in the dimly lit saloon; the murmur of voices held low as if they are in a library or a church.

The Cotton Tree is one of those pubs that has a double life. At this stage in proceedings it's an old-fashioned boozer for those who don't like loud music, still read newspapers, will speak if they're spoken to but otherwise not bother and who don't see any point in sharing a drink with their wife or girlfriend – if they have one. Older men of a certain type. Not the ones who are clinging onto youth by furious diet and exercise and still getting away with skinny jeans and designer trainers. This is the refuge for those who are resigned to old age, who are ready to embrace it as a kind of release from the need to justify their lives because now they're nearly over and nobody expects much of them any more. No one bothers or questions them here or suggests they could be doing something better with their time. This is what acceptance feels like. When the sun fades, the lights will brighten slowly and the music will start to crank up, gently at first but building to a thumping barrage soon enough. Then it will be time for these customers to slip away and make way for the next shift.

Taylor settles himself by a small oak table in the corner where he has a good view of the front door and the bar and looks at the full glass in front of him, glowing golden in the evening sun. That first pint is always the best, he thinks; shaving the top off your thirst as you take a deep swallow and savour the smooth, almost silky sensation as it slides down so easily into your gut. And you aren't too full yet so there is no strain, none of the uncomfortable bloating that will come later. You taste the flavour fully and run it round your mouth a little rather than just knocking it back, and it lingers like a comforting thought at the end of a hard day. And you take a second sip, not quite as greedy this time because you've broken the fast now, and you notice, even then, so early in the evening, that it's not quite as good as the first. But it's alright. If you come back tomorrow it will be waiting for you again. And it's still peaceful, so you want to hang on to that good feeling for as long as you can.

There is only one woman in the pub, Trish, behind the bar. She nods at Taylor as an elderly man with a prominent beer belly hobbles in, acknowledges a couple of the other regulars and sets himself with some difficulty on a stool. Taylor watches as the two of them chat while Trish is pulling him a pint. The man turns round to look at him, has another quick word with Trish and then slowly makes his way over to the corner table, settles himself on the banquette under the window and holds out his hand.

'Harry Lomax. You wanted a word?'

'It's about Gerry Bradshaw.'

'What about 'im?'

'I represent a local firm of solicitors – Curtis and Curtis?'

He hands over one of his cards. Harry reads it and looks back at Taylor as if he were a door-to-door salesman he was keen to get shut of.

'Matthew died not long ago, didn't he?'

'His daughter, Sarah, has taken over the firm.'

'Oh aye.'

Harry sucks the top off his beer leaving a foamy smudge on his upper lip that he wipes away with the back of his hand.

'I understand that you and Gerry are old friends, from your playing days?'

'Known 'im since I was a kid.'

'Well, we're trying to find him.'

Harry slurps an impressive draught of beer, emptying about half his glass.

'You could always go round 'is house. That might be one way.'

Taylor smiles warmly. Need to keep him onside. Can't afford to draw another blank.

'Yes, his wife is worried about him. Not been seen for a few days. That's why they called me in.'

'Not like Gerry.'

'No, that's what Mrs Bradshaw said. I don't suppose you know where he might be?'

Harry examines his fingernails in some detail.

'See, the thing is… I used to be the landlord 'ere. Got used to sizing people up pretty quick. Whether you can trust them or not. Spot if they're likely to cause trouble.'

Harry knocks back most of what's left in his glass and gives Taylor a disdainful look.

'Not from round 'ere, are yer?'

'Not originally, no. Born in Oldham.'

Harry pauses before draining the last of his beer.

'Nowt good ever came from Oldham.'

He rolls his empty glass in his hands as if he were warming a vintage cognac. Taylor decides not to rise to the bait.

'Nobody's perfect. Can I get you another?'

'Like to be sure who I'm drinking with.'

'Like I said, I'm a private investigator working for Mrs Bradshaw's solicitors.'

'I'll tell you what you are, son. You're a fucking debt collector. Can smell one a mile off.'

'No, no, no. Honestly. I'm trying to help.'

Harry is looking down his nose at Taylor as if he were some mess that had been trodden into the carpet.

'Look, you can ring the solicitor's and check. Jim Glassbrook? He's been there for years. Or Matthew's daughter?'

Harry gets up with some effort and grimaces as he walks stiffly back to his perch at the bar.

'We think that his life might be in danger.'

Harry pauses but does not turn round.

'I need to find him before they do.'

Harry wheels round slowly, gives Taylor the once over and then holds out his glass.

'Bitter.'

Taylor watches Harry from the bar as Trish refills their glasses. He's on his phone, standing by the window looking out at the moors. When he finishes the call Taylor's heart sinks as Harry moves towards the door, but he is only stretching his legs and is waiting for his pint when Taylor returns to their table, leaning over to one side, rubbing his hip.

'Waiting to get this replaced. Knee's gone as well.'

He raises his glass in a toast.

'Bloody football.'

They sip their beer in tribute.

'When I was the landlord, folk were always asking me what I remembered most about when I were playing. They want to go over matches they were at or get the gossip about other players. So, I told 'em what they want to hear. Good for business. But do you know what most sticks in my mind? Pain. You couldn't let on you were injured in them days or you'd be out the team and your pay would drop right down. So you'd get the trainer to give you an injection on the sly, get you through the next match and just hope it'd sort itself out.'

Taylor bides his time. Waits for Harry to come round to it.

'Then you get to be thirty-three, thirty-four and your body just won't do it any more. So you walk away. Limp away in my case. And these days getting out of bed in the morning is like a full training session. Knees popping like firecrackers, clicking joints back into place, unlocking my back...'

Harry glances up at Taylor who is listening patiently. Just checking. He's after sympathy but doesn't want pity. Reassured, he takes another drink.

'Spoke to Jim. He vouches for you.'

The slightest of nods from Taylor. A tall man with a full head of snow-white hair stops by and places his hand on Harry's shoulder. They exchange pleasantries ('Awright?' 'Not so bad.' 'Liz OK?' 'She's fine.' 'See you later.' 'Right.') and the man continues his rounds, stopping off at the other tables, getting a few amiable grunts from the rest of the drinkers but not lingering long enough to disturb the equilibrium, and finally ending up at the bar. Harry watches for a while and then turns back to Taylor.

'Who's they?'

'Sorry?'

'You said they were after Gerry.'

'We don't know.'

'Not much of a detective, are yer? What do you know?'

Oh, to hell with it, thinks Taylor. I've got to take something back to the Elephant Man.

'He left his house a few days ago after a threatening phone call. His wife is frantic but says she doesn't know what it's about. So, I'm contacting his old pals to see if they can throw any light on what's going on. But no one seems to have seen him for a while.'

'If Eileen's that worried, why hasn't she called the police?'

Taylor shuffles in his seat and looks as if he is suffering from indigestion.

'I'm sure she has her reasons.'

'They do alright, don't they, 'im and Eileen? Bought a new house not long ago. And he runs a Mercedes. 'Ow do yer think he manages that on a pension?'

'I'm not sure. I… err… didn't know about the… err…'

'You're sure you're a detective, are yer? Who've you spoken to so far?'

Taylor explains about Denis and Ronnie.

'Wasting yer time there, son. You'd have been better off talking to Don Bradley.'

'Was he another footballer?'

'He were on t'books for a while but never made it. Bright bloke, though. Went to college. Became an accountant.'

Oh shit, thinks Taylor. Why didn't I think of that? What does Deep Throat say in *All the President's Men*? Follow the money.

'Was he Gerry's accountant?'

'There you are. Got there in the end.'

'Do you know where I can find him?'

'Overdale.'

'Near the crematorium?'

'In the garden of remembrance. Someone shot him while he were doing his roses. Looks like you've got a real case on yer hands, Sherlock.'

SIXTEEN

'League Cup tie, September 1967. Bolton 3 Liverpool 2.'

Sarah slaps the match programme on the desk in front of Jim who is snacking on some raw beetroot. Full of vitamin C he's been led to believe. He wipes his mouth with his handkerchief, leaving a bloody smear behind, and picks the programme up.

'Oh aye. First time they'd beaten 'em for years. Whole town was in raptures.'

'Dad's favourite match. He used to go over it in detail when he'd had a few.'

Jim flicks through a few pages and hands it back to Sarah.

'Hmm. Seem to remember they lost the next round three-nil. Been having a clear out?'

'I remembered what Dad told me about the match. Said that Gerry Bradshaw ran the game in midfield. Best game he ever had for the Wanderers.'

Jim leans back in his chair. She has that look on her face. Like when she was a little girl and stole one of the lollipops they kept on reception for customers. Sarah has a secret sweet. All he has to do is to wait. She is bursting to show him.

'I was sitting in his study, and it came to me. All those football programmes. Hundreds of them.'

She brandishes an envelope like a conjuror giving the big reveal.

'That's where he'd stashed Gerry's instructions.'

Now she has his attention. There is that flicker in his eyes.

'What does it say?'

Sarah hands him the typewritten letter. Jim reads it through carefully. Sarah notices that his lips move slightly as he picks out the content.

April 2017

Dear Matthew,

If you have opened this letter, then I must be dead or missing. Whichever it is, Eileen is going to need your help.

We agreed that it was best you didn't know too much about my financial affairs, but I've been putting some money aside for a rainy day, just in case.

Only I've had to keep it where no one could find it, if you know what I mean.

Get in touch with Don. He knows how to access my account and get the money to Eileen safely.

Tell her to be careful. Best not to splash out. Might be a good idea to start again in a new area.

And tell her I'm sorry. I was hoping it wouldn't come to this.

Thanks. You're a pal.

Gerry

Jim turns the letter over hoping there would be more on the other side.

'Nothing else?'

'I went through the other programmes but that's all. Do you know who Don is?'

Jim shakes his head, belches discreetly and studies the letter again.

'Whatever's happened, he saw it coming a long time ago.'

'Looks like Eileen's been telling the truth. It's pretty obvious that he's involved in something illegal. And this Don character is in on it.'

Jim hands the letter back.

'Probably a tax fraud. That's the main reason someone hides their money.'

'OK – but the Inland Revenue don't usually threaten to torch your house. Not at first, anyway.'

'Point taken.'

'So who are these people? And what made Gerry decide it was time to go underground?'

Sarah starts to pace around the room. She'd been on a management development course last year and a video had shown different models of leadership in action. The one that stuck in her mind was where the boss (a man in the film, irritatingly) inspired his team by energy and ideas, throwing them in all directions for others to pick up and nurture. The idea appealed to her but there was a downside (she couldn't remember exactly what) and so she'd decided not to try this at work – given that she was not actually a boss. But here, in her own firm? Why not?

The man in the film had done a lot of gesticulating to hammer home his points. We'll have a bit of that as well, she thought.

'So where are we?

Gerry starts getting phone calls a few weeks ago but the one last week spooks him so much he pops out for a pint of milk and doesn't come back.

Eileen doesn't know what the calls are about...'

Jim interrupts, dangling a piece of beetroot tantalisingly close to his mouth.

'Says she doesn't know what they're about...'

Sarah sweeps round on another circuit of the office.

'Alright, but she gets another call threatening to reduce her dream house to ashes if she doesn't produce Gerry...'

Jim again, his mouth half full and his lips now a worrying shade of crimson.

'Says she got a threatening call...'

'Yes, alright Jim. You're interrupting my flow.

She remembers that Gerry told her to go and see Dad if anything ever happened to him, so she comes round to us in a state.'

She sees Jim raise his hand slightly as a prelude to another intervention but shuts him down and motors on.

'We now have corroboration of her statement in the form of Gerry's letter to Dad.

The letter also tells us that Gerry has been salting money away in a secret account – almost certainly crooked earnings – and working some sort of scam with this guy, Don.'

Jim makes another attempt to butt in but Sarah drowns him out by turning up her volume control.

'THEREFORE, we can presume that whoever is after Gerry are likely to be associates in his illegal activity after a bigger share OR the victims of whatever scam he's been pulling – and they aren't the kind of people who resolve their grievances by a nice, civilised law suit.

And the reason they want their hands on Gerry is to get the money that's in this account.

So, if we can find out who Don is, and where Don is, we'll find out what this is all about and probably find Gerry as well.'

Sarah thrusts her hands on to her hips and stands triumphant.

'Questions? Comments?'

At this point in the video the assembled staff look on in awe at their charismatic boss and start firing off brilliant ideas inspired by his intellectual tour de force. Sarah looks over expectantly at Jim, but his head has disappeared. All she can see are his shoulders and back. He seems to be rummaging through the drawers in his desk. She calls his name a couple of times and he surfaces at last.

'Sorry. Thought I had a bit of yeast in here somewhere.'

'Well… what do you think? Do you agree with my analysis?'

Jim pulls his waistcoat back into place, pushes the remnants of beetroot to one side and sits up straight in his chair.

'I take your point that the letter appears to back up Eileen's version of events.'

Sarah isn't having that.

'Appears to…!'

Jim raises his hand imperiously as if he were stopping the flow of traffic.

'Please, Sarah, you're disrupting my train of thought.

Let's assume that Gerry has been up to something lucrative and illegal.

My best guess is that it's some kind of investment fraud – duping people into handing over their money in the hope of quick return that turns out to be an illusion. That would explain how Gerry and Eileen came by that new house of theirs.

Gerry would've left school at fifteen so I think it's unlikely he was the brains behind any financial fraud. That must be where this Don comes in.

Why did he flee? Perhaps he was worried that he was going to be found out and arrested? I think there's a strong possibility he's disappeared with all the proceeds and is trying to throw Eileen off the scent, leaving her to carry the can.'

Sarah sits down again to process Jim's version of events.

'What about the threatening phone calls?'

Jim is calmly sorting out the pens and pencils on his desk back into the right order.

'Could have been anybody on the line. Could have been his friend Don.'

'But why did Gerry tell Eileen to come and see Dad if he was in trouble? Why send her to us so she can get help?'

Jim feels he has the upper hand now and has difficulty suppressing a smug grin.

'That was Plan A in the event of the investors catching up with him and wanting their money back. I reckon this is Plan B – make a clean break and say bye bye to Eileen. Gerry was at your father's funeral. He probably thought Eileen would draw a blank if she came here now.'

Sarah is quiet now, her role as fantasy boss over for the time being. She is thinking about Gerry's letter and Jim's idea of Plan A.

'Do you think Dad knew?'

'Knew what?'

'He must have done, mustn't he? He'd have known that Gerry couldn't afford to buy that house without some shady dealing. And he knew about Don. And Gerry says he didn't want to know any details so that means he knew something illegal was going on and he...'

Sarah breaks off and takes a deep breath. Jim leaves his desk and sits next to her on the small sofa set aside for informal chats with clients.

'We're just speculating. We don't know anything really. But I did know your father. And he wouldn't have gone along with any crime.'

'I've got to get to the bottom of this, Jim.'

'Yes. I know.'

'We need to find this Don bloke.'

'And interview Eileen again. She knows more than she's letting on.'

Sarah is calmer now. She nods her head.

'Any word from Taylor?'

Jim purses his lips.

'Not a sausage. He's due in this afternoon for his daily report, but I wouldn't hold your breath if I was you. Odds on he's given up and pocketed the fee.'

'Up to us then. We need to talk to Eileen again. You've always said she was lying to us.'

'Not necessarily lying. Just not telling the whole truth.'

'Right. Get your coat. My car's outside.'

'I don't think we should draw attention to the house. Probably not even a good idea to bring her back here. We should wait. Find a different location.'

'Suit yourself.'

Sarah bounces up off the sofa and heads for the door.

'I'll let you know how I get on.'

The sun had been struggling to break through thick cloud all day, leaving the town shuddering in a stiff breeze, but now, as evening has almost arrived, it finally wins the battle and Sarah feels a pleasant glow as she steps out into the street. Better late than never, she thinks, and crosses to her car. The shops are closed and the nightlife is beginning to take over. A few hard-bitten smokers have been drinking outside the pub opposite and their bad habits are rewarded by some late sunshine. She can hear them chuckling at their good fortune.

As she is about to slot her car key into the lock two men in balaclavas suddenly appear from a nearby alleyway and crowd in either side of her. One shoves a gloved hand over her mouth and the other grabs her wrist.

'Make a noise and I'll break your fucking arm.'

The one with his hand over her mouth reaches into his pocket and shows her the knife.

'Now you can either bleed to death here or you can come quietly with us.'

They pull her away from the car and start to shove her towards the alleyway. Sarah's arm is now up her back and it feels as if they are going to wrench it from its socket. The pain is excruciating but she forces herself not to cry out. The men are tight to her sides so she can't wrestle free and she feels the panic take over as she realises there is nothing she can do.

They are almost in the alley when a drunk staggers out and confronts them. A shabby figure, half bent over doing up his flies and clutching a wilted roll-up. He brightens as he sees Sarah and the men heading for him and forces himself upright.

''Ey up, lads! Got a light?'

The men hesitate, unsure what to do.

'Out the fucking way!'

'Alright, alright, pal. Just asking. What about the lady? Have you got a light, love?'

The man on Sarah's right slips his hand down from her mouth moves in on the drunk and shoves him up against the wall.

'I said move.'

The drunk is stunned at first but then rages back, screaming at the top of his voice.

'Hey, hey. Get yer 'ands off me, yer bastard. Who the fuck do you think you're shoving?'

There is a murmur of interest now from the smokers outside the pub. Their luck's in. First a bit of sunshine and now a punch-up. Some of them start to wander over for a closer look.

The man still holding Sarah spots the drinkers heading their way and pulls on the shoulder of the one who has the drunk pinned to the wall. He looks round and loosens his hold while they size up the situation.

The drunk lurches forward and throws his arms around Sarah's neck.

"Ow about a kiss, love?'

Sarah recoils at the stink of stale beer on his breath as he puts his mouth to her ear and whispers,

'When he lets go run for it back to the office.'

He rears back and starts bellowing.

'Hey – what's going on 'ere? What're you doing with this girl?'

It takes a moment for the smokers to realise what's happening but then they start running towards them. Sarah feels her arm go free as both her kidnappers leg it down the alleyway and into a black van at the far end. The rear doors slam shut behind them and the van screeches off, round the corner and out of sight.

The smokers are milling around, uncertain about what to do next. A broken conversation jangles round the group ('Is she alright?' 'What the fuck was that?' 'Did you see who it was?' 'Somebody should call t'police'). And while they are kicking this about, the drunk shepherds Sarah across the street and back into the safety of Curtis and Curtis.

She leans against the wall, head in her hands, relief cascading through her whole body. She is sobbing, her legs are shaking and she can hardly speak. So all she can manage when the drunk asks her if she is OK is,

'Thanks, Taylor.'

Seventeen

A sparkling new, metallic blue BMW with shaded windows is parked on the street near Matthew's house. It doesn't feel right for that neighbourhood where the vibe is more Range Rover, Volvo estate or Ford Galaxy people carrier. Too fast, too sharp, too pushy.

Taylor tells the taxi driver to go past the house and pull over. He and Jim had both decided to see Sarah back home safely and he'd spotted the car straightaway as they drew into the road. All three of them crane their heads back to get a better look.

'Do you recognise it, Sarah?'

She shakes her head.

Jim's face is even more hang dog than usual.

'Maybe you should go and stay at your mother's.'

'All my stuff is in there.'

'What do you think, Taylor?'

'Jim's right. Best not to take a chance. They could easily have followed you home one time.'

He is about to tell the taxi driver to move off when they see a window in the BMW go down. Whoever is in the car is checking them out. Within seconds the door flings open and a tall, athletic-looking black man steps out, raises his arm and starts sprinting towards the taxi. Taylor yells,

'Go. Go now!'

The taxi driver panics and stalls the car as he turns on the ignition. There is a whirring, screaming noise as the engine tries to fire up. They can see the man clearly now, only a few yards away and shouting out Sarah's name.

Taylor realises there is nothing else for it but to try and tackle him although he is built like a rugby forward and looks as if he could tear the car door off with his bare hands.

'For fuck's sake!'

He starts to open the door as Sarah shouts out.

'Oh my God! It's Marcus.'

*

They have a hard job persuading Jim and Taylor to go home. A combination of Jim seeing himself as some sort of guardian now that Sarah's father is dead and Taylor enjoying his new role of knight in shining armour means they are both reluctant to leave her with a stranger.

'We'll be fine,' she assures them.

Marcus can see they aren't at ease. It's a look he is accustomed to, but he tells himself that all three of them are probably in shock so best not to jump to conclusions.

'I'll look after her now.'

After they have been put into the taxi Marcus raids the drinks cabinet for a couple of large brandies and pulls Sarah's head onto his shoulder as they sit back on the settee. They stay like that for a minute or two. He tries to match his breathing to Sarah's, tuning himself back into the rhythms of her body, feeling his chest fall and rise in time with hers. And then Sarah raises her head, smiles, pecks him on the cheek and shuffles away slightly into her own space.

'You should have called.'

'Hmm. Not had much success in getting hold of you, have I?'

'It's all been a bit mental the last couple of days.'

'I'm not having a go, I'm just saying.'

He slides his hand over to hers and gives it a gentle squeeze.

'I was worried about you.'

She pats his hand.

'I know.'

'So I thought, fuck it. Got the train to Manchester and picked up a hire car.'

She nods her head slightly in acknowledgement but then inclines her face away and rubs her eyes.

'You're not sorry I came, are you?'

'No… 'course not. I'm glad you're here.'

She gives him a peck on the cheek and Marcus is relieved to find that this feels good and is enough. He takes a good look round the room.

'You never lived here then?'

'No, Dad bought this house after he left Mum. I stayed with her till I finished at uni.'

'It's like a set for one of them period dramas. You know, *Adventures of Sherlock Holmes* or something.'

'Dad preferred the past to the present. Easier to manage, isn't it?'

She shivers. Marcus rubs her shoulders.

'Do you want the heating on?'

'No, I think it's just… you know… it's all been a bit…'

The tears begin to trickle slowly down her face and then her breathing starts to come in jerky spasms until they break into a continuous flood of sobs and wails.

'Oh God, oh God! I don't… Oh my god!'

He holds her until the heaving subsides and she is quiet and can be led upstairs and helped into bed. He lies by her side in the night, unsure whether to hold her, not wanting the intimacy to be misunderstood, until he hears her breathing evenly in sleep and knows that he can rest now as well.

Next morning they are both quiet. There is definitely an atmosphere, as if they'd had an argument the night before or one of them had been caught out doing something they shouldn't. Perhaps it's just that we've been apart for a couple of weeks, and we need to get used to each other again, thinks Sarah. But there is something else. She can tell by the way Marcus is continually stirring his coffee and staring intently at the tabletop. He is holding back, not saying what is on his mind. This is his way. She would rather get things out in the open even if it means a stand-up row. Clear the air and move on works best for her. But he prefers to let things simmer but when they do come to the boil it's much worse and harder to pretend it never happened.

He's still paying too much attention to his coffee when he asks, 'What actually happened yesterday?'

She tells him about Gerry's disappearance; the threats to Eileen; finding the letter and then the attack; who Taylor is and how he saved her. Marcus rubs his hand over his face as if trying to wipe it clean.

'But you're going to drop this now? Hand it over to the police?'

'It's not that simple.'

'Someone tried to kidnap you in broad daylight. If that's not a matter for the cops, then what is?'

'Eileen is frightened that if she involves them, they'll kill her and Gerry.'

'And what are you and the Chuckle Brothers going to do to stop that?'

'I said I'd help her.'

'You didn't even know her until a couple of days ago.'

'Dad was their friend. They trusted him and so she came to me and… I… I can't just…'

Marcus looks if he's swallowed something unpleasant and can't get the taste out of his mouth. Lips tightened, eyes screwed up.

'Baby. Can I ask you something? What the fuck are you doing?'

Sarah recoils. It's as if he'd slapped her in the face. She tries to splutter something in reply but nothing coherent comes out.

Marcus puts out his hand across the breakfast table, but she draws hers away and stares at him in confusion.

'Sorry. That didn't come out right, but you know what I mean.'

Sarah is starting to recover herself, the initial shock shifting into anger.

'No, I don't.'

'Getting involved in all this. You could have been killed or tortured or God knows what. Why put yourself in danger like that?'

'We didn't know what it was really about until yesterday.'

'You just told me they threatened to burn that woman's house down.'

'Yeah, but we didn't know that was true. She could have been making it up.'

'You're in over your head. You know that.'

'I thought you'd come here to support me.'

'I have. I'm only thinking of you.'

'I can look after myself.'

Marcus shoots her a quizzical look.

'Look, I know you can… usually. But these guys are dangerous. Professionals. And you can't rely on that Taylor bloke to protect you. One punch and he's gone.'

'He saved my life yesterday.'

'He got lucky. Listen. I love you but this has got to stop. Promise me that you'll give this up.'

'Don't tell me what to do.'

'You're not thinking straight. Your dad's only just died and… and your… err… emotions are…'

He falters as he sees that Sarah's face has frozen. She's sucking in her cheeks and her nostrils are slightly flared. He's seen that look before. Don't push me too far.

'I'm scared, Sarah. Scared something's going to happen to you.'

Her face softens slightly.

'Yeah. Me too.'

He stretches out his hand to hers and this time she does not pull away.

'Will you think about what I've said?'

She squeezes his hand.

'How long can you stay?'

'I can work from here for a couple of days. I'm supposed to be in Guildford on Thursday – been some problems on site – but I can put that off if you...'

'No. It's fine. I can do this.'

She starts to clear the plates and cups from the table.

'I need to go in and see the others. Talk it through. You're right, I know, but... don't look so worried!'

Marcus gives her a huge grin in response, like a child asked to smile for the camera.

'OK. That looks a bit mad, but it'll do.'

As she turns to put the breakfast things in the sink his face drops again and he feels that weight he used to get in his stomach when he set off to school, running the gauntlet of the local estate: knowing there was something bad waiting up ahead and not being able to avoid it.

EIGHTEEN

Taylor has slept well. Eddie's couch was as lumpy and unyielding as before but after rescuing Sarah he was feeling good about himself for the first time in a long time. He hadn't even needed a drink to take the edge off. The sleep of the just. Nothing like it. And when he wakes he finds a rare day of summer waiting for him. For once, the low clouds that always seem to sag over the town have evaporated leaving a sky so bright it hurts his eyes to look at it.

On top of that, he is relatively solvent. Jim had handed over his bonus without any debate and thrown in another fifty pounds. He could see the relief in the old man's face when he brought Sarah back into the office and explained what had happened. There was no bluster and no sign of that air of weary contempt he'd shown after the interview. Jim had fussed over Sarah like an indulgent grandad, putting his jacket round her, organising a cup of tea, making reassuring noises and even treating Taylor to a reluctant smile which he took to mean, "I didn't think you had it in you but well done all the same".

They'd all agreed to meet at eleven the next morning – give Sarah a lie-in – and take stock of where they were. As it is such a glorious morning, Taylor decides to walk into town. The fresh air and exercise would do him good but also give him the chance to spot some more car number plates on the way in.

There is a definite spring in his step and perhaps even a song in his heart. Today feels like the start of a musical, one of those uplifting, show stopping overture numbers that gets the juices flowing and the feet tapping. What would fit best? Not the opening sequence of *West Side Story* – he can't see himself soaring into the Bolton skyline like Russ Tamblyn. How about the one from *La La Land* where all the motorists get out of their cars to celebrate another day of sun? Too smoggy – he can taste the petrol fumes. No, even though Bolton bears little resemblance to the rolling plains of America, today feels like the opening of *Oklahoma!* The corn may not be as high as an elephant's eye, but it is a beautiful morning.

He gets there early and finds Jim waiting for him in his office. The warm, self-satisfied glow starts to fade as soon as he sees the look on Jim's face. The sourness and suspicion have returned.

'Sarah will join us in a while. She's been delayed. Give us a chance to talk.'

This is not what Taylor had in mind. He was hoping for a little spot of back-slapping from Jim while Sarah looked on, her heart too full of gratitude to speak, a tear welling in her eye. But Jim's expression reminds him of his old headmaster who would summon guilty boys to his study and confront them with silence and a pitiless stare that told them, "I know what you have done".

Taylor can see that his day in the sun is going to be very short-lived as Jim starts to set out his case.

'Thought I'd ring a mate of mine in the police given what happened last night.'

'Oh, yes?'

Keep it light. He may just be fishing.

'Seems that somebody did ring it in but by the time they got there everybody from the pub had buggered off and they couldn't get any further, so they've put it down as a prank call.'

'What did you say?'

'You heard Sarah. Didn't want to report it. 'Course she might have changed her mind – we'll see when she gets here – so I told him we'd heard some commotion but didn't see anything.'

Move it away from the police. Shift the attention. It might work.

'She's probably still in shock. Now she's had a chance to think about what might have happened – that's when it really hits you.'

'We'll see. Now then…'

No. He's not buying it.

'While I was on the phone, I mentioned you. Said you were helping us out with some enquiries. Didn't recognise your name so I described you and then it came back to him.'

This is the point at which his headmaster would have expected the victim to own up to their crime and seek penitence, but the spirit is oozing out of Taylor, and he remains silent.

'"Oh," he said. "That scruffy git. The one who edited the staff magazine".'

It is supposed to be a relief when the truth comes out, a sense of a weight being lifted off the shoulders, confession being good for the soul. But Taylor feels none of that. Only a sick feeling in the stomach and an overwhelming desire to run and hide in the toilet.

'He remembered a few other things about you. Waste of space, he said. Pissed every lunchtime. Never at your desk when you were wanted. Always had a firm grip of the wrong end of the stick.'

Taylor plonks himself down in a chair and puffs out his cheeks. As they say in the comics – it's a fair cop.

'I never actually said I was a police officer. Just with the police.'

Jim obviously feels that this is not worthy of a reply and continues to regard Taylor with disgust.

'OK. I realise that you were likely to think that.'

More silence from Jim. Taylor wriggles with discomfort, a tiddler thrashing about on the line. He rubs his hands along his thighs to stop his legs from jiggling with nerves.

'But isn't it all about results? What about last night?'

Jim appears not to be paying full attention and Taylor thinks he can hear some gurgling noises from across the table. Jim presses his hand to his stomach but can't shift the trapped wind. He arches his back, raises himself slightly in the chair and there is a loud, prolonged, stuttering escape of gas from below as a massive fart of relief finally comes. Some of the tension leaves Jim's face but none of the contempt.

'Better?' asks Taylor.

'We're not a high-flying law firm. Couldn't say that anyone here is bursting with brains. But we do expect one thing from those that work for us. Can you tell me what that is?'

Jim pauses for dramatic effect. Taylor is now firmly back in the skin of his fourteen-year-old self. In those days he would be looking at detention and a revocation of whatever privileges he was supposed to have. This looks like the sack.

'Honesty?'

'That would be nice, but you have to be realistic about inquiry agents. No, I was setting the bar a bit lower.'

Taylor feels unbearably weary. This is not going to stop until I say it, he thinks.

'The truth?'

'Did Matthew know you'd never been a copper?'

'Not sure. He never made a big point of it.'

Now that Jim has cleared out that wind he is feeling a bit peckish so he pulls out a small box of crackers from his desk drawer and breaks into one. The crumbs tumble from his lips and settle on his waistcoat like dandruff.

'Alright, Jim. I get the picture.'

He reaches across the table to shake Jim's hand.

'All the best anyway.'

Jim does not take his hand and Taylor thinks he can see a sly smile being smothered, a brightness in the eyes.

'You don't want my report then?'

'Send me an email. I presume there won't be much in it.'

'You might be surprised. I think I know who was behind whatever Gerry was up to.'

He is almost out the door when Jim calls to him.

'Alright, let's hear it.'

Taylor turns to see Jim crunching on another cracker but there is no mistaking his suppressed eagerness. Taylor has come up trumps once, perhaps he can do it again.

'So… are we…?'

'We've paid for this so let's have it.'

'Please would be nice.'

'Have you actually managed to find out anything?'

This could be Jim's idea of fun, seeing Taylor squirm for a bit longer, but maybe all is not lost. Perhaps he can pull this back, so he fills him in on the meetings with Gerry's old teammates. Jim takes a few notes and grunts along the way to show he is paying attention. Not that he seems very impressed.

'Anything else?'

'Anything else? Harry Lomax has given us a good steer about this Don Bradley bloke. You know what they say. Follow the money.'

Taylor can see Jim is a little distracted, as if he is flicking through the files in his head, placing the information in the right place, waiting for the connections to be made. But he doesn't want to give much away to Taylor. He's not putting him back on the team yet.

'Your brief was to find Gerry Bradshaw. Remember?'

'None of his Bolton mates have heard from him. I could try the ones who live further away. Ring them, maybe?'

'Time's running out. They're getting desperate or they wouldn't have tried to snatch Sarah. I don't suppose you've had any luck in finding Gerry's car.'

'I've been keeping my eyes open.'

Jim stops in the middle of scribbling something in his notebook.

'Hang on a minute. If you don't have any live contacts with the police, how are you doing that?'

Taylor realises that he now looks exactly like that boy who had desecrated the cricket pitch at school after he'd been told he was too crap to be allowed to practise on the wicket. Found out again in his sin.

'Well… you know… I thought I might… errm… you know… see it on my travels.'

'Sorry, your plan for finding Gerry's car was to drive round Bolton until you spotted it parked up somewhere?'

'Err… I don't have a car at the moment… but I have been on the bus a lot and you get a good view…'

Jim starts to shake. At first Taylor thinks it's the start of a stroke and tries to remember what the rhythm is for giving mouth to mouth resuscitation. It's to the tune of "Staying Alive" isn't it, he thinks? Or is it "Waterloo"? But before this is put to the test, little snorts start to pop out of Jim's nose, and these give way to wheezes that in turn become chortles until his whole body is pulsating with laughter.

Taylor has only two choices. Turn on his heels and leave with what little dignity remains or sit there while Jim creases up. He needs the money and has been feeling useful since last night, so all that is in favour of sucking this up. But if Jim keeps on milking this, he might forget which side his bread is buttered.

Jim is giving it the full music-hall treatment, dabbing his eyes with a rather grubby looking hankie, and occasionally pointing at Taylor in delight. Just as he feels he can't endure it any longer, that even his humiliation threshold has been breached, Jim starts to calm down, his shoulders cease to shake and the guffaws subside into gleeful sighs.

'You… you may be the worst detective in the world but you're bloody good entertainment value.'

'Thanks. Remind me to get you to put that in a reference.'

'So, last night, you were hanging round town doing a bit of car spotting?'

'Well, yeah… I mean errm… I was going to come in and give my report but then I saw those guys get out of the van and there was something about them. So, I decided to hang around.'

Jim straightens up when he hears this.

'You saw the van? Did you get the number?'

The sick look on Taylor's face says it all. Jim flings himself backward in his swivel chair and lets out a growl.

'For fuck's sake...'

At which point Sarah scurries in, looking a bit flustered, pushing her hair back over her ears. She pulls up short by the door.

'You two fighting again already?'

Taylor is looking distinctly shifty, and Jim looks like a kettle coming to the boil.

'The Boy Blunder here has just been giving me his report. He saw the van those men got away in but didn't get the bloody registration number. You couldn't make it up!'

Jim is spitting crumbs across his desk in his haste to bring the guilty verdict in.

'And another thing. He's never been a copper. He was a civilian, working on their press releases.'

And now the coup de grâce, each word given due space as he spells it out.

'He lied to us.'

Sarah is standing behind Taylor, so he can't see her face and how she is taking this. Just when he was starting to get his life back together or at least collecting up some of the pieces. Stupid. If he'd been thinking straight, he'd have got the number while he was watching those blokes. As soon as he saw them, he knew they were trouble. Both wearing black woolly hats that hid their hair and exaggerated the whiteness of their faces. Both looking purposeful, unlike the loungers outside the pub, and yet hanging about, waiting. Then Sarah stepped out of the office, and he could see them come to life, stepping back into the alleyway, just out of sight. He had to think quickly. He couldn't take them on physically, they'd have trampled over him and kicked his head in for good measure. So he had to play it smart, use his brains. And it worked. He'd saved her. There wasn't time to get the number as well... was there?

Jim is looking past him, expectantly, at Sarah and he can hear her breathing, absorbing what she'd been told. Finally, she says,

'OK but that doesn't change the fact that I wouldn't be here now if it weren't for him.'

She takes a seat next to Taylor.

'What else?'

Jim is stunned. He's not just out of his comfort zone, he's lost track of it altogether. Each day since Sarah arrived has taken him further away from all the lessons he'd learned alongside Matthew. Stick to the facts, don't speculate. Proceed as quickly as you can but as slowly as you must. Savour the detail, that's where the treasure is to be found. Trust only those you know to be truthful and keep a beady eye on the rest.

'You're not proposing to keep him on? Not after this.'

Sarah does not reply but turns to Taylor.

'Any news on where Gerry might be hiding?'

Jim is not giving up and for a very good reason. This is crazy.

'Sarah… you're not thinking straight.'

'Wow. It's not even lunchtime and you're the second person to say that to me.'

Back to Taylor.

'Well? Anything?'

'No one's seen him, but Harry Lomax mentioned an accountant who was shot dead in his own home a couple of months ago. Police have been treating it as an armed robbery that went wrong. Seems the house was stuffed full of valuable antiques.'

'What's the connection with Gerry?'

'He was on Bolton's books as a player before he packed it in and retrained. Seems he was a close friend of Gerry's and handled his financial affairs. Name of Bradley. Don Bradley.'

'Don! That's the name in the letter Gerry left with Dad.'

Jim puts his arm out towards Sarah, the palm of his hand raised in warning but too late to stop Taylor coming back to life again.

'What letter?'

Sarah hesitates, confronted by Jim's glare. He takes the opportunity to jump in.

'Sarah and I need to consider our next move. What's in Eileen's best interests. You can leave it to us now.'

None of them moves. In the silence they can hear a forty-a-day man coughing his guts up as he passes by outside. He leans against the office wall, and they can hear the tar bubbling in his windpipe as he tries to get his breath, a death rattle if there ever was one. With a final heave he clears it and stumps off and out of their hearing. And now they are back in the room waiting for someone to make the next move.

Taylor knows they expect him to get up sheepishly and slip away without causing any further embarrassment. Disappear. Get lost. What he usually does. But he remembers what it felt like to get up this morning and have a reason to get washed, get dressed and get going. He's not giving that up without a struggle.

'Is that what you want, Sarah?'

She is thinking of Marcus, who is back at the house, pretending to work but worrying what might happen to her today. Will those men be watching her, waiting for another chance? And her mother, still trying to come to terms with the reason she now lives a solitary existence and no longer able to ask the only person who could have told her why. And what is it that she wants?

'I don't know.'

Jim is only just holding it together. He likes Sarah, even though she is a nightmare to work for. There's a vitality and passion about her that he hadn't realised he was missing until she walked back into the office. He'd settled into a life where all the rough edges had been rubbed away, causes of friction minimised, no grit in the engine. And so each day was manageable. He'd needed that after Marion died. But the days had also become predictable. Counting out how many were left. Same old, same old. No variation. This last week he has been flying by the seat of his pants, and he's not sure he wants to stop.

But there is a line over which he cannot cross.

'How can you trust a liar?'

Taylor's mentor when he was a young journalist, Mr Naylor, had offered him advice about interviewing politicians. The clever ones, he said, will not answer any question that doesn't suit them. Instead, they'll point out that you should have asked a different question and then give you an answer to that instead. Of course, he added, that works both ways.

'I think the real issue is what we do next, Jim. We know that Gerry was enjoying a standard of living that should have been way beyond his means, but we don't know how. We need to interview Eileen again.'

'We?' asks Jim. Taylor presses on without acknowledging him.

'Odds are she knows more than she's letting on, because however they came by the extra cash it's almost certainly illegal. Which brings us to Don Bradley. Doesn't sound like the police have any active leads but you could put money on those guys who tried to snatch you being the same ones who murdered him. The question is why?'

He sees the fear flickering in Sarah's eyes, but he can't stop now.

'It's always about money or sex and this wasn't a crime of passion. My guess is that Don had some money that belonged to someone else, but they couldn't get it out of him, and they ran out of patience. Then they turned their attention to Gerry. He knew what had happened to Don so he legged it.'

Jim has let Taylor have his head and, he had to admit, that wasn't a bad summing up. However, he's damned if he's going to give any satisfaction to the deceitful little sod.

'Now you've told us what we already knew have you anything else to add before you leave?'

But he can see that he's not connecting with Sarah. Her face is more animated now as she juggles the facts in her head, sifting out what matters.

'So what are we saying? Jim and I thought that it could have been some kind of financial scam that had been rumbled and the investors were trying to get their money back. Presumably Don would have been the brains behind that.'

Now it is him and Sarah again, Taylor feels more at ease. He can feel that she isn't ready to give up yet, not with so many loose ends.

'OK – could be. But how would some small investors who'd lost their life savings club together to hire some hitmen? You can't just do a search on Check-a-Trader.'

Good point thinks Jim but he keeps that to himself. Taylor is up and running now.

'And what would Gerry be bringing to the party? Football was his whole life so far as we know, so why would Don need him?'

Even Jim is starting to get into the mood now, despite his best intentions.

'Alright. You have a better idea, do you?'

'Money laundering. Seems to be a very popular pastime. And lucrative. The downside being that the real owners of the money are exactly the kind of people who know where to find a contract killer.'

'That could be how Don Bradley came to a sticky end but where does a clapped-out wing half fit into it?'

'Not sure, but maybe someone else knew what was going on besides Eileen. Someone who was able to give valuable advice.'

Taylor turns to Sarah, who is rubbing the bridge of her nose as if she's trying to clear her head. He waits for her to say what he has been thinking since he heard about the letter.

'Dad, you mean.'

'Jim said they were close. Maybe he told your father more than he lets on in that letter.'

Jim is not having this. Some malodorous twerp having a swipe at Matthew.

'What the hell are you suggesting? That he was in on this?'

'I'm not saying he was involved but Gerry could have confided in him. Put him in a difficult position. Torn between his friendship and the law.'

Jim is revving himself up to come back at Taylor when Sarah says quietly,

'It's possible, Jim. We can't rule it out. But we won't get any further unless we can trace that bank account. And for that we need to find Gerry.'

The hesitancy starts to leave her as she speaks, a sequence of events now coming more clearly into view.

'Taylor. See if you can get hold of some more of Gerry's mates. He might have decided to go further afield. Jim, you and Kelly interview Eileen again. We all reckon she knows more than she's letting on. Best not mention that someone tried to kidnap me – she's frightened enough already.'

Jim can see that she's made her mind up. No point in arguing the toss for the sake of it.

'And what about you?'

'I'm going to do what I should have done at the start. Go and see the police.'

Nineteen

1963

I'd always been shy of girls and Mam wasn't exactly encouraging.

When I was a teenager, she'd say I hadn't time for courting. I needed to concentrate on my football and get myself in the team.

Then, when I got in the team, she changed her tune. Once a girl got to know I was a footballer then she'd be bound to try and trap me because, now the maximum wage had been abolished, I was on good money.

So I couldn't win either way.

Looking back, I can see Mam was scared of losing me but I was nearly twenty-one and in those days you got wed younger. Several of the lads had already settled down and you could tell from the smile on their face on Monday mornings that they were getting their share at the weekend.

I was starting to feel embarrassed about still living with my mother. There'd be plenty of banter about girls when the lads got together for a pint, but I had to pretend I knew what I was talking about. Truth is, I didn't know what a girl's body was really like and even if I had been lucky enough to get my hands under some lass's dress, I had no idea what I was supposed to do if I managed to get that far. I think the other lads knew I was covering up; they'd smile to each other and nod like they were old married men who had all the answers.

The club was sort of on my side, though. They reckoned that the sooner a player got married the better. Young lads with a bit of money in their pockets were bound to get into trouble. Once they had a wife to go home to – and probably some kids – they'd calm down and be out of temptation's way. That was the theory, anyway. The backroom staff were all middle-aged, brought up in a different world, and it took a while for the sixties sexual revolution to reach Bolton, so it didn't really cross their mind that you could have sex with a girl unless you were going to marry her.

The best place to meet girls was at the Palais. We weren't supposed to go out on Fridays but Saturday night, after the game, that was different. If we were at home, or hadn't that far to travel back, I'd meet Ernie and Frank, and Harry sometimes, and we'd have a few pints in town because they only had soft drinks at the Palais in them days. Then we'd stroll up to Bridge Street.

Trouble was, they were nearly as shy as me. Harry had something more about him but that weren't much help to me if he clicked with some girl and left me on my own. Most of the time we'd just be hanging around at the edge of the dance floor or on the balcony watching the dancers. I think we always hoped that somebody would recognise us and ask for our autographs and that would attract the girls. But I can't remember that ever happening. We were in the same boat as all the other lads stood there looking on.

They had a bakery at the Palais so you could get a cup of tea and something to eat. I was always starving after a match and as the beer wore off I'd nip down and get a pasty or summat. That's when I met her. She was serving behind the counter. I'd spotted her a few weeks before and there was something about her that stuck in my mind. Most people were a bit sweaty with dancing, even the girls, but she seemed above it all somehow, all neat in her little pinny and uniform. And her hair was nice. Blonde and curly and bouncing on her shoulder when she moved.

'You must have a worm,' she said to me one night as I ordered a pasty and piece of cake.

People were shouting all round me, so I wasn't sure what she'd said to me.

'You what?'

'You're always hungry.'

I nodded. This was my chance.

'I'm a footballer. Gives you an appetite.'

I was hoping this would spark some interest, but she didn't seem impressed. I found out later that she'd been asking about me and knew who I was but wasn't going to give me the satisfaction of letting me know that.

The queue was building up behind me and I could feel they were getting fed up waiting so I had to be quick. I knew the café closed at midnight.

''Ow about a dance when you've finished?'

And she gave me a little smile. Like she knew all along I was going to ask her.

Some bloke behind me gave me a shove.

'Come on, pal. We're gasping 'ere.'

The queue heaved and I had to move away down the counter towards the till. Her eyes were still on me.

'Eileen,' she called after me. 'My name's Eileen.'

Twenty

Sarah is lounging on a low-slung scarlet sofa in the glazed, sunlit atrium of an office block on the North Manchester Business Park. The design is what she takes to be typical of the Lego school of corporate architecture beloved of multinational information and communications technology equipment and services companies the world over.

From the outside there appears to be no substance to the building, an interlocking grid of enormous glass panes, some crystal bright, others sapphire blue, reflecting the sky and the manicured lawns that surround it but showing nothing of what lies within. The interior gives few clues. Plain white walls and grey driftwood flooring create a feeling of calm assurance without revealing any character or identity. From this perspective she could just as well be in Palo Alto, a bit of Silicon Valley parachuted into Newton Heath.

Step a few hundred yards from the park and the crammed red-brick terraces and the open spaces sprouting giant weeds where intended developments had never materialised alongside the six lanes of clogged traffic on the Oldham Road tell a different story. The broad, sunny uplands of opportunity have not trickled down that far, where life expectancy has stalled and is starting to drop back.

But this is not in evidence where Sarah is seated. This is where dreams can come true and problems can be solved. There is a productive hum around the place as the employees buzz about their duties and when she gazes upwards, she can see floor after floor hanging in the air above her, each teeming with its dedicated workers. Corporate logos are in evidence but discreetly so and more prominence is given to inspirational slogans from historical figures. Nelson Mandela, Martin Luther King, Gandhi, Confucius and so on. More bloody men, thinks Sarah. On the wall above her, in scarlet font, are the words:

A person who never made a mistake never tried anything new

Albert Einstein, apparently. Good job he was a physicist and not a heart surgeon, she thinks.

The receptionist signals to her and calls her over. Mr Timpson will see her now. Tenth floor. Someone will meet her at the lift. She must wear her visitor badge at all times. Sorry about the security, but you can't be too careful these days. After all, this is a police station.

Assistant Chief Constable Alec Timpson might be on his way out, but he isn't overly concerned. His time had come and gone. That's life. Nowadays the minimum requirement to get to the tenth floor is a degree (preferably in the social sciences although criminology was still acceptable) and an MBA (although that was now seen as a little passé and doctorates were preferable) – neither of which he possessed.

This made him a bit of an oddity. He'd come up through the ranks and served his time as a sergeant, then an inspector, on through superintendent and district commander, and finally to ACC. As the ceilings in this building seemed to be one of the few things not made of glass he knew when he was banging his head on one. This was as far as he was going.

Sometimes he wondered if the Chief Constable had promoted him as a kind of mascot, a nod of respect to the old ways of working. A traditional copper who could ground the technocratic high-flyers in the senior team by reminding them what the world outside the conference circuit was really like. This led to inevitable banter which he had decided to tolerate as the longer he hung on the better his pension would be. *Is that how they did it in the Bow Street Runners, Alec? What was Doctor Crippen actually like? Any new leads on Jack the Ripper?* Occasionally, he would demonstrate a detailed knowledge of police procedure that would create a gratifying if silent appreciation from his peers, but such little victories had become few and far between. His current, and final, portfolio was operational support, which mainly consisted of human relations, IT, press and public information, admin and estates management. A chance to take things a bit easier, the Chief Constable had told him, wind down a little.

Fair enough. He was tired. He had to admit that. Energy levels weren't quite the same as they used to be. And he was bored. Fed up. Angry. Yes, mostly angry. More than thirty years' experience in the field, working some of the toughest patches in the north-west, and now he had to feign interest in a spreadsheet setting out the benefit realisation targets for the new customer services interface. How the fuck had it come to this?

So, when he got the call from Sarah, he was only too glad to sidestep a meeting on water penetration issues at Wigan West Divisional Office and find a space in his schedule. He'd been stationed in Bolton for several years and come to know Matthew Curtis well. They'd had few professional connections but had been in the same lodge and always hit it off, even though Alec was a United fan, so he'd kept in touch as his career continued onwards and upwards. He had attended the funeral and was genuinely moved to leave his friend to slide down the conveyor belt and on to the furnace. Not many left like Matthew.

Sarah, he didn't really know. She'd only been a student when Mathew's marriage folded, and Alec had moved on to Manchester long before that. She hadn't wanted to say too much over the phone, but it seemed to be something to do with threats to one of

Matthew's clients. He ought to have told her just to phone it in like anyone else but... maybe it was something in the tone of her voice, a hint of panic underneath the otherwise assured pitch she'd made to see him. Maybe it was a favour to Matthew, something he could still do for an old friend. Maybe he thought it might be a bit of real police work for a change.

Whatever the reason, there she sits, balancing a cup of coffee on her lap and thanking him for seeing her at such short notice. Alec tries to locate the awkward, gangling kid who hung about on the edges of conversations when he used to visit Matthew, but she isn't really visible any more. In her place is, to be frank, a rather sexy woman in the prime of life smartly turned out in a two-piece suit and white blouse, designer handbag and painfully high-heeled shoes. Every inch the corporate lawyer which she had told him she now was.

Alec notes this without getting carried away. He's known several senior officers who had lost all sense of perspective when confronted by a pair of shapely legs in a short skirt. Some had even gone so far as to end up suspended or forced into early retirement – which meant it must have been pretty extreme or it would have been hushed up in the time-honoured fashion. But when your pension is within reach it isn't worthwhile taking silly risks for a quick grope. In any case, times had changed and as the father of two daughters himself he was happy about that. However, he makes a conscious effort to keep his attention on Sarah's face and not let it wander lower down. He's only flesh and blood, after all.

He commiserates about her loss, shares a few memories of her father, and then moves on to business.

'How can I help?'

'Can we treat this as a confidential conversation?'

Alec's antennae start twitching. It's always bad news when a lawyer wants something kept between just the two of them.

'Depends, doesn't it? If you've got some expired parking fines that need sorting, then perhaps. But I don't think you'd have come all this way just for that. So… No. We can't.'

'OK. Then I hope you'll bear with me if I don't mention any names.'

No more than five minutes have elapsed, but Alec is already regretting agreeing to this meeting. What the hell is she about to tell him?

'One of Matthew's old clients, you said?'

Sarah gives him the potted history but leaving out details she doesn't want to be questioned about – the possible link to the murder of Don Bradley; the attempt to kidnap her; shifting Eileen to a new address. She'd rehearsed this in the car on the way over and thought it sounded plausible, but she starts to get a sinking feeling as she sees Alec fiddling with his expensive fountain pen, seemingly unconvinced by what he's heard.

'What makes you think there's any real threat to this couple?'

'We've not heard any of the telephone calls, but they've put the fear of God into her. And her husband never returned home the day after one of the calls.'

'But is there any evidence that they'd carry out their threat? Have they actually done anything to suggest they would?'

'Well…'

'And wherever he is, these people, whoever they are – they haven't got him, have they?'

'No.'

'So you don't know he's in any danger. He might have some other reason for walking out. Men often do.'

'We don't think he's that type.'

'Although, you've never met him, have you? So it's hard to say what type of man he is.'

If this were a court case and Alec were the judge, Sarah would be thinking of changing her plea. This was not going as she had intended.

'We think it must be about money.'

'Probably. But you don't have any evidence about that either. Maybe you're right and it's some sort of scam or even money laundering but you'd have to give us all the details if you wanted us to look into that. And you don't want to do that, do you? Now why is that, Sarah? Don't you trust us?'

'I've not got permission from my client.'

'Hmm. Then there's this letter given to your father. Is that what's worrying you? That Matthew might have been involved in something dodgy?'

Sarah is flustered now. He's going too fast.

'No, of course not.'

'Maybe you should be.'

'What's that supposed to mean?'

'Let me spell it out for you then. This friend of his has been up to something he doesn't want people to know about. In fact, it sounds to me like Matthew specifically told him not to share the details – so as not to compromise himself. So, we can presume it's not above board. And he knows that there is money salted away somewhere and consents to hold some details on his friend's behalf.'

Alec waits to see if there are any comments, but Sarah is tongue-tied. She can't say more without mentioning Don Bradley and that would open a much bigger can of worms. He continues.

'I knew your father for many years, and he was a good man. But...'

She knew the inevitable but was coming.

'... he was a practical man with a good head for business. Isn't it possible that he may have come to some sort of accommodation with this friend in return for advice and support? A retainer? Or simply a cut? We don't know what this bloke was up to. Perhaps your father was careful to ensure that he didn't either. That way he could tell himself that this was a normal arrangement, a fee for services rendered.'

Sarah finally finds her voice.

'I don't think Dad would have done that.'

'But it's possible, isn't it? And if you go digging around in the dirt you're likely to get your hands filthy. Is that what you want? Is that what your mother wants?'

'So I should forget about it, you mean. Walk away.'

Alec bristles at this.

'I'm trying to help, you know. You may be a hotshot when it comes to tying companies up in contractual knots but you're way out of your depth on this. Stop playing at detectives and get back to what you understand.'

'What about his wife? You're saying I should just ignore the threats to her.'

'Alleged threats. And if they're real she should come to us. But we'll need the whole story. We'll need to know what her old man has been up to.'

He pauses momentarily for effect.

'And anyone else who might have been involved.'

So there it is. Either spill the beans and hope that her father was as strait-laced as she'd always thought him to be, or let it lie.

Alec softens a little. He can see that his point has hit home.

'Look, don't worry. This guy's probably got a gambling debt and some bookie who's seen too many crime shows fancies himself as a hard case and is trying to put the wind up an old lady. Once they realise that her husband's deserted her, they'll leave her be. In any case, it's not your problem.'

He gets up from the desk and starts to usher her to the door. They are standing by a vast sheet of glass that makes Sarah feel she is floating in mid-air, with nothing to hold her up. Alec looks across the park to the building opposite. It is similar to the police headquarters but has touches of emerald in the glazing and some brick detailing.

'When I first started, police stations were next to fire stations, near to pubs and local shops. Part of the community. We have new neighbours now.'

He points across the road.

'That's the Fujitsu Corporation. Where their offices are – underneath them in fact – is the field where Newton Heath Football Club used to play.'

No reaction from Sarah.

'The club that became Manchester United. Moved on a bit since then. These days they have more than twenty global partners. Some of their fans even come from Manchester.'

He turns back and offers Sarah his hand.

'Onwards and upwards, eh? Give my best to your mother. One of the constables will show you the way out.'

TWENTY-ONE

After the incident with Sarah, Jim had decided it would be best to meet Eileen on neutral ground. The office was safe enough in itself, but he didn't want anyone following her home to her hideaway. Kelly suggested the café at a garden centre in Darcy Lever where she used to take her nan.

'Very nice scones but you need to steer clear of the Eccles cakes.'

Jim is sitting at a table in "The Bothy" waiting for the others to arrive. He's had a quick stroll round the nursery and is now taking in his surroundings and the other customers.

Normally he feels at home with nature. He's had his allotment for over thirty years and is pretty much self-sufficient in vegetables. This is just as well given that his consumption of tubers, bulbs, leaves, stems, flowers, fruit, fungi and seeds approaches industrial proportions. He has a particular passion for the brassica family, which can result in some noxious build-ups of wind, but as it is more than five years since Marion passed away this is, for the most part, no one else's problem but his. Having his own office at work is also a godsend for all concerned.

So, he should be in his element but there is something a bit odd about this whole set-up. "The Bothy" is the size of a large motorway service station on the M1 and it seems that every Bolton resident old enough for a bus pass has fetched up for lunch. Wall-to-wall pensioners as far as the eye can see. Signs in the car park proudly announce that the new extension is complete and that a full range of hot and cold meals, snacks and beverages are there for the asking. Bookings are also being accepted for Christmas, which is only six months away. This would explain why the nursery area seems so small and the plant range so limited. Green space has had to be sacrificed in the interests of getting more covers for luncheon and tea. This is a big eatery with a small garden centre attached, not the other way round.

In fact, he can't see much sign of anyone actually buying plants. There is a large sales area devoted to knick-knacks associated with gardens – imitation stone ornaments with inscriptions on them, chiming bells to hang in a tree, tea-lights in bottles to illuminate evening drinks – as well as heavy-duty items such as benches, umbrellas, gas-powered barbecues and (a new one on Jim) clay Mexican chimeneas. His fellow diners have picked up greetings cards, dried flowers, packs of shortbread biscuits from Scotland and packets of cream fudge from Devon but very few have opted for plants and flowers unless they are in a bunch and wrapped in cellophane.

And people aren't being put off their lunch by the décor, which surprises Jim a little as it appears to have been designed by a committee of delusional individuals who could not agree on what the theme of the café should be and so decided to chuck a bit of everything in to keep the peace.

By the entrance there is a thriving community of garden gnomes who live in large toadstools (the ones with neat white polka dots on top) and suffer from morbid obesity due to the fact they spend all day sitting down holding a fishing rod. Along one side, a tropical jungle bulging with lush vegetation and hanging vines dominates but this has become entangled with a nearby scale model of an idyllic English village complete with village green, duck pond and church spire. Consequently, life-size plastic chimpanzees and gorillas are placed uncomfortably close to tiny houses and cars making it look like the set for the as yet unmade film classic – King Kong versus Camberwick Green. At the far end, someone has boldly gone for a science-fiction vibe, but it seems to have run into budget issues and remains an unrealised dream. A cardboard cut-out of Darth Vader has fallen over on top of the Starship Enterprise in an intergalactic pile-up while E.T. looks on with indifference.

Jim cannot see what any of this has to do with either a café or a garden centre but he knows it isn't giving him much of an appetite. In fact, he feels a little queasy and has settled for an Earl Grey tea and nothing else thank you despite being implored by the young woman at the till to push the boat out and try the chocolate fudge cake. He spots Kelly shepherding Eileen past Gnomeland and half rises with his hand in the air. Kelly nods and steers through the tightly packed tables and settles Eileen down opposite him.

'What will you have, Eileen?' he offers.

'No, it's alright, Mr Glassbrook,' says Kelly. 'We've ordered. They'll bring it over.'

Eileen is fussing over whether to take off her coat and where she would put it if she did. Kelly eases it off her shoulders and onto the back of the chair.

'Thanks.'

Eileen takes a good look around at the other customers, plates piled high and shouting over the top of each other. She wrinkles her nose.

'The way some folk eat. You'd think they'd never seen toad-in-the-hole before.'

A waitress brings over a large pot of tea and places a toasted teacake in front of Eileen. She glances up at Jim.

'It's all I've had all day.'

She scrapes a thin layer of butter on the teacake and begins to nibble the edge.

'You've not heard anything then?'

'No. Not yet. But we don't think Gerry's in Bolton, so Taylor is making some enquiries further afield.'

'You don't think he's dead, do you?'

Kelly reaches over to pat the back of her hand.

'Now, don't start thinking like that. We'll find him, won't we, Mr Glassbrook?'

Eileen breaks off a fragment of teacake and places it delicately in her mouth, taking care to wipe her fingers on the serviette afterwards.

'I miss him.'

Jim wonders for a moment if she is going to cry but the tears are blinked away as she stirs her tea and then pushes the teacake to one side.

'Why can't I have Treacle with me?'

'We've been over that.'

'I'm lonely.'

She looks meaningfully at Jim.

'Maybe you don't mind being on your own, but I do. He'd be company for me.'

'You need to be careful. It won't be for long.'

'You're sure he's alright, Kelly? He's not pining for me, is he?'

Kelly, who has not seen Treacle conscious except at mealtimes, nods vigorously.

'He seems quite happy.'

'And you've got his basket? He can't rest without it.'

'Yes, I told you. Sarah brought it with him.'

Reassured, Eileen drags the teacake closer permitting herself a tiny bit more.

Jim drains the last of his tea, removes his glasses and polishes them with his tie. Kelly has seen him do this many times before. It's invariably the prelude to a series of awkward questions.

'Now then, Eileen. We were wondering if there was anything more you could tell us that might help.'

There is the slightest hesitation as she prises another morsel off the teacake.

'I've told you everything I know.'

'Hmmm.'

Kelly knows that it is not a good sign when Mr Glassbrook goes "Hmmm". This is what he says when he's unhappy about something, like finding a slug in his salad or being told a case file is missing. She can sense him stalking Eileen like a cat circling a sparrow.

'When you first came to see us, you said Gerry took off the morning after he received another phone call. Do you know what was said that made him decide to disappear?'

Eileen is concentrating on her teacake. Not eating it, concentrating on it. And not looking at Jim.

'No.'

'Gerry didn't tell you what it was about? That's a bit strange, isn't it?'

'I suppose he didn't want to worry me.'

He's painting her into a corner, thinks Kelly. She feels sorry for Eileen but she's been told very clearly that this has to be done if they are to get to the bottom of things and so she says nothing.

'I can understand that,' continues Jim, 'but by going off like he did, no word, well... that's not fair on you, is it?'

'Gerry must have thought it was for the best. I don't know... if he was gone, maybe they'd leave me alone.'

'And he didn't say anything before he went? Where he might be going?'

Eileen has taken her hankie from her handbag and is twisting it round her fingers.

'Or leave you a note?'

She presses the serviette to her mouth.

'I don't feel well. That butter might be off.'

Kelly dutifully sniffs it and makes a non-committal face.

'I think you should take me back now, love. I don't want to be sick here.'

Kelly flashes a look at Jim who looks unperturbed as he carries on.

'Of course, Eileen. Just one more thing before you go. When did you last see Don Bradley?'

Eileen has screwed the hankie so tightly round her forefinger that it is glowing red and looking ready to burst.

'Don? Errmm… I'm not sure. Why?'

'He worked with Gerry, didn't he? Financial adviser?'

'Gerry was retired. He wasn't working with anyone.'

'Oh. I was told they were very close.'

He pauses to let that sink in.

'Must have been a terrible shock when you heard he'd been shot.'

Eileen picks up the serviette and retches into it. A thin trickle of bile slithers down her chin. Kelly shoots a furious look at Jim and helps Eileen tidy herself up before escorting her to the Ladies and leaving Jim to pick up the bill.

She knows, he thinks to himself. She knows.

After dabbing Eileen's face with cold water and wiping any traces of sick from her dress Kelly links arms with her back to the car. Eileen is silent on the short ride to the nan's house.

'You sure you can manage?'

'Thanks, love. I'll probably have a lie-down. You get off back to work now.'

Kelly watches her to the door and leaves the engine idling for a few minutes, wondering if there is something more she could do to help. Typical Mr Glassbrook. Push and push until she couldn't stand it any more, leaving her to clean up the mess. And where has it got them? Can't he see the poor woman is frightened to death?

She sees the front curtains being drawn so pulls away and decides to go home first and then get back to the office. All is quiet in the cul-de-sac when she gets there; children still at school; most parents still at work. And it's just as quiet as she turns the key, enters the house and hangs her coat by the front door. No sound from Treacle but that's nothing new so she wanders into the kitchen and sees the washing on the garden line.

Be dry now, she thinks as she grabs the laundry basket and steps outside. She unpegs the double sheet and folds it neatly. That's when she sees him, dangling like a little doll, his tiny body swaying in the breeze. Treacle's head is bowed over his chest, the neck broken, his lifeless body sagging on the line.

Kelly screams and drops the basket. But no one hears her because no one is there.

She gulps and reaches out to brush her fingers over Treacle's coat but then immediately withdraws them in horror. This sets him swinging like a condemned man on the gibbet.

There is a luggage label tied to one of his back legs with a pink ribbon. On one side is a mobile telephone number. On the other are the words:

Ring us when you get this message.

Twenty-Two

One thing Taylor has learned about retired footballers is that they like nothing more than talking about their old exploits. Open up a conversation about their most memorable game, most feared opponent or the best goal they ever scored, and they are willing to give you whatever time you want.

But they are also a suspicious lot. Each time he's mentioned that he is a private investigator he's felt like a man who has outstayed his welcome in the pub. 'Let's be 'aving yer.' 'Time please.' 'Aven't you got no 'ome to go to?'

So when he rings Bill Chadwick, he decides to revert to his old life and pose as a freelance journalist researching a piece on the "Golden Age" of football, a "Where are they now – the glory boys of yesteryear?" sort of article. Sure enough, Bill is more than happy to meet and relive his magic moments. The National Football Museum opposite Victoria Station? Yes, he can do that. Tomorrow? I suppose so. See you there.

Taylor arrives early. He doesn't want to get caught out in conversation about the history of the game, so he starts browsing the exhibits. He soon realises that this is just like going to any other museum. Too much damned stuff. After an hour he can't remember what was in the display case he had just been looking at and has started to feel unaccountably exhausted. By the time he joins Bill in the ground-floor café the only things he can recall are a replica of the Jules Rimet Trophy that England won in 1966 (the original being in Brazil) and the shirt Geoff Hurst wore in the final. The rest is a blurred montage of grainy Victorian photographs, several footballs from famous matches and a pile of old boots. Oh well, he thinks, I'll just have to wing it. Not like it's the first time.

Bill Chadwick is different from the other old players he has interviewed. A little younger, full head of neatly trimmed, wire-wool hair, double-breasted blue blazer over a white shirt and club tie, grey flannels with a razor-sharp crease and shiny black brogues. He looks fit as a flea and Taylor feels his bones crackle uncomfortably when they share a handshake.

It doesn't take long to get him chatty and at ease. A few open questions about his childhood, how he broke into the first team and the surprise move to City.

'Came out of a clear blue sky, you might say.'

He allows himself a chuckle at a joke he has probably used many times before.

'So, you didn't ask for a transfer?'

'Never entered my head. To be honest, when they called me into the office, I thought they were going to send me down to the Reserves. Things hadn't been going too well. We were losing a lot of matches and I think I'd lost interest a bit.'

'But City obviously saw something in you.'

'Don't forget, I'd played for England Under 23s a couple of times but with the Wanderers dropping into the Second Division there were no chance of me getting a full cap. But somebody must have remembered that and thought I might still have it in me.'

He smiles to himself, enjoying the warmth of a happy memory, a real piece of luck.

'And then we won the League Cup. Full house at Wembley. Dream come true.'

'I can't understand why Bolton let you go.'

'Desperate for cash. Off-loading me were perfect for them. They thought I was on the way down, see, so this were a last chance to make a bit of money.'

Taylor has been conscientiously jotting down all of Bill's yesterdays and he notes how relaxed he is looking, gratified to be the centre of attention again for a short while.

'Thanks, I enjoyed that. I were a bit surprised when you rang me. Not that many folk interested in the old days. Most can't remember much before last week. I mean, come on, can you tell me who won the FA Cup last year?'

Taylor shakes his head. This is something about football that he is definitely sure of.

'There you are.'

Bill shakes his head ruefully at the way the world has gone.

'By the way. Who was it that put you on to me?'

'Gerry Bradshaw.'

Taylor sees Bill stiffen at the mention of Gerry's name. The easy-going slouch is gone, the half-smile sliding off his lips. He checks his cuffs and then leans over to pull up his socks. When he is back upright, he is fully on guard.

'Oh aye. How is he?'

'That's the thing, Bill. He's disappeared. Went out for a pint of milk a few days ago and hasn't been seen since. You haven't heard from him, have you?'

The shutters are firmly down now but Taylor can see that Bill is rattled.

'No, but err... give him my regards when you see him. Right. I need to make a move.'

He starts putting on his raincoat. Last chance to hook him, thinks Taylor.

'Whatever it is he's been up to, it's got out of hand. They've threatened to kill his wife. Burn his house down.'

Bill drops back into his seat, a look of horror on his face.

'Oh God!'

'We need to find Gerry before they do. There's not much time.'

Bill is looking around nervously, all the composure gone.

'Who are you?'

'I'm working for Eileen Bradshaw. She's terrified. Can you help her?'

He sees Bill weighing up his options. Walk away and hope for the best or do the right thing. Abruptly, he stands up and strides towards the exit.

'Not here.'

The cathedral is smaller than Taylor expected. Given that "Mancs" are always crowing about how everything in their city is bigger and better than elsewhere, as if they were the Texas of the north-west, this feels surprisingly intimate and on a human scale. There is a soft, golden glow from the stain glass windows that percolates the fluted grey-brown columns sprouting like a row of carefully planted trees in the nave, dappled in late evening sunlight. The organist is taking a few choir members through their paces on the other side of an ornate screen behind a modern styled altar around which the rest of the building radiates. There are soaring passages as the singers hit their stride and the harmonies circle above them, the high notes pinging about the roof timbers and causing a tingle of awe and delight on those listening, only to be abruptly halted by a mistake no one but the choir leader can detect until the whole thing is attempted again.

Taylor is feeling unexpectedly peaceful. He does not see himself as one of those whom his old editor called a "God-botherer" but there are times when he feels himself reaching out for something more. Whenever he sets foot in a church, usually for a funeral, he feels the building is trying to convince him that there is a purpose to the universe which is still being played out, a manifest destiny of which he is a part even if he does not realise it or refuses to accept it. And when he hears the choir, imitating songs of praise from the celestial host, there is a part of him that wants to believe. Because it is harder to believe in nothing, and he is getting tired of it.

If Bill's thoughts are similarly elevated, he is showing little sign of it as he casts his eyes about nervously, checking for anyone who looks out of place. A few solitary penitents are already there, kneeling in silent prayer, and there is a group of excitable youngsters setting up a charity stall near the porch, trying to balance their delight at being together out of school with respect for where they are. Other than that, there is a smattering of older people skirting the aisles, trying to decode the tombs and memorials that coat the walls, but they all look like the English Heritage type, at ease in their natural environment.

Bill seems to be reassured and sidles along to the middle of a row of seats halfway down the central aisle, making sure he is a suitable distance from any of the other visitors. Taylor joins him. For a few minutes they sit in silence looking at the altar screen and listening to the choir, hidden from sight, going through their paces. Taylor decides to bide his time. Some instinct tells him not to push this man. When Bill does speak it is little more than a whisper.

'How do I know you're what you say you are?'

Taylor peels one of his business cards from his wallet and hands it to Bill.

'Means nowt. Anyone can get one of them printed.'

Taylor keeps his eyes fixed on the altar.

'I want to find Gerry while he's still alive. If there is something you want to tell me, now is the time.'

Bill nods his head slowly several times.

'Gerry's that bit older than me. When I got into the first team, he sort of took me under his wing, like a big brother. Made sure nobody took any liberties. I've never forgotten that.'

'When did you last speak to him?'

'He rang me, I dunno, six maybe eight weeks ago. Something had happened, he didn't say what, but I could tell from his voice that it was something bad. He was scared. Gerry's a tough bugger so it takes summat to knock him off his perch. I found out later that somebody had shot Don. Anyway, Gerry said it was all off. Finished. Too dangerous.'

'What was?'

Bill is hunched over now, head bowed, hands clasped together between his knees.

'Do you believe in God?'

'No, I don't think so. Not really.'

'Me neither. Pity. Might come in handy.'

'What was too dangerous, Bill?'

'It came as a relief to me, Gerry calling it off like that. I'd wanted to get out for a while but... it's not easy. You can't just ask for a transfer.'

His shoulders shake slightly but he is not laughing. Taylor tells himself to be patient. He's seen enough spy films to know this is a man who has held a secret for too long and wants to spill his guts and get the poison out of his system. But, force the issue now and you could drive the truth back down deep, where it can't be got at. Move away from closed questions. Get him to open up.

'How did it all start?'

'We'd allus kept in touch. Gerry were a great one for reunions. Get the lads together for a dinner – bit of a piss-up. He were sort of like the social secretary. Sorted out the dates, booked the hotels, reserved the tables. We'd been doing it for years but then the numbers started to fall. Couple of the lads died or got too frail to come any more. Then this dementia thing started. That's what put the idea in Gerry's mind.'

Now we're coming to it thinks Taylor. One more little nudge.

'You mean, do something while you still can?'

'Aye. Players today, well... some of 'em make enough in a couple of years to last the whole of their lives. Never 'ave to work again. Weren't like that for us. Some of the lads went back to the jobs they'd had before they started playing – brickies, factory workers... even a milkman. But if you could, if you were lucky, you got a job in football. A few of us made it on to the coaching side but some o't lads were physios, kitmen, scouts – anything to stay involved.

But we were all struggling for money, worried about our pensions. Worried we might end up like Denis. That's how it all started.'

The choir have finally mastered the Gloria and the cathedral is ringing with their praise, the top, piercing notes from the sopranos reverberating in their heads.

'How what started, Bill?'

'Most of us that were left were still in the game, just about. And we all had contacts, lads we'd worked with or trained. And Gerry said, now it's our turn to make a bit of money while we still can. Get our fair share for once.'

He rubs his forehead with the tips of his fingers, pressing hard as if trying to erase the memory.

'I never liked the idea, but Gerry said it would happen anyway, without us, so what's the difference.'

A thundering crash breaks the mood as two men blunder into the church. There is a disturbance by the charity stall and voices are raised. Staff hustle down to the porch, trying to calm the situation, making shushing sounds and holding their fingers to their lips.

The choir comes to a dead stop.

Bill looks around in panic.

'Just a couple of drunks,' Taylor says. 'Ignore them. Go on.'

But Bill is already on his way, striding towards the altar and the exit by the side chapel. Taylor watches hopelessly as he slips out of reach.

The staff behind him have restored some order by now and the two men are sitting down. Cups of tea are being offered. The discordant voices are subsiding. No problem. The men are regulars it seems. Taylor waits a while to see if the choir will start up again, but they've had enough practice for one day and the brief glimpse of the soundtrack to Paradise has melted away. He lingers, not sure what he is going to do next and knowing that once he leaves the church he'll have all those unsolved problems to face again. But there isn't any choice, so he picks up his coat and heads back to the train station.

Twenty-Three

Sarah has plenty to think about on the drive back to Bolton after her meeting with Alec Timpson. As luck would have it, she has the perfect opportunity to chew things over in her mind because she's been stuck at the same spot on the M60 for the last twenty-five minutes. The junctions around Worsley are like the confluences of several major rivers, all pouring their contents into the same narrow channel. Chaos and disastrous overflows are the regular result as traffic tails back for miles waiting to trickle through the bottleneck. Might as well make the most of it, she thinks.

On the face of it, this has been a pointless journey and a colossal waste of time. So much for all the earache she'd suffered from Jim and Marcus about handing the whole thing over to the professionals. Alec couldn't have been less interested if she'd been a fundraiser from Amnesty International.

As for the interview – more like an interrogation – it had been much briefer than she had hoped. The haste with which he saw her off the premises bordered on rudeness, and he hadn't offered one scrap of help. Even so, if she strips away his irritating tone of condescension and his apparent indifference to Eileen's fate, there was something behind his cynical analysis that was worth considering.

She surveys the lines of cars that stretch beyond her sight in all directions, each sending up a haze of effluent to attack the ozone layer, and switches her engine off. Every little helps, she thinks, and we're not going anywhere soon.

Alec hadn't taken the threats to Eileen very seriously. That wasn't surprising given she had held back most of the information that might have made him sit up and take notice. No mention of the threat to turn Eileen's house into a sacrificial pyre nor of the two thugs who had tried to bundle her into the back of a van. Why had she done that? She'd told Alec that she could not disclose details without the permission of her client but wasn't that just a smoke screen? The truth was that she didn't want to hand things over to the police, wasn't it? That despite the real threat to her own safety she wanted to see this through herself.

And what was that all about? Jim, Marcus and now Alec (how she loved the men in her life telling her what to do) had all said that solving Eileen's problems was not her responsibility. Just because her husband used to have a few beers with her dad back in the day did not mean she had to put herself and her business in jeopardy. And yet, she did feel a sense of obligation towards Eileen. It wasn't that she even liked her that much – too proper and fussy – but when she'd repeated that Gerry had always told her to go and see Matthew if she was in trouble, that struck a nerve. Her father had made a promise and maybe it was her duty to see it was kept. But – she might as well admit it to herself – the men had a point when they said she liked playing the part of the detective, unlocking the crime, bringing the bad guys to justice, protecting the innocent. Also, it had to be said that, along with the bowel-loosening terror she'd experienced when those two men had grabbed her, she got off on the thrill of danger. It gave her a buzz, made her feel more alive, and she liked it. Her father was never a risk-taker but maybe she was. And that was another reason for not handing it over to the cops. She wanted to get even herself.

The red brake lights of cars in the far distance begin to go off in a slow sequence, one by one, the wave moving steadily towards her. Movement at last. She restarts the engine and levers down the handbrake but the cars from another road, over to the left, are quicker off the mark and start to creep into the spaces. Within a couple of minutes she sees the brake lights turning red again and she switches off the engine. This would test the patience of a saint, she thinks. A Buddhist saint – if there is such a thing.

There was no getting away from it. She had to consider the question of how much her father knew. Jim would never entertain the idea of Matthew becoming involved in shady dealings, but Taylor was on to it as soon as he heard about the letter from Gerry. She knows her dad had his head screwed on tightly enough to work out what was going on. At best, he would have known that Gerry's money was dirty but decided to turn a blind eye out of friendship. At worst, he was up to his neck in it with Don, acting as the legal adviser on how to recycle the money securely.

And that's what Alec Timpson was getting at. Be careful what questions you ask because you might not like the answers. It was all very well living out a fantasy life as a sleuth but not at the expense of trashing her own father's reputation.

The car immediately in front of her suddenly jolts forward. She hadn't noticed that the log jam ahead had shifted again and this time the cars on her stretch of road were not giving an opening to anyone else. Each driver inches forward in first gear, perilously close to the ones in front and behind, blocking off any chance for any vehicle to sneak in from the other road, until she passes the junction. And then, like a sudden clearance in a blocked drain, the traffic begins to flow more quickly, everyone accelerating to put the blackspot behind them and wondering what had caused the delay as everything on the road ahead seems clear now. She puts her foot down to make up for lost time but the thoughts that have been buzzing round her head since she left the police station don't get blown away no matter how fast she goes.

It is past five o'clock as she finally approaches Bolton, and she is feeling too tired to go into the office so decides to call it a day and see if she can make things right with Marcus. His flashy BMW is parked on the driveway but is obscured by a familiar white hatchback. Sarah's spirits slip a little lower. This is all she needs.

Marcus must have found the key to the shed with the garden furniture in it because when she walks round to the back of the house she finds him leaning back on a rattan chair clinking glasses with her mother who brightens at her arrival.

'Hello, love. We weren't expecting you till later.'

Helen is looking very relaxed. As if you've got one over on me, thinks Sarah, getting Marcus on his own and pumping him for information. Maybe I got back just in time.

But the way Marcus jumps up and rushes over to peck her on the cheek makes him look like a man who has been caught at it with another woman. In this case his pseudo mother-in-law. They've been talking about me, thinks Sarah.

'We've just been talking about you, haven't we, Marcus?'

The way her mum uses his name. Drawing him into her orbit, recruiting him to her side. Marcus shifts from foot to foot. He can see he's going to get mown down in the crossfire if he's not careful.

'Gin and tonic?'

'Why not?'

This gives him what he was hoping for, a chance to sneak off into the house before the hostilities begin.

Helen is eyeing Sarah, waiting for her to make the first move but there is no way she is falling for that one. You've come to me. Say what you've got to say.

'Marcus told me about what happened to you last night.'

'Nearly happened.'

'Don't split hairs. You could have been killed.'

'It wasn't like that.'

'If they'd got you into that van God knows what they would have done to you.'

'But they didn't, did they?'

'You could have been raped, tortured...'

'That's enough, Mum...'

137

'Sarah!' screams Helen.

She flinches. Her mother hasn't shouted at her like that in years, but she can remember the tone and it takes her back to being a little girl of five or six stepping away from her when she saw a cute dog on the other side of the road. Putting her foot off the pavement to cross over and give the dog a pat when she hears her mother bellowing out her name, feels the biting pain of her hand gripping her shoulder and hauling her back and the rush of wind as the car surges past her, only inches away. That's what she hears in Helen's voice now. The desperation of a mother who thinks she may be too late to save her child.

Sarah sees the fear in Helen's eyes. Please, they are saying. One death in the family is enough. She leans forward and rubs her mother's back, puts her head close to hers.

'It's alright, Mum. I'm fine.'

Helen gulps in some air. She isn't sobbing. She doesn't do that. But she can't quite trust her voice yet and it cracks slightly as she says,

'Why didn't you tell me?'

Sarah pulls back.

'Why did I have to hear it from Marcus?'

'I'm sorry. I wasn't thinking straight last night. I just sort of... crashed out.'

'Marcus said you went into the office this morning. Saw Jim Glassbrook. Told him.'

Sarah looks back at the house, willing Marcus to return with her drink and divert the spotlight from her. But he is nowhere in view. She bows her head slightly.

'What can I say? I should have rung you. I don't know why I didn't.'

'When you were a little girl, you always liked to keep a secret from us. Hide something in your room. We had to pretend we didn't know.'

'I'm not a little girl any more.'

'Some things don't change though, do they?'

'I've said I'm sorry, Mum. What more do you want?'

'Just a quick call to let me know you're safe. That's all I need. Instead, I have to hear it from a man I hardly know.'

'Whose fault is that?'

'You never bring Marcus to see me.'

'It wasn't exactly a roaring success the only time I did.'

Helen hunches her shoulders, drawing her neck in and wrinkling the flesh under her chin.

'I wasn't really myself that weekend.'

'You could have visited us.'

'You know I hate London…'

'It's never your fault, is it? It's always someone else…'

Their voices die away as they hear the sound of fizzing, crackling ice as Marcus picks his way carefully down the path, brandishing a full tray of drinks like an Edwardian butler.

'Thought I might as well get another round in.'

He looks up hopefully as he places the tray on the table but can see from their expressions that things have not been going well while he's been away. Helen compresses her lips into what looks like it might become a smile, but this quickly degenerates into a grimace of regretful disappointment.

'Not for me. I'm driving.'

Sarah sighs loudly, reaches over and grabs her mother's drink and upends it into hers. The tonic fizzes up and gushes over the side of her glass and puddles onto the table.

'Cheers!'

Marcus spots another chance to make a getaway – 'I'll fetch a cloth' – but Sarah presses down on his shoulder as he tries to rise.

'Leave it.'

The conversation has drained away and the three of them sit with plenty on their mind but nothing to say. There is a persistent whirring, whining noise as the man from next door attacks his borders with a strimmer.

Helen directs her gaze to the middle distance as if she were on a country estate with a panoramic view instead of in a suburban garden fenced off from encroaching neighbours. She is pointedly not looking at Sarah as she downs half of her inflated gin and tonic in one go. There is no audible tutting sound as yet but her lips are pursed and ready.

Marcus feels his sense of unease mutating into low-level panic as he desperately tries to think of some topic of conversation that would lower the tension. This is just how it was when he made the first of his only two visits to Bolton to be introduced to Helen and Matthew – separately, of course. He had been nagging Sarah for weeks beforehand and whilst she had never actually said 'No, that's not a good idea', neither had she made any move to arrange a date.

'What are you worried about? They've seen photos of me. It's not going to be a shock, is it?'

'It's not that. Well… it's partly that. I mean… you know… it's not like they have any friends who are black. Certainly not any neighbours.'

'OK – so they might be a bit awkward at first. I get that. But, you never know – they might like me. Some people do.'

She had squeezed his arm then.

'Course they'll like you. Dad'll be glad to have someone to argue with about football and Mum will enjoy making a fuss over you.'

Marcus heard the words but was not picking up any conviction in them.

'It's OK. I understand. I mean, if they decide to turn on the fridge, you know, give me that traditional English frosty welcome, I can handle that. I've had it plenty of times before.'

'They won't be like that.'

'What then?'

'It's Mum. She'll want to know things. I haven't brought anyone home for years, so she knows this is serious and she'll start probing you for information.'

'So what? I've got nothing to hide. She wants to know about me and my family – that's fine. She's got the right to know what kind of bloke I am.'

Sarah had shaken her head emphatically.

'No. Not about you. About me.'

Which is pretty much how it had turned out that weekend. Over lunch, Matthew had been perfectly polite, carefully choosing his words, keen to hear Marcus's views on the topics of the day and respectful of his opinions. But there was no spark of connection, no spontaneous laughs that signalled the beginnings of mutual trust. He could have been entertaining anyone and would have shown the same impersonal courtesy.

'I might as well have been the new vicar,' Marcus remarked as they left. Looking back, all of Matthew's attention had been on Sarah and her work. How is she finding the new firm? Is she having to work long hours? Any chance of a partnership? Doesn't she find company law a bit dull? Wouldn't she like to return to more general practice? Outside London maybe?

The focus was even more pronounced at dinner with Helen that night. She had adopted what Sarah called her "Queen Mother" persona with Marcus. And what work do you do? (Senior accountant for a business development company.) I don't really know what that entails. (He had done his best to explain but could see her attention wane quite quickly.) And your father is an accountant? That must be interesting. (Hardly.) And your mother, does she work? (No.) Well, running a home must be a full-time job... with a family as big as yours.

It wasn't long before Marcus's jaw was aching with the effort of maintaining a fixed smile. Meantime, Sarah had demolished most of a bottle of red wine and her eyelids were starting to droop. Any questions from Helen directed at her – and there were many – were deflected with a mixture of 'I don't know', 'Couldn't say', 'Maybe' and the like. After a number of failed attempts to extract information Helen decided to wear down Marcus instead.

'Of course, Sarah's always been very ambitious. Job first with you, isn't it, love? Puts a lot of strain on your relationship I expect.'

A mutinous stare from Sarah as Marcus stuttered to respond, his eyes flitting from one woman to the other as he tried to pick his way a safe path through the landmines.

'Errm… I suppose we both work quite long hours…'

'But there are other things in life other than work, aren't there? Not that Matthew ever seemed to realise that. What do you think? No one ever went to their death-bed wishing they'd spent more time at the office. Isn't that what they say?'

Sarah had not been able to resist commenting on that, addressing her remarks to a half-empty glass of Shiraz.

'That's so deep, Mum. Never heard it before. Must make a note of that.'

Helen ignored this and turned her attention back to Marcus, moving in like a boxer cornering their opponent. By this stage in the evening he had realised that he was on his own. Sarah was ringside but he needed to keep his guard up or Helen would put him on the canvas.

'I think we do alright, don't we, Sarah?'

No response. Keep going.

'Errm… we go to the theatre when we can.'

'Do you?'

Helen was back in regal mode again.

'And we get to the gym twice a week.'

'I was thinking of something more… umm… personal. Meaningful.'

He was struggling now, hanging on the ropes, half wondering whether Sarah was going to throw in the towel and half wondering whether Helen was going to take the gloves off and go bare knuckle instead.

'Errm… Oh… we try to get out for a meal at least one night a week. There's a good Italian not far from us. And if we can, we might get out of town for a walk…'

He ran out of steam when he saw in Helen's expression that this was not what she was getting at. Sarah slowly raised her head from the table.

'She means kids. Have you got me pregnant yet and, if not, when are you going to get round to it?'

Helen looked as if she had swallowed a pickled onion in the belief it was a liqueur chocolate. Pure disgust.

'No need to ask whether you're pregnant when you're knocking that wine back like there's no tomorrow.'

That was when the remainder of the bottle went flying across the table as Sarah swiped it aside, leaving a red gash across the linen tablecloth and a pool of wine on the cream carpet. Sarah had staggered off to bed at this point leaving Helen and Marcus to see whether salt would soak up the bloody mess (as recommended on the net) or whether it was better to apply cold water liberally.

Neither the tablecloth nor the carpet ever recovered, and the evidence was there to confront them over a largely silent breakfast, after which they left as quickly as decency would allow. And here I am again, thinks Marcus, waiting for the ruckus to kick off. And yet, it feels different this time. Helen looks more anxious than irritated, glancing over at Sarah with a softer expression than he has seen before. He can see sadness in her eyes, pity even, and a kind of longing. Maybe she's not in the mood for a fight today, he thinks.

Helen's arrival had startled them both. She had let herself in, thinking Sarah would be at work, and wandered into the living room where Marcus was stretched out on the settee, wearing only his shorts, laptop open and crunching some numbers.

'Fucking 'ell.'

'Oh God!'

Both had put their hands to their chest as if their heart were about to give out. Helen leaned forward on the back of the settee and took some deep breaths while Marcus jumped up, embarrassed to be found half naked, nervously crossing his arms over his chest like a schoolboy coming out of a cold shower.

'Sorry, I didn't hear you come in.'

Helen cast her eyes about the room, maternal instinct kicking in.

'Where's Sarah? What's happened?'

Marcus found a T-shirt, made himself decent and explained about the attempted kidnap. He had expected Helen to go into meltdown, but she received the news very quietly. Not calmly, but quietly and that was when he decided that a G&T would be more help than a cup of tea. Sitting on the patio he went over all the details he had, watching as she took it all in. Bit by bit, the initial shock turned into disbelief. This was utterly beyond her experience. She and Matthew had spent most of their lives insulating themselves against the problems that beset so many others. But these were piddling issues compared to this – living in a safe neighbourhood, paying off the mortgage, finding the right school – that sort of thing. Not steering clear of thugs in balaclavas who held a knife to your throat. How had their lives crash-landed into some kind of cheap cop show?

At first, Marcus was on his guard, wondering whether Helen was somehow going to blame him for this mess but, as she asked more about how Sarah was coping and why he thought she was so hell bent on helping some woman she scarcely knew, he realised they were beginning to find common ground. They had to find some way of getting Sarah to give up this stupid case. Last night had been a warning. She wouldn't get off so lightly the next time. But they had to be careful. They both loved Sarah, in very different ways, and so it was only natural, they reasoned, that they should do everything they could to keep her safe. But they knew that she was likely to see this as a conspiracy, the two of them ganging up on her, which would only make her even more determined to carry on.

This was as far as they had got when Sarah turned up and any feelings of disloyalty Marcus had about plotting with her mother seep away when he sees her polish off the remainder of her engorged drink, holding the glass upside down and sucking the last of the gin off the ice cubes.

'How are the supplies holding up?' she asks him.

'I think we might make it through the night.'

Helen is encouraged by the friendly snort Sarah gives in reply and the faint smile that follows. She decides on a slightly different tack.

'Marcus told me you'd been to see Alec Timpson.'

'Did he?'

'Haven't seen him for years. Big man these days. How is he?'

'That's two questions, Mum. Three strikes and you're out.'

So Helen withdraws and Marcus takes over.

'What did he say?'

'Not much.'

'I mean, are they going to follow it up? Let you step back?'

Sarah can feel the gin taking effect already, a bit of fuzziness round the edge, a feeling of distance between her brain and her body, but when she sees the two of them glance at each other, Helen willing Marcus on, she knows.

'Oh my god. You two have been getting on well, haven't you?'

'Sarah...'

'Let's see. Mum is Bad Cop – obviously – so that means you're Good Cop. As usual.'

'Was he any help? That's all I'm asking.'

Sarah shifts uneasily in her chair and swirls the ice cubes in her glass.

'No... he wasn't interested.'

'That can't be right. An old lady is threatened with arson and someone pulls a knife on you in broad daylight – and the police aren't interested!'

'Any chance of another drink?'

Marcus watches as she belatedly starts to take a keen interest in the spilt drink and begins to dab the table with a paper hankie.

'Sarah – you did tell him everything... didn't you?'

'Errm...'

'Jesus! Why not?'

Sarah mumbles something about "client confidentiality" but her heart isn't in it. She's visibly crumbling now, defences collapsing, ready to raise the white flag. Marcus is fuming, taking deep breaths, not trusting himself to say what's on his mind so Helen sees her chance to come in as the peacemaker.

'Why don't we go inside and I'll make us something to eat?'

Helen rustles up an omelette and some salad while Sarah takes a shower. She returns in a dressing gown and a blue towel wrapped round her head which she just about manages to keep in place as they eat another meal together in strained silence. She is waiting for the next barrage of questions to begin but the other two keep the conversation light and general, Marcus apparently keen to hear about Helen's new kitchen and she in turn taking an intelligent interest in network solutions for small and medium-sized companies.

Sarah thinks she may start screaming if this goes on much longer. She can see what they are up to, deliberately not referring to the only topic that is on all of their minds. It's a war of nerves. They think that by not bringing the subject up Sarah will have to say something herself and tell them what the hell is going on. It's so transparent but knowing what is happening and being able to stand up to it are two different things. The shower has sobered her up but has also sapped her energy. She could feel it going down the plughole with the shampoo. It isn't that she doesn't want to fight any more, it's just that she hasn't got the stamina for it. And there is something else. She is no longer sure that they aren't right.

'I've been thinking...'

The other two carry on eating, showing no air of expectancy.

'If I took Eileen to see the police...'

She sees Marcus pause, a piece of lettuce dangling precariously from his fork, until he recovers himself and pops it into his mouth. They're determined not to make this easy for me, she thinks.

'... then they'd have to sit up and take notice.'

Helen takes a delicate sip of water. There is a conspicuous absence of wine on the table.

'But it won't be easy to persuade her. She's terrified of what they might do.'

Helen puts her knife and fork down, slowly wipes her lips with a serviette and puts her hand on top of Sarah's.

'What if I come with you? She might listen to someone more her own age. And we did know each other all those years ago.'

Sarah nods.

'Maybe. I'll ring Kelly now and tell her to let Eileen know to expect me.'

'I'll call round for you about ten tomorrow, shall I? The sooner she gets police protection the better.'

Sometimes you just have to accept that you're beaten. Sarah readjusts the towel on her head and pushes the remains of the omelette to one side.

'OK.'

Wisely, Marcus has still not said a thing, but she can see a twinkle of satisfaction in his eyes.

Twenty-Four

It is only a fifteen-minute drive from Matthew's house in Smithills to Moses Gate. About four miles. But Sarah and Helen feel they have come a long way by the time they get to the terraced house where Eileen is holed up.

Matthew's house is surrounded by a loose, flowing network of wide, tree-lined roads, each home discreetly positioned at a respectful distance from its neighbour. There is room to breathe and open countryside is just down the lane. As they head into Bolton the trees disappear and by the time they hit St Peter's Way they are sweeping along four lanes of tarmac sunken below the level of the surrounding town, hemmed in by identikit industrial units that seem to stretch all the way to Manchester. There is no longer any sense of place or people. This is just somewhere to pass through on your way elsewhere.

But as they near the turn-off to Moses Gate, there is a tantalising break in the sprawl on their left-hand side. The car showrooms and building depots give way to a straggle of unhappy trees choking in the car fumes, and beyond them the prospect of open space. Not beautiful, perhaps. Scruffy and maltreated, still recovering from the first industrial revolution but untended and wild. A glimpse of how it was before the motorways ploughed through.

It doesn't last long. As they veer onto the old Manchester Road the houses begin to close in on either side, narrow strips of identical red/black terraces fronting directly on to the road. No room for gardens or greenery. This is where people are packed in without such fuss.

Kelly's grandmother lived just off the main road. Handy for what few shops there still are. Her street is part of a grid of two-up, two-down terraces, thin houses without any adornment, where the front door is hard by the pavement and you step straight into the living room. There will be a galley kitchen beyond and two small bedrooms and a tiny bathroom upstairs. They know this without stepping inside the house as each looks exactly the same. Seen one, seen them all. Some owners have painted their doors a brighter colour or put some diamond-shaped leading on the PVC windows but it's no use. It doesn't register. There isn't any way of breaking out of the overwhelming uniformity.

'Never been here before.'

They are sitting in the car outside the house. Helen is angling her head to get a view up and down the street.

'I don't think I've been missing much.'

'Dad was brought up in a house like this, wasn't he?'

Helen opens the car door and steps out.

'Before my time, love.'

'Mum!'

Sarah is right behind her.

'Remember. I'll do the talking. You just come in if Eileen starts to wobble. OK?'

'You're in charge.'

No bell, so Sarah bangs the door with the side of her fist. No reply. Another set of thumps. Still nothing. Sarah crouches down and shouts through the letter box. A response at last. But from next door.

'You've missed her, love.'

A woman in her fifties with a small child peering round her leg.

'We saw her go out, didn't we, Amy?'

'When was this?'

'Oh – not long after your Mam dropped you off, was it?'

Amy doesn't reply but shrinks back behind the woman's legs.

'About half past eight. Two fellers came for her. In a van.'

Sarah glances at her mother. Say nothing.

'Nowt wrong is there?'

'No, no. We just called round on spec. Thanks for letting us know.'

Excitement over, the woman ushers Amy back inside. Helen and Sarah get back in the car.

'What do we do now?'

'I don't know.'

'It's got to be them, hasn't it? The same ones who tried to get you.'

'Probably.'

'Who else could it be?'

Sarah is staring down the street as if she could will Eileen back into view, see her toddling round the corner, fussing with a bag of groceries as she comes back from the shops.

'We can't just sit here. We have to call the police, don't we?'

Before Sarah can answer, her phone rings.

*

It was Kelly who had told Jim the news. She had come to see him first thing in his office that morning.

'Apparently Sarah got nowhere with the police on her own so she's taking Eileen in. I suppose that's what made her mind up.'

Kelly's face had crumpled, and she had begun to sob.

Jim didn't keep a box of hankies on his desk. The clients he saw weren't the weepy type, so he had to make do with putting his arm awkwardly round Kelly's shoulder in the hope she'd stop all that of her own accord.

'Now, now. What's to do? It's not the end of the world.'

'It's Eileen. What's going to happen to her now?'

'Might be for the best. Let her tell them her tale. See if they can get the whole story out of her.'

Kelly had flashed him an angry look.

'I don't know why you've never taken to Eileen. What's she ever done to annoy you?'

This wasn't like Kelly, who normally would cross the street, take a taxi and catch a long-distance train to avoid an argument.

'I'm only saying. They're best placed to find a missing person. We should never have taken this on.'

'Sarah didn't think so. She knows what her father would have done if he'd been here. I would have thought you'd agree with her.'

And with that she had stormed out of his office crashing the door shut behind her and leaving Jim to contemplate his shortcomings.

An hour later he is still pondering what Kelly has said and whether he has got this all wrong. If someone asks you for help, you're supposed to help them. That's what they taught him at chapel when he was a boy.

But why exactly?

Marion would have had an answer for that.

Because you can.

She was always one for what Jim regarded as lost causes – "waifs and strays" he called them. 'What's the point?' he asked her. 'There's so many folk in trouble. You can't help them all.' But she had an answer for that. 'No, love – that's true. All the more reason to help the ones you can.'

Dead so many years now and still telling him what to do.

Marion wasn't his only teacher. As he stares out the window, he remembers first coming with Matthew to look at the offices… what… must be thirty-five years ago at least. They were occupied by a rundown accountancy firm who had failed to move with the times and couldn't afford the lease any more. Jim wasn't keen on moving into a Victorian building. Back then he saw himself as a moderniser and favoured taking a new suite of custom-built offices with all the facilities laid on. That way they could appeal to a new set of customers. Those who knew how to prosper in hard times, picking up bankrupt firms and stripping their assets, moving in quick and then out again even quicker and who wanted advice on how to hold on to what they had grabbed. But Matthew was adamant.

'Our clients want to know they can trust us. That we're not some fly-by-night wide-boys who are more interested in taking their money than providing a service. No. If we smarten this place up it will do wonders for business. It reeks of tradition and respectability. We'll take it.'

In the end they had both been proved right. And wrong. The customers who wanted to turn a swift profit by all means possible without ending up in court took their custom to the solicitors who walked and talked like them. There was money to be made but the risks could be high, and you had to leave your conscience at home when you came to work.

The customers they kept were those who did not feel comfortable with the bitter medicine the government was administering to sort the economy out. The ones who wanted to keep their businesses going if they could and ride out the storm. They weren't necessarily sentimental. If they had to sell up and sack all their staff, they would do the necessary but at least have the decency to feel guilty about it. And not to crow too much about what they'd been able to set aside for themselves.

But over time these customers had retired, sold up, cashed in or simply died, leaving Curtis and Curtis with a shrinking client base. By then both he and Mathew were too old to fully grasp the new ways of working. They had computers installed but couldn't use them properly. Still insisted on dictating their letters. Clung to their paper files. Like the band on the Titanic, they played on with the same old tunes because they didn't know what else to do.

That's when Matthew had started talking about Sarah coming into the firm some day. There had been an estrangement after he divorced Helen. That was a strangely bloodless affair, thought Jim. Matthew seemed curiously detached from the whole business and left Jim to sort out the details. No other parties where involved – he'd never known Matthew to show much interest in women – so it wasn't messy like most divorces he'd dealt with. Matthew had never confided in him why the marriage had hit the rocks but didn't seem very upset by it. Perhaps this was what infuriated Helen, that it all seemed so unnecessary.

Naturally, or so it seemed to Jim, Sarah had taken her mother's side and after she went to university in London there wasn't much contact. But Matthew had kept up a keen interest in her career taking some hope from the fact that she had opted to study law. He was jubilant when she graduated with a First and then bagged a place with a prestigious commercial firm in the City. For some reason that Jim never understood, Matthew became increasingly convinced that Sarah would tire of London life and opt to move back up north and take up his reins.

'It'll be the shot in the arm we need. She'll know how to modernise the firm and bring in new clients and you and I can ease up and take a back seat. We have to keep things ticking over until then.'

On Matthew's instructions they changed the name to Curtis and Curtis and waited for the call from Sarah. Jim was sceptical from the outset. Why would Sarah choose to swap a lucrative career path in a snazzy metropolitan law firm to take over a sleepy little business in a town where the local economy had been flushed down the toilet? But somehow Matthew held on to an unshakeable belief that she would not let all his hard work go to waste, building up the practice from scratch, completing the long journey his parents had set him on, becoming the person they had dreamed he could be. No. She couldn't turn her back on that. They had to be patient. Matthew would soften her up every chance he got until the penny dropped and she saw for herself what she had to do.

Of course, Matthew thought he had more time on his hands. His heart had different ideas and had run its course.

But you have to make the best of things. Find the joy – that's what Marion had told him to do – but it was an uphill battle after she'd gone. To his surprise Jim had retained a small helping of his old friend's optimism that Sarah might step into her father's shoes. It didn't take long for that to evaporate. He was shocked to see how indifferent and even hostile she was to the notion. It took meeting that silly woman Eileen to make her see things differently. Something about her stirred up feelings of obligation to her father and that had given him hope again. It wasn't just Matthew who had invested in Curtis and Curtis. He had given most of his working life to it and, apart from his allotment, this was all he had left.

And there was something about Sarah. Her mood swings were unpredictable; her temper was always one spark from bursting into flame; she was too impetuous; she didn't listen to advice; her swearing was unfeminine. And she wore her skirts too short. On the other hand, she was full of life; her laugh lifted the room; her energy was boundless, and her heart was big and in the right place. In fact, pretty much the opposite to Matthew, and Jim was gradually getting used to the change. He was no longer in control of every aspect of the business and never sure what she was going to do next but somehow that didn't matter to him as much as he thought it would. Coming to work had ceased to be predictable, something he had tried hard to maintain through order and routine, and he was finding that letting go wasn't as awful as he had feared.

And then there was the attack. He'd always had the feeling that whoever was after Gerry would be keeping a watch on Eileen's house and trying to track her down. He should have been more insistent with Sarah about not going back to get that bloody dog! Someone must have followed her to the office and then spied their chance to nab her and get her to tell them where Eileen was hiding. If it hadn't been for the Boy Blunder they would have succeeded. To be fair, Taylor had handled that pretty well even if he was a deceitful toe-rag, but it should have been Jim who had kept Sarah safe, not him. That's the least Matthew would have expected. To step into his shoes and keep any eye out for his little girl.

So he was disappointed – no, more than that – upset, that Sarah had not phoned him to say she had decided to throw in the towel and take Eileen to the police. He had thought she regarded him like a partner in the firm, the way her father had. Someone to be confided in, consulted. Someone whose opinion counted for something. Perhaps even a kind of uncle or godfather. Not just another member of staff to be given a cursory message by one of his juniors.

What had he been thinking? He'd allowed himself to become sentimental and imagine that his relationship with Sarah was personal when it was really just a commercial transaction.

So he isn't best pleased when Sarah barges into his office without knocking, bringing Helen with her.

'We need to talk. Can you get hold of Taylor and get him down here now?'

Jim is on the point of telling Sarah that he is not her bloody secretary when he takes in the expressions on the two women's faces.

'Where's Eileen?'

'That's what we need to talk about.'

TWENTY-FIVE

'What exactly did they say?'

They are all assembled in the conference room. Helen seems to have become an honorary member of the team and is being fussed over by Kelly who has been offering her a bewildering choice of teas and coffees and her pick of the biscuit tin. Taylor is more than normally creased and bedraggled, his hair in a bird's nest tangle as if he has just got out of bed with a crashing hangover. Which he has. Except it was yet another settee.

Sarah looks pale and is tight-lipped. Her hands are laid on the table and her fingers are drumming furiously on the polished surface. She hasn't spoken since they sat down. Jim can't read her. Is she about to collapse under the strain or is she setting herself to do whatever is necessary? She'd told him about the phone call as soon as she got back to the office but insisted on waiting until Taylor arrived before going into any detail.

Jim's question causes her to raise her head and look each one of them in the face before answering.

'These may not be the exact words, but they're close enough.

You're too late, love. Eileen's staying with us for a while.

Now listen. Don't even think about going to the police. Even if you can get them to take you seriously this time it won't do any good. First sign of coppers we'll be away. You know what that means for Eileen.

All we want is Gerry. You get him to come to us and we'll let Eileen go. It's as simple as that.

I told them we hadn't found Gerry yet. Didn't know where he was. They weren't having it.

You're on the right track. Keep going. One of his mates must know where he is. You've got forty-eight hours.

I told them it wasn't enough time.

It's all there is. We can't hang around. After that we cut our losses.

We'll ring you in two days. And don't try ringing this phone. I'll be taking a hammer to it when I hang up.'

Silence as they absorb what has happened. Helen is stony-faced and hands a tissue to Kelly who is shedding quiet tears.

'After that we cut our losses,' mumbles Jim, and Sarah immediately thinks of the knife they held against her that night.

Jim is on the point of asking a question when Taylor unexpectedly comes to life.

'Anything else?'

Sarah hesitates and reddens a little.

'He told me I looked sexy in this dress and that maybe we should meet up when all this is over.'

Jim mutters 'Bastard' but Taylor is keeping his cool.

'So they could see you.'

Sarah shifts uncomfortably in her chair. Helen puts her hand on top of hers.

'You were right, Jim. They must have been watching Eileen's house when I went there to fetch Treacle. Oh God! They must have been following me ever since. First, they try to get me, then they get Eileen.'

Helen rubs her back as if she's trying to massage the pain away.

'It's not your fault.'

'Then whose fault is it?'

Silence again. Jim is taking in the room, scrutinising every face, gauging the mood.

'If we take these people seriously...'

Helen makes as if to interrupt him, but he ploughs on.

'... and I think we have to, then we've got less than two days to get Eileen back in one piece.'

He pauses for effect to drive the point home giving Helen the chance to jump back in.

'Sorry, but what the hell are you talking about, Jim? You've got two days to get that poor woman back? This nonsense has to stop. Now.'

She gives the rest of the group the withering look she used to serve up regularly to errant kids in Year 9.

'If you lot had taken her to the police right from the start none of this would have happened. Messing about in things none of you understands. Grow up! This isn't some stupid detective novel, it's real. Eileen's life is in danger.'

'I've tried that, Mum. They didn't want to know.'

'But you didn't tell them everything, did you? Thought you could do it all on your own. They've got to act now. They're threatening to kill her.'

Kelly has been sniffling continually since Sarah began but now her shoulders start to pulse, and she bursts into a piercing keen of grief that rips through the room. Helen is stunned at first but puts her arm round Kelly and eases her up out of her seat. She signals to the others to carry on as she shepherds her away making the comforting noises parents save for small children. Jim closes the door behind them.

'She's got very close to Eileen.'

Taylor has caught a faint reflection of himself in the window and is vainly trying to straighten his hair as he speaks.

'Too close?'

Jim bristles.

'Meaning?'

'They know Sarah went to the cops and got the bum's rush. Which, by the way, is more than I did until now.'

Sarah has been slouching ever lower over the table as the discussion has gone on but now draws herself upright.

'Go on.'

'And they know that I've been seeing some of Gerry's old mates.'

He turns to Jim and raises his eyebrows.

'I know you don't think I'm much of a detective, but I'd know if someone was following me.'

Jim swallows down the impulse to challenge that.

'And your point is...'

Sarah butts in before Taylor can respond.

'Who told them?'

Taylor nods.

'Precisely. I'm not offering a spot prize for this, and I won't be asking for a bonus either cos it doesn't take too many little grey cells to work that one out.'

Jim is shaking his head.

'She's worked here nearly twenty years. She wouldn't do that.'

'Think about it. None of us has been to that house before today. So how did they know Eileen was there?'

'One of the neighbours could have seen her. Mentioned it to someone else. Word got round...'

Jim's voice trails off as he listens to what he's saying. That won't wash.

Taylor opens the door to the office slightly, checking there is no one in the corridor outside, and then closes it again.

'They've always been one step ahead of us. Now we know why.'

Jim feels empty inside. This was the place where he had always felt in control. He and Matthew had created an environment that was constructed to suit their personalities and make their working lives as accommodating as possible. A tiny, functioning world built in their image. Now Matthew has gone, the business is almost on the rocks, and he is having to face up to the fact that their longest serving employee has betrayed them.

Sarah's emotional reaction is less complex.

159

'Shit!'

'They probably followed you to Kelly's house and then spied their chance to get at her. Offered her a dollop of cash if she fed them information about Eileen. Maybe even convinced her it was in Eileen's best interests. Get this whole thing over as quickly as possible.'

A low, rumbling growl of disagreement from Jim.

'No. Not Kelly. She's fond of that old fusspot. Look how she was crying just now. You can't put that on. No, they must have threatened her and her family. Forced her to help them.'

'Makes no difference, either way.'

'It does to me.'

Sarah is pacing round the room now, hoping that movement will clear her brain and help her see the way through.

'OK – if we assume you're right...'

'Any better ideas...?'

'... then what are our options?'

Jim throws his head back and slowly rotates his neck. Sarah winces as the bones make a cracking, splintering sound.

'Oh God, Sarah. You're not going to start again with that business of throwing your hands in all directions and shouting out any thought that comes into your head, are you?'

'Come on, Jim. We don't have much time. Mum might bring her back any moment.'

'Alright, alright.'

He rubs circles round his eyes and stares intently at the table top.

'We could all march down to the police station, hand Kelly over and get them to find out what she knows. 'Course they are not going to be best pleased with us given we could have done that with Eileen when Gerry first went missing.'

'But we still don't know what this is all about. Or if Dad was involved.'

Taylor chips in.

'I've got an idea about that. When I met Bill Chadwick, he talked about how Gerry was like a kind of social secretary to the old boys' club. Organised regular meetings kept everyone in touch. He also said that he was bitter about having missed out on the kind of pay checks players get today.'

'So what are you thinking?'

'I reckon that's what Gerry brought to the party. Don had the financial nous, but Gerry had the contacts.'

'Contacts for what?'

'I'm not sure yet, but I think that several of his old teammates were in on this. Bill was about to cough it all up, but something spooked him and he legged it before he could explain. I need to get hold of him again.'

Jim begins growling, like a dog whose dinner has been taken away from him.

'We're past all that now. Forget about Gerry. He's alright, thank you very much... wherever he is. It's Eileen we've got to worry about.'

'Yes, but if I can find Gerry...'

'There isn't time...'

Sarah raises the palms of her hands and signals for them both to calm down.

'Alright, alright. Option 1 – hand this over to the cops. What else?'

'Do we have any other choice now? You heard your mother.'

'Dad left this firm to me, not her, Jim.'

'This isn't just about you. If Eileen dies, we'll all be responsible for not contacting the police.'

Jim relaxes his shoulders and sighs.

'I know... I don't want to give up now either. It feels personal now. But we have to be realistic. Forty-eight hours.'

Taylor is looking deeply into his long-empty paper coffee cup as if he could conjure some more caffeine from the dried remains. Jim is staring at him defiantly, daring him to make his case.

Sarah has perched herself on the window ledge, watching them as if they were two tennis players trying to smash the ball past the other.

'If I found Gerry, we could persuade him to surrender himself to them. If the money is all they want, then they might let both of them go. Or Eileen, at least.'

Jim snorts. Just the kind of useless contribution he'd expect.

'You've had five days to find him and we can't even narrow it down to Great Britain. So what's going to change in two more? And even if you did, how do we know he'll agree to come quietly? You going to kidnap him so we can rescue his wife from some kidnappers? We'll end up with a longer jail sentence than they do.'

'And what makes you think the police will do any better? They're coming into this cold. And if they don't find her in time she's had it anyway.'

Sarah nods in agreement.

'Taylor's right. And remember. If they find out that we've involved the cops they say they're going to disappear. Handing it over now could be the most dangerous option for Eileen.'

Jim isn't having that either.

'But they won't know the police are on the case unless we tell Kelly. And we can control that.'

'He's got a point there, Taylor.'

Jim sees his chance to go on the offensive.

'And to be completely safe, we can hand Kelly over as well. Once she's in custody then the line will go dead. No more inside information. They'll never know.'

Jim sits back, content that he has clinched the argument, but Taylor isn't finished yet.

'If they stop hearing from Kelly then they'll know something's wrong. That's the quickest way of getting Eileen's throat cut.'

No fetching that one back. But Jim chases after it anyway.

'So you'd just leave Kelly be, would you? Let her carry on telling them every move we plan to make?'

'Exactly. That's option 3.'

Sarah has a pained expression on her face.

'Are you actually recommending that?'

'Think about it. It's like the Enigma code. The enemy doesn't know we've broken it.'

He ignores Jim's plea to "God Almighty" and focuses on Sarah.

'We can use Kelly to our advantage in a way the police never could. Get her to tell them what we want them to know, not what they want to know.'

Sarah's eyes are still narrowed in suspicion, but he can see unmistakable signs of interest.

'You're right, Jim. The chances of me finding Gerry in the next two days aren't great but it doesn't matter. We just tell them I've found him and when they check with Kelly, she confirms it.'

Sarah responds hesitantly.

'O… K. What then?'

'We arrange to deliver Gerry to them. Get them out into the open.'

'But we don't have him.'

'Maybe they've never met Gerry. So, as long as we show them an elderly man in a car…'

Taylor can't resist a little smile as he turns his face towards Jim.

'Any old man would do…'

'Oh my god. Now he's on about a hostage exchange. Well, you can forget that. I'm not having myself chained to a radiator for anybody.'

'Jim's right. That won't work. But you might be on to something about Kelly. Do you really think she has a soft spot for Eileen?'

Jim blinks in agreement.

'Maybe we can get her to come back to our side.'

Taylor is loving it.

'Like a double agent, you mean?'

'Don't encourage him, Sarah. He's off on some espionage fantasy now.'

'No, seriously. This might work.'

It is time for Jim to be the adult in the room. Again.

'So let me get this straight. We're going to tell them we have Gerry and arrange to meet them to exchange him for Eileen. And we get Kelly to convince them it's true. Only we can't actually produce Gerry and I'm certainly not going to be his stunt double. And presuming they fall for that, the three of us – sorry, four – I forgot your mother – we're going to overpower a gang of career criminals who have already shot Gerry's accomplice and are handy with a knife. That's your plan, is it?'

'It needs more work, I'll give you that. But... in a nutshell... yes. And I think I know where we might be able to get some helpers.'

'You're not actually considering this, are you, Sarah?'

She has turned to the window again and is gazing down the street. She screws her eyes a little to make the picture hazy and imagines that she is a little girl again and her father is showing her proudly round his office and its window on the world. At the time it seemed unimaginably huge and luxurious, and she remembers lying in bed at home thinking about the day when she could move into one of the offices and work alongside him. The memory remains but that little girl has gone, and her father is now dust in a jar. And the offices have shrunk in size and look run-down and tired – like Jim, who is looking imploringly at her, willing her not to make things worse than they already are. Taylor also has his eyes on her hoping she is brave enough to give him one more chance to make a success of something.

She moves back to the desk, places both her hands on the edge and leans forward but before she can deliver her verdict, Helen slips back into the room. Her scolding, schoolmistress manner has gone and been replaced by a look of anxious hesitancy.

'What's up, Mum?'

'It's Kelly. She wants to tell you something.'

TWENTY-SIX

1968

Things were drifting at Bolton, and I felt I was just marking time there. We'd had a big win against Liverpool in the Cup the year before and I thought that might be the spark for a good run in the league and a real push for promotion. But we ran out of steam and ended up in mid-table again.

It felt like the club had lost hope about getting back to the First Division and all the board seemed to care about was making sure the books balanced at the end of the year. Crowds were down, money was tight, and Bolton had become a selling club, willing to let players go to the highest bidder. Frank Goodall had gone to Tottenham and now there was talk of him playing for England. And we had a really good little winger in Ronnie Shepherd but when Chelsea came along with a chequebook, they let him go as well. I could see there was no way we'd be getting out of the Second Division if they couldn't hang onto the best players.

On a personal level I was doing well. The press had agreed I was Man of the Match against Liverpool and there'd been a lot of paper talk about a big club coming in for me off the back of that. I waited for the offers to come in but instead, all I saw were other players moving on.

I missed Mam then, not being able to talk it over with her. I'd lost her the year before. Breast cancer. But Eileen had picked up where she left off. She reckoned I needed pushing, just like Mam always had.

'You're too soft, Gerry. They know how loyal you are to Bolton, and they take advantage.'

'Since when did loyalty become a bad thing?'

'Since it stopped you getting on. You should be playing in the First Division. Everybody says so.'

'Then how come no bugger's come in for me?'

'Maybe they don't know you'd be willing to move.'

I started to argue with her some more, but she stopped me short.

'You're to go in tomorrow and ask for a transfer. That'll shake things up.'

Tom Clark had been manager since the early fifties, and the board had kept faith with him after we got relegated four years earlier, but time had passed him by. Elsewhere there were young managers with progressive ideas, but we were stuck in the same old ways, hoping that if we kept doing the things that had worked before we'd somehow get back to where we used to be.

He was a distant figure to us players. Left all the training to Joe Turner and the other backroom staff. But the board still trusted him, and he had the final say on which players stayed and which could go.

He must have known why I'd come to see him because he were all over me when I went to his office. Couldn't have been nicer. Sat me down. Offered me a drink and a cigarette. Told me how well I'd been playing. How much the club valued me.

'I'm glad you've come to see me, Gerry. I'd been wanting to have a word. Been thinking about next season. We need to have a right good go this time and I think you're the feller to lead the team. How do you feel about being captain?'

He were a crafty sod. Took the wind right out of my sails.

'Oh... err... well... err... that'd be great, Mr Clark.'

'That's settled then. I'll let Joe know and you can tell the lads in training.'

He got up then and started to show me out.

'Err… there was something I wanted to ask you, Mr Clark.'

He stiffened a bit but was still smiling. He knew what was coming.

'I've been thinking about my career.'

He nodded.

'So have I. There's not many left like you, Gerry. A one-club man.'

He wasn't going to make this easy.

'But that's the thing. I want to play at the top level. I think I'm good enough.'

''Course you are, Gerry. That's why I want to build the team around you. With you as captain I think we can go all the way.'

'But I've been thinking, maybe I need to move to another club to do that.'

He put his arm on my shoulder and sat me down again.

'Now. What's brought this on? Aren't you happy here? Haven't we always treated you well?'

'It's not that, Mr Clark. But when I see what's happened to Frank since he left. Being talked about for England. You only get that when you're at a top club.'

He didn't like that.

'There's been plenty of lads played for England while I've been manager. And I happen to think this is a top club.'

'All I'm saying is, you've let other players go. I'd like to go as well.'

'What makes you think we wouldn't let you leave?'

That shocked me.

'You mean you would accept a bid for me?'

He leaned back on his chair and rested his hands on his paunch.

'See, that's the thing, Gerry. No one has put in a bid for you. We got good money for Frank and there were plenty of offers for Ronnie. But you? Not a sausage.'

He had me then. I was too stunned to reply.

'I know what it's like. You have a good match, the papers sing your praises and you start thinking you're God's gift. But the truth is, Gerry, nobody but us wants you.'

'You don't know that. How can you know that?'

He beckoned me over to the other side of the room and brought out a hefty file full of typed sheets.

'See that? It's a list of all the footballers who are out of contract and looking for a new club. Dozens of 'em. We get sent them in the close season, see if we'd be interested in taking any of them on. But it's getting late and most of this lot won't find a club. Or else they'll have to drop down a league or two and take a pay cut.'

He banged the file down on the table to make the point.

'Don't let the papers turn your head. You're wanted here. We all love you. But if it gets out that you want a transfer... well, I could hardly make you captain, could I? And it's funny how quickly the supporters can change when they know somebody wants away. Think about it, Gerry. You don't want to end up running down your contract in the Reserves and then finish up on this list.'

He could see he'd won because he started to speak more softly to me, like he were my uncle or summat.

'Listen. Don't worry. This is just between us. If you're going to be captain, then naturally I'll talk to the board about lifting your wages a bit. That'll make things easier at home, won't it? I know what it's like when you first get married.'

When I got home that night, Eileen took one look at my face and walked off to the kitchen in disgust.

'Your mother was right about you. Too easily satisfied.'

I knew she was right, but the truth is I was too scared to take the risk and push for the move. I signed a new contract and they made me the skipper.

'The start of a new era,' Tom Clark told the press at the start of the season.

Three months later, after a bad run of defeats, he was sacked.

TWENTY-SEVEN

The platform at Burnage station is raised above the surrounding roads, at the summit of a criss-cross of aluminium steps, giving a panoramic view of... well, not much really. The crane-clogged skyline of Manchester is too far off to see so the passengers have to be content with gazing down on rows of identical pantile roofs and watching the cars scooting past the fast-food shops on Fog Lane. Not that they want to linger too long. The station's elevated position means that there is nothing to hold back the gusty wind which has fought its way from the Atlantic, whooshed across Ireland in no time, hopped over the Irish Sea and is now threatening to blow Taylor off his feet.

It is quiet mid-morning, just three other customers huddled in the shelter of an unattended ticket office, all paying close attention to their phones, seemingly oblivious to anything going on around them. Taylor had suggested meeting Bill Chadwick at Piccadilly. Too crowded he said. Too much of a chance of being spotted. Better a few stops up the line. Now he can see why Bill chose this station for a rendezvous. If he stripped off all his clothes and cavorted up and down the platform in goose-pimply splendour, there is a chance that one of the other passengers might notice and remember him. Otherwise, he is invisible. A non-person to his fellow travellers.

The train from the airport pulls in and scoops up everyone but Taylor. Only Bill gets off. He walks purposefully past Taylor without acknowledging him hissing 'Fog Lane Park' as he heads for the steps and down to the road.

Taylor finds him by some scruffy cages not far from the main entrance.

'Used to be birds of paradise in 'ere at one time. They had parrots and chipmunks and monkeys as well. Came to feed 'em when the kids were young.'

They stare into the empty cages. Bill looks down at the hand by his side, searching for a child who is no longer there ('Look at them, Dad. What they called?'). Taylor remains silent, waiting for the mood to shift. Without warning Bill turns away and heads off towards some waterlogged football pitches. The signs of neglect are obvious. Bare stretches round centre spots given over to rutted mud and the penalty areas looking like Flanders Field after a battle. Some of the pitches have wonky goals, the posts leaning towards each other for support, others stand naked and unmarked. Back to basics here. Coats for goalposts and skins versus shirts.

'I remember when this place were packed on a weekend. Might be half a dozen games going on at once. Kids of all ages, mums and dads cheering 'em on. Now look at it.'

They do. Two dogs slither across the field chasing one another, wheeling round, losing their feet, nipping at each other's necks. Play fighting. They yelp away and out of sight into some bushes.

'Councils are skint,' offers Taylor. 'No money.'

Bill hunches his shoulders and inspects his still shiny shoes.

'It's not just that. Nobody can be bothered any more. Rather be sat indoors watching than playing.'

I need to move this on, thinks Taylor, or he'll sink so low I'll never get him back.

'In the cathedral. What was it you were going to tell me?'

Bill trudges off along the side of the pitch, hands thrust deep into his raincoat pockets leaving Taylor to trot behind.

'You said Gerry got you involved but you could never stand the stuff. What did you mean?'

Bill stops and Taylor can hear him gulping for air. He's about to leg it. Last chance.

'They've kidnapped Eileen.'

'What!'

Taylor lets that sink in for moment or two.

'They say they're going to kill her if we don't hand Gerry over to them.'

'Jesus!'

'We've only got forty-eight hours. You've got to help us.'

'I can't... don't know where he is.'

'I don't think they're bluffing. Not after what happened to Don.'

Bill is breathing heavily now, weighing up his options.

'We know something but not enough. You need to tell us what this is all about before it's too late.'

Taylor steers them to a nearby bench, backing onto what used to be decorative flower bed but has now become hopelessly overgrown by weeds, grass sprouting in all directions in a losing battle with thistles and brambles. A sign says "Wild Meadow" – virtue signalling arising from necessity. Bill peers into the middle distance. He looks his age now. A thin man in his seventies frightened to face up to what lies ahead of him.

'Was it Don who started it all?'

Bill nods.

'None of us knew him that well, apart from Gerry. Weren't at the club that long before his knee went. All over for him before he were twenty-one. Wasn't much they could do in them days.

He started coming to the reunions. He'd retrained as an accountant and become some sort of financial adviser, you know, helping people with their pension and suggesting investments. Done very well judging by the car he were driving. Lot better than the rest of us.

You've had no word from Gerry then?'

Taylor shakes his head.

'How did it begin?'

'Can't remember when exactly. It were near the end of one session, and we were moaning about how much they get paid these days and how we could retire happily on what some of 'em earn in a month. And then we got going on our aches and pains, dodgy hips, arthritis – how we were never looked after properly. I know Gerry got really fired up about it. Said we'd been exploited and thrown on t'scrap heap when we weren't needed any more.

He had a point, but I thought that were too much. A lot of us have still got jobs at clubs. Nobody's thrown us away yet.

But Gerry weren't having it. Told us we were still being taken for a ride. What we got was a pittance compared to the handouts for agents and hangers-on. We deserve better than that, he said.

I didn't think much of it at the time. We often started feeling sorry for ourselves by the end of an evening; when we moved on to shorts and got to reminiscing.'

Bill stops to look at some sparrows and tits that have gathered by their feet, pecking around hopefully. Somebody must have been feeding them from this bench, but they soon realise it isn't these two. After a short while one bird breaks ranks and the others scatter into the air and zoom off in search of richer pickings, squabbling noisily as they fly out of sight. Bill continues staring at the ground where they were.

'So, what was different about that evening?'

'Normally it would just peter out. Nowt we can do about it. Just the way things are. Anybody want to share a taxi?'

'But not that night?'

'Gerry said it didn't have to be that way. It wasn't too late to get our share. There was something we could do. Then he asked Don to speak about an idea he'd had. Must have planned it in advance. He had it all off pat. Gave us the hard sell.'

'So what was it? Something to do with money laundering? Re-routing dirty cash into legitimate businesses and then drawing it out again?'

Bill looks confused.

'What?'

'Or was it dodgy investments? Getting friends and relatives to put money into get-rich-quick schemes that went belly up?'

'What are you talking about?'

'The scheme Don suggested to you all. Some sort of financial scam, wasn't it?'

'Nothing complicated like that. Import and retail is what he called it. He had some backers who needed new ways of getting their products into growing markets. That's how Don talked. You couldn't be sure from the way he spoke what it was all about. But we knew. We all knew from the start.'

'Knew what?'

Bill kicks out at two pigeons doing a courtship dance too close to his legs.

'Drugs.'

There is an open-air café at the other side of the park so they head in that direction. It's a school day so no older kids are hanging around, just a smattering of bleary-eyed young mothers pretending to take an interest in what their toddlers are up to in the sandpit or the playground but really catching up with pointless distractions on their phone and swigging some much-needed caffeine from a paper cup. No one pays any attention to the two men who grab a drink – cappuccino (of sorts) for Taylor, tea for Bill – and settle at a table as far from the hub-bub as possible.

'How did it work?'

'Easy enough. A lot of us are still working for big clubs – scouts, kit men, match-day ambassadors – or we have friends and relatives that are on the staff somewhere. That's where Gerry came in. He knew everybody.

These days clubs are travelling all over Europe, more or less every week at some times in the season. There wouldn't be many games where we didn't have someone, or knew someone, who was on the plane.'

'What then?'

'Somebody would find us – usually just before the game – and give us a parcel. Most likely in a boot bag or something that would look right with the rest of the kit. Nothing too big – like a few of bags of flour – and we'd stash it away with the rest of the gear – usually when the game was on and everybody else was busy.'

'What about customs?'

'You're normally going back about one or two in the morning on a private plane. There's hardly anyone about at the airports. Anyway, they just wave the footballers through. They're like film stars these days – red carpet wherever they go.

Then we retrieve the package at the other end. If the kit man isn't one of us, we cut him in, and he makes sure it gets back to us.'

Taylor finally gives up on his cappuccino and tosses it into a nearby bin. It misses and there are some disgusted looks from the young mums as a frothy, mud-brown pool forms on the patio. He decides to pretend this never happened.

'How did you get rid of the stuff?'

'Oh, that was down to Gerry or Don. We'd get the package to them and they'd do the rest. We never had any contact with the… err…'

'Criminals? Drug dealers?'

'Distributors. That's what Don called them.'

Bill sucks on his tea and looks past Taylor who is trying not show his disapproval. He isn't making a very good job of it.

'I know. But that's how it was. If we didn't say the word, it was easier to think we weren't doing anything wrong.'

He glances at Taylor who is looking sad. Like he expected more of a man like Bill.

'I did try to back out once.'

'Made enough by then, had you?'

'I didn't want to be part of it any more. But Don wasn't having it. Said I was too important a contact. Couldn't be spared. And anyway, the distributors wouldn't be too happy about it. I got the message. He didn't have to spell it out.

Don had an answer for everything. If we weren't doing it, then somebody else would. There'd still be drugs so long as there's people who want them. So what difference does it make?'

'And is that what you think?'

Bill rubs his eyes and sighs heavily but says nothing.

'How long has this been going on?'

'This was our fifth season.'

'Bloody hell!'

'I know. I kept thinking, this can't go on. Somebody will make a mistake. Somebody will talk. But it never happened. We all stuck together, like when we were playing. And after a while...'

'You get used to it.'

'Aye. It becomes a kind of routine. And the money comes in regular as clockwork. Cash. And you get used to that too.'

'And then they shot Don.'

Bill stands up and stretches his shoulders.

'Let's walk.'

They wander over to the bowling green which, in contrast to the rest of the park, looks in tip-top condition. Two groups of ladies – definitely ladies rather than women – are having a match. White tops and grey skirts. There is a steely silence about the game, both teams concentrating hard, and then discreet murmurs of approval as they see one ball scatter their opponents into the gully. They stroll round the perimeter, half watching the contest.

'Gerry rang me. I think he'd been on the phone to the others as well.'

'How was he? Shit scared?'

'You don't know Gerry. He were always good under pressure. Never saw him rattled in a game. No. He were shaken, obviously. But not panicking.

Said something about Don having taken it too far. Told me to keep my head down and he'd get back in touch.'

'When was this?'

'Couple of months ago. Never heard from him again.'

Bill pulls on Taylor's arm and stops him in his tracks.

'Do you think he's dead?'

'I don't know. Nobody's seen him since he walked out on Eileen. But they're still trying to find him – so they haven't killed him.'

'But you reckon they would? Eileen's a bit of a stuck-up cow but she doesn't deserve this. How're you going to find her?'

There is a loud cheer from the bowlers as the final ball caresses the jack with a delicate kiss and ends the match.

Taylor can sense the change in Bill. The slump in his shoulders has gone and his expression has altered. Teeth clenched, cheeks sucked in, eyes bright and focused. He has his match face on.

'No idea,' replies Taylor, 'but I do know we're going to need some help.'

TWENTY-EIGHT

Twelve of the forty-eight hours gone, and they are taking stock in Helen's living room. Given the ticking clock, they have decided against getting hopelessly drunk, blacking out and forgetting the whole damn thing. There will be plenty of time for that later if everything goes belly up.

Helen is in the kitchen processing an assortment of frozen food trays through the microwave. None of the dishes go together (prawn masala and shepherd's pie) but no one cares about what they eat at this stage. Jim has been told there is a cauliflower cheese somewhere so that will have to be his ration for the day.

He is nursing a tepid cup of Earl Grey tea and Sarah is doing her best to pretend that her tumbler of tonic water with ice, lemon and a dash of Angostura bitter also has a healthy jigger of gin.

Marcus has brought along a couple of packs of alcohol-free beer but no one can see the point of drinking them. For his benefit they have been bringing him up to speed about Kelly's confession a few hours before.

*

There had been tears, of course.

Plenty of them. Sarah had begun to wonder whether Kelly would shrivel away due to dehydration. And although "Sorry"

177

seems to be the hardest word for many people, Kelly had no problems with it.

'I'm so sorry, Sarah.'

'Yes. I can see that.'

'I can't tell you how sorry I am.'

'Yes...'

'Letting you down... and your father. After all he did for me. And now Eileen... I'm so sorry...'

Jim had found the whole spectacle upsetting and disgusting in equal measure. The sight of Kelly blubbing continuously and uncontrollably and the slobber of snot dripping from her nose turned his stomach. He had known Kelly for over twenty years but now he realised he'd never known her much at all. He had presumed that she felt the same loyalty to Curtis and Curtis that he held. In this he had been badly mistaken. And the fact that it was that gobshite Taylor who had spotted this and not him really got his goat.

Helen had also been on hand, making comforting noises, feeding a chain of paper hankies to mop up the streaming eyes and the runny nose.

Jim was not a violent man, he didn't feel like slapping Kelly for her treachery, but he was inclined to sling her out on her ear. But they had decided to take Taylor's advice and "turn" Kelly. So it was a case of an arm round the shoulder rather than a boot up the backside. He felt that Sarah and Helen were better suited to this, but he was on hand if the tactics changed. Each to their own.

Kelly explained about the calling card they had left on her washing line. Sarah felt tears welling at the back of her eyes and a catch in her throat. It wasn't that she loved Treacle – she wasn't sure that was possible – and it had to be admitted that he was treading a fine line between life and death. But he was harmless. And the fact that someone had taken the trouble to lift him from his basket, probably still half asleep, and wring his neck until the life was squeezed out of him and then calmly hang him out to dry like a pair of old knickers – that made her feel like joining Kelly in a good weep.

'What did they say when you phoned them?'

'They didn't want to hurt Eileen, but Gerry had something that was theirs. And if they didn't get it soon then she'd have to suffer for it. Unless I helped them.'

'And you went along with them. Just like that?'

More tears. Helen rubbing her back and telling her she'll feel better when she's got it all out. Finally, she had calmed down enough to continue.

'I didn't have a choice. The dog was just a warning. They could get in the house whenever they wanted and next time it would be me – or Chris. And the police would never find them if I told them. But they would find me.'

'So you told them what we were planning, all that we talked about?'

Kelly nodded.

'They were worried when you went to the police. They thought they'd connect this with some other crime they were investigating. I think they were on the point of packing up then, giving it up.'

She had paused then, hesitating before adding what Sarah knew was coming.

'But you didn't tell them everything, did you? So they never put two and two together.'

Kelly let that lie there for a moment.

'I'm sorry, Sarah. But that made them feel they were safe.'

'Until you told them I'd changed my mind and I was going to take Eileen to the police?'

'They knew they had to act quickly then, or they'd lose her.'

Jim had kept a lid on it until then but couldn't control himself any longer.

'So what was all that rubbish about you caring for Eileen? Feeling sorry for her.'

'I do. I do.'

'Didn't stop you handing her over to have her throat cut, did it?'

Helen had turned her body half round as if to shield Kelly from him. Kelly had curled into her like a child trying to avoid a beating from an angry father.

'That's enough, Jim. That's not helping.'

'I suppose you feel better now do you, Kelly? Now you've got that off your chest. How do you think Eileen feels right now?'

'JIM!'

Sarah had fixed him with a look that said, just one more word. Just one.

He sat back and shut up. Sarah kept one eye on him. In case.

'What else can you tell us, Kelly?'

'Nothing really.'

'We have to find Eileen – you know that. Anything you know – anything – you must tell us.'

Kelly turned to Helen to help her, panic in her eyes.

'Did they mention anything that might help work out where they've taken her?'

Kelly hung her head.

'We didn't meet face to face. It was just on the phone. Always a different number. And it wasn't like it was a conversation. I told them what I knew, and they told me to carry on listening to what you were doing and keep my mouth shut.'

Helen had placed her hand under Kelly's chin, touching only by her fingertips, and then tenderly lifted her face to look into hers.

'Any snippet. The odd word. A reference you didn't understand. Think.'

Silence while Kelly turned the reels over in her head, searching for something to offer in atonement. Jim saw it was hopeless. A frightened, middle-aged woman who had wandered into someone else's world and was stunned into incomprehension. He could see Sarah was also on the point of giving it up. No use flogging a dead horse.

Then, gradually, they could see Kelly's eyes liven and her neck become tense as if she was looking for something she knew was there but couldn't put her hand on it; flicking through index cards one by one in her mind until she came across the one she was after.

Helen gave her what she hoped was her best welcoming and expectant smile.

And suddenly it popped into Kelly's head.

'Jackie.'

'What?'

'In the background. On the last call. I heard one of them say Jackie.'

Sarah and Jim had hung back, not wanting to break the spell, leaving Helen to cajole her a little more. Like landing a fish, thought Jim. Most likely to slip off the line the nearer you bring it to the net.

'Was that all, Kelly? Just Jackie? Or did he say something else as well?'

Kelly's face was set now, and her eyes were focused on an object just out of sight. The tearful hesitancy suspended for the moment. Back to the file index. Flicking through the cards at high speed. Another fragment was there if she could only find it. Like going back to a dream and trying to remember what had been so clear before but was now lost in the fog.

'Something about a house, I think.'

'Go on.'

'It wasn't very clear. Somebody was speaking, not knowing I was on the phone. One of the others told him to shut up.'

'What else, Kelly? What about Jackie and this house?'

'I'm not sure. That it was ready? Jackie's house was ready? Or sorted out? Something like that.'

Jim had been the first to say it.

'Who the hell is Jackie?'

'Don's widow.'

Taylor had slipped into the room without any fuss and had

been standing by the door listening to Kelly as she racked her brains. He stepped forward and joined them at the table.

'Jackie was the wife of Don Bradley. Until someone put a bullet in his head.'

And then Kelly had thrown up all over the carpet tiles.

*

Kelly had crashed out not long after they got to Helen's house and it was agreed she might as well be left to sleep as it wasn't likely she had any more to tell them. Nothing more she can do to help. For now.

There is a lot for them to digest and none of it is easy. Especially the partially defrosted bao buns.

Marcus feels he is intruding; out of place. It isn't exactly an unusual sensation. For a lot of his working life he spends time as the only black man in a room of white executives. Usually, it is fine and people are, for the most part, courteous and respectful. But not exactly warm either. There is a sense of distance; his world and their world. They touch and overlap from time to time, but they are in different orbits. He's gotten used to it. Tells himself that he's overcome more obstacles to get where he is than they've had expenses claims. And he's almost certainly better than they are at his job or they wouldn't have drafted him in. So, stuff it.

Not that this group is too intimidating. While he was being briefed on Kelly's confession, he took time to survey Team Curtis. This is the group who are going to overcome a gang of hard cases who have already killed one person, tried to kidnap another and are now holding an old lady to ransom. A septuagenarian macrobiotic fanatic with dangling jowls like a pair of kangaroo pouches; a clapped out sofa-surfer with body odour problems and leaky shoes; an elderly, retired schoolteacher still coming to terms with her ex-husband's desertion and death.

Oh – and him. A thirty-something freelance corporate accountant who does weights on the weekends.

Hardly the A-Team. What's my role here?

But then there is Sarah. Delightful and maddening at the same time. He is feeling very tender towards her since she nearly got hauled off in a transit. Protective. But he also knows that she would knee him in the balls (figuratively speaking, he hopes) if he tried to wrap her in cotton wool and stop her doing what she is determined to see through. She has energy to burn and that gives him some hope even though the sensible part of him, the bit that can see when a company is a lost cause and all you can do is shut it down and get the best deal you can, knows this is a car crash in progress. He has decided to stick around to be sure no harm comes to Sarah. If he can help the rest of Team Curtis then he will, but that's not his priority.

Taylor has filled them in on his meeting with Bill Chadwick. The realisation that they are dealing with a drug-smuggling racket has taken the oxygen out of the room. If there is any remnant of optimism still alive it is now gasping for air.

Sarah has been rubbing her eyes and her mascara has smeared leaving her looking washed out and weary, all colour drained from her face.

'We were over-thinking it. Got carried away that it was some sort of sophisticated financial scam that had got out of hand. But it's just an ordinary everyday story of illegal drugs and gangland murders. Happens all the time.'

'Not to me,' Jim adds unnecessarily. 'Not to Gerry or the others, either. And certainly not to your...'

He sits back, his mouth still open but the word unspoken. Helen finishes his sentence for him.

'Not to Matthew, you mean. But who knows?'

She turns to Sarah.

'Since he left me, I've had plenty of time to think about your father. More and more he feels like a mystery to me. You'd think you'd know someone by the time you get past your silver wedding, but nothing would surprise me now.'

She braces herself for a sharp comeback, but Sarah shows no reaction, and this depresses Helen even more. If Sarah has lost hope, then Eileen really has had it. When she does respond it is quiet and directed at no one in particular.

'It seems different somehow, doesn't it? Swindling someone out of their life savings or taking dirty money and making it clean. I mean that's despicable but it's... oh, I don't know...'

'White collar? Middle class?' suggests Taylor.

Marcus pitches in to help. He can see Sarah grappling with what her father was caught up in.

'You know what Sarah means. It's like cyber-crimes or telephone scams. It's cruel but you're not, you know... physically... I mean... you're not actually...'

'Looking at them in the face as you ruin their lives?'

'It's not the same though, is it? People exploited abroad, casual violence, lives flushed down the toilet. Drugs. It's different to other crimes.'

Taylor gets up and wanders round the back of the sofa.

'Feels much the same to me. I had a client. Couple of years ago. They got on to her. Letters. Phone calls. Besieged her. Cut her off from her family. Took all her savings. Mind you, she still had enough kept back to make up an overdose. Wasn't just the loss of money that killed her. It was shame. And embarrassment. And there weren't any highs along the way to take the edge off.'

Jim decides it is time to come in and bring them back to business.

'It's different in this way, though. Scammers don't threaten to actually cut your throat if you don't pay up.'

Taylor sits back down again.

'OK – but the fact that it's drugs doesn't change anything.'

"Course it bloody does.'

'Not really – just because this somehow seems a less respectable crime doesn't make them any more dangerous. We knew they were capable of murder before. It's still the same problem.'

'But the kind of people we're up against...' adds Helen.

'I think that helps us.'

Marcus rocks back in his chair in disbelief.

'What the fuck are you talking about? How can it help us that we're dealing with guys who are used to killing people to get what they want?'

Taylor leans forward to stress his point.

'Career criminals. This is their business. And you're right, they'll do whatever they need to do to protect it. But what did Kelly tell you? That they were prepared to pack it all in when they thought the police might be on to them.'

No one looks directly at Sarah who is now huddled in one corner of the settee, half-crouched with her arms wrapped round her chest.

'The point I'm making is that they don't just do things without thinking of the consequences. When they tried to snatch Sarah, they legged it rather than risk getting caught in the crowd.'

Marcus still looks unconvinced.

'They executed Gerry's mate. Took him out without hesitation. And now they have Eileen. Why wouldn't they dispose of her?'

'If they shot Don Bradley there was a reason for it. And they'll need a reason to kill Eileen. What we have to do is give them a reason not to kill her. Not to make it worth their while.'

'OK – that sounds clever but what does it actually mean? How could we do that? I mean, look at us! Tell me one thing we have going for us.'

'Well, I think we know now where they're holding Eileen.'

Taylor fidgets with his phone.

'It's all on the net. News sites were full of it for a few weeks. Now it's just another unsolved crime. Join the queue. Mmm. Oh yeah, here it is.'

He turns the phone to them to show a photograph of an attractive older woman standing outside an imposing Victorian pile that can be glimpsed through the high wrought-iron gates behind her.

'Jackie Bradley. The grieving widow still looking for justice for the unknown killers of her husband, Don. Pictured outside their grand home – Elswick House. That was six weeks ago.'

He flips the phone closed.

'Just outside Garstang. Looked it up. Isolated position. In its own grounds and surrounded by walls. Perfect place to hide someone, wouldn't you say?'

Marcus checks the faces of the others. Are they buying this?

'You saying this Eileen woman is being held there? You can't know that for sure.'

'Where else could it be? You heard what Kelly said. Jackie's house. Got to be.'

Marcus turns to Jim and gives him a pleading look. Help me out here. Pour some cold water over this before it really catches hold. He nods slightly. Leave this to me.

'Let me get this straight. Don Bradley was shot in his own home by a professional gunman. Almost certainly because of some fallout with the same gang who have kidnapped Eileen and tried to snatch Sarah.'

'Yeah – that's right.'

'And now Jackie is so well-disposed towards these people that she has invited them into her home so they can hold an old friend hostage. In you come, lads. Treat the place as your own. No hard feelings about Don. I know it's only business. Nothing personal.

Is that what you're telling us?'

Before Taylor can reply they hear Helen's voice. She doesn't look up from her task of clearing up the dirty plates while the debate has been going on around her, but she hasn't missed anything.

'Maybe she's not there. She can't bear to stay in the house after what happened, so they know it's empty.'

Taylor chimes in.

'Yeah. Or maybe they've threatened her as well. Said she'll get what her husband got if she doesn't cooperate.'

Jim swallows uncomfortably as if he were trying to digest a whole dill pickle without slicing it.

'You still can't be sure that this is where they're holding Eileen.'

Taylor shrugs his shoulders.

'Time's running out, Jim. What else have we got?'

Marcus can see Jim is faltering so he steps back in.

'OK. Let's suppose you're right. How are we going to get Eileen out of there? I mean, look at us. We can't do this on our own.'

Taylor hoovers up the remnants of some cheese and onion crisps before Helen sweeps them away.

'Ah, but we're not on our own, are we? Gerry Bradshaw has friends. Lots of friends. And I know where to find them.'

TWENTY-NINE

1973-76

You know when you're done. The trouble is, you don't want to admit it and it takes someone else to spell it out for you.

When I'd signed that five-year contract in 1968 I'd kidded myself that there was still a chance of Bolton getting back into the big-time. But each year we got a little weaker and gradually dropped down the table. Any player with a transfer value was moved on and by the start of the seventies I was surrounded by promising but untried youngsters who'd been promoted too early from the Reserves. In the end it became embarrassing. We couldn't score at one end and couldn't keep the ball out of the net at the other. And so, I was the captain who led the team down into the Third Division for the first time in the club's history.

I was thirty when my contract came up for renewal. By then, only Harry Lomax was left of the lads who had been in the team when I started. Denis had retired and taken over his dad's building business. Ernie had been snapped up by Liverpool for next to nothing and Bill had somehow managed to get himself to Manchester City when it looked like his chance had gone.

We'd had a succession of managers since Tom Clark finally stood down. At first it seemed like the club was a "sleeping giant" and that the right man could act like a blood transfusion that would bring it back to life. A couple of experienced men came and went without doing much to stop the rot and then the board turned to recently retired players with a good pedigree looking for their first job in management. The thinking was that this would bring a bit of prestige back to the club and also that inexperienced managers tended to be a bit cheaper.

In came Jimmy Reed, a former Scottish international who'd had a good career playing for Aston Villa and Wolves at centre half. When he told you something, you listened. Not just because he was six-foot three but because he knew what he was talking about. For the first time in years, I felt we had someone in charge who could actually succeed and move the club forwards.

I sat down to discuss a new contract with him. Jimmy was a Glaswegian. He didn't beat around the bush.

'You're getting on, Gerry. Not sure you've got that much left in your legs.'

'Come on, boss, I'm only thirty. I've still got plenty to give.'

We were in his little office under the main stand. His desk was covered in piles of paper scattered haphazardly across the surface. He shifted a couple of stacks to one side and started doodling on a notepad while he spoke to me.

'I believe in being honest with my players.'

'I appreciate that.'

He glanced up at me and then carried on drawing some intricate geometric pattern.

'If I had a young lad now who was capable of filling your position, I'd let you go.'

My heart sank.

'You've lost a yard of pace and you've scored... what is it...?' He flicked back a few pages in his pad. 'Oh yeah – seven goals in the last three years. Not exactly tearing up trees, are ye?'

Bugger this, I thought.

'It's not been easy.'

'It's not supposed to be easy.'

'You're my fourth manager in five years. The heart of this team's been ripped out and kids shoved in to take the place of men. If it weren't for me and Harry holding it together in midfield, we'd be a damn sight worse off than we are. So don't go laying this at my door.'

He pushed the pad to one side.

'I never said it was all your fault. I just said you're not the player you used to be. And you're not, are ye?'

'I've still got a lot to offer this club.'

'You can do a job for me. I'm not disputing that. But I want you to be realistic.'

I knew what was coming then. He dipped into the desk drawer and pushed a contract across the desk.

'Two years.'

'I was hoping for three.'

'You'll be thirty-three by then, Gerry. Same year as our Lord was when he died.'

Jimmy was a Catholic.

'No, son. Two years is all I can give ye. I want you to help me bring these youngsters on. There's some good prospects here but they need time to learn and a good example to follow. That's where you come in.'

'I thought you said my legs had gone.'

'That's OK. They can do the running for ye.'

I signed. What choice did I have? But this wasn't a bad decision. Jimmy turned out to be a natural as a manager and by the time my contract ran out again, we'd been promoted back to the Second Division. I'd played most of the games that season but missed out on the run-in when I twisted my knee late on in a game at Port Vale. That's when I knew it was over for me but I kept hoping that Jimmy would give me one more year.

No chance. You can't kid an old pro.

'I've sat in your seat, Gerry. I know what it's like. But this happens to all of us. Question is, what are you going to do next?'

'What can I do? Football's all I know.'

'The board have said they'll give you a testimonial. So that'll cushion the blow a bit.'

'I need a job, Jimmy.'

He started running his fingers up and down the biro he was holding, turning something over in his mind.

'You've been good with the kids. Helped them grow up. Learn good habits. How would you feel about helping the next generation?'

'What are you saying, Jimmy?'

'Reserve team trainer. Would you fancy that?'

In them days, trainer was a fancy description of the real job. You did spend time coaching the youngsters, but you were also responsible for mopping the dressing room floor, scrubbing out the toilets, washing out the baths, cleaning the boots and any other dirty job as required. I'd be going straight from club captain to general dogsbody.

I thought of Archie Wilcox all those years ago limping round the touchline asking me if I wanted to end up like him.

I thought of the other players, the lads I'd skippered for the last seven years, watching me unblocking the toilets.

I thought of Eileen and the expression on her face when I told her.

And I wasn't sure I could bear it.

'Well?' said Jimmy. 'Yes, or no?'

'I'll take it.'

THIRTY

'They've found Gerry.'

Kelly was shaking and her voice was quavery, sweaty fingerprints showing on the glass of her phone. She hoped this wouldn't seem strange to them as this is the way she has been every time she has to ring with information. With any luck they wouldn't notice the difference on this occasion. That she is lying through her teeth.

It hadn't been easy to persuade Kelly to make the call but with Helen and Sarah at her side giving silent support and Jim securely out of sight in another room she'd eventually agreed.

'It's the least I can do.'

'Yes, it is,' Jim had added before he was bundled out to the kitchen.

She really wanted no more to do with this, to be able to walk away and try to forget it had ever happened. Forget what she had done. But she also wanted to help Eileen. Always had.

'But what if they come back for me?'

'They won't,' Sarah told her. 'If everything goes according to plan they'll disappear and go back to what they were doing before. Give it up as a bad job.'

'And what if the plan doesn't work?'

Helen had squeezed her hand.

'We can't live on what ifs. We've got to try this and hope for the best.'

Kelly had stared at Helen's hand for several seconds before gently easing it away from her.

'You'll have to tell the police, won't you? Are you going to hand me over to them? As an accomplice?'

'You were threatened. You had no choice. But if you do this it shows that you wanted to make it right. And we'll stand by you, won't we, Sarah?'

It was just as well that Jim was working his way through some dried apricots and walnuts at that moment and not on hand to hear this, as he would have exploded, but Sarah closed her eyes and smiled thinly in assent.

So Kelly made the call.

'Do you know where he is?'

'They've not said. With one of his old teammates, I think.'

'Which one?'

'I don't know. They don't tell me everything. Sarah's going to ring you.'

'You need to find out where they're hiding him. I don't trust that bitch.'

Sarah made a slashing movement across her throat.

'Someone's coming. I have to go.'

And she had wept then, with relief and gratitude, because Sarah told her that her part was over. They would take it from here.

*

Harry Lomax is standing outside the Cross Keys pub, casting an eye up and down the street. He's chosen this for the rendezvous because it has a function room at the back, slightly separate from the rest of the pub, so they should be able to meet up without causing too much attention. A tattered banner on the wall proclaims the Cross Keys to be "Perfect for Weddings, Christenings and all your catering occasions". Harry smiles to himself. He has been here before. Perfect if you're not too keen on your intended, couldn't give a shit about your kids and don't mind what you stuff down your throat.

He's known the landlord, Brian, for years. Shifty bugger but he can keep a secret. And the room is cheap, because no one else wants it.

'Used to have a salsa class two afternoons a week,' he tells Harry, 'but we couldn't sort out the smell from the drains, so they fucked off to the Lord Nelson.'

It's only just gone eleven o'clock so there aren't many customers in the bar as the others arrive and are shuffled into the back room. They don't want to be recognised today but part of them is also disappointed that nobody looks up from their pint to pay them some heed. They used to be local heroes but now they look just like lots of other old men. At a loose end and looking for some way to pass the time before they get the final whistle.

'I'm talking about love, ladies and gentlemen.'

Harry turns to watch a middle-aged black man with impressive greying dreadlocks sitting down on a plastic crate on the opposite side of the road.

'Not the love of a woman. Not the love of a man. Not even the love of a child or a baby.'

He is shouting out his message to the world and the world appears to think it can take it or leave it. One or two early shoppers slow down as they pass by, momentarily diverted by the curiosity value. Others quicken their pace in case he's a busker or a chugger and might thrust a collection bucket in their face.

'No. We all need such love in our lives. But this is deeper. This love sustains us. Lifts us up on eagle's wings high above the earth.'

Harry notes that he is a handsome man. Tall, slim and dressed entirely in black with a rollneck sweater decorated by some clunky looking beads, he looks like a rock star fallen on hard times. His voice is rich and warm and cuts through the chuntering traffic boom. But most people seem to be tuning him out, walking past without even giving him a glance. Which is odd, thinks Harry, as there isn't much else to remark upon along Deansgate on a Thursday morning.

There is a portable speaker by the man's side, and he bends over to switch it on. Then he stands up in an attempt to get some sort of reaction. He is well over six-foot tall and, Harry notices, is sporting a pair of snazzy, stitched cowboy boots that make him even more imposing.

'I'm talking about Jesus, ladies and gentlemen. The Saviour of the World. The Prince of Peace.'

The speaker sparks into action. Harry is expecting a deep bass and a reggae beat to back up the message. Maybe a bit of Bob Marley. Instead, he hears the Beatles giving it some welly.

'"All you need is love." Altogether now. "All you need is love, love. Love is all you need."'

Harry becomes conscious of someone close by his side and turns to see Bill Chadwick, also staring across the street at the preacher, who may be fighting a losing battle but is not about to give up. He's in harmony with John and Paul and belting out the redemptive power of eternal love.

'Pity he's talking about peace, love and understanding. Looks like he could be a handy lad in a fight.'

He nods towards the open pub door.

'Are they all here?'

'You're the last. Come on.'

They head on into the bar and leave salvation for another day. The preacher gives them a parting shot.

'Don't turn your back on him, ladies and gentlemen. He will save you if you only listen. It's your choice.'

They are a mixed bunch, gathered in the back room. As Harry and Bill enter, they can see obvious signs of tension and unease. Not surprising given what they've been told over the phone about Gerry and Eileen. The rotting stench from the drains isn't helping to lift the mood much either.

They make their way to the back of the room where there is a top table for close family of the bride and groom, pressing a few hands as they pass their old mates. Bill does a quick head count. Everyone who was asked has turned up – Ernie, Frank, Stan and Gordon. All of them in pretty good nick considering. And each has brought at least one other relative with him – son, nephew, grandson, whatever. Not a bad haul; a dozen of them in all. Full team and a sub. Some likely looking lads out there. Harry nods at Bill. You do the pre-match talk.

'Thanks for coming at such short notice. I think everyone's here.'

A few murmurs as they look around, checking who is in the squad.

'I didn't ask Denis or Ronnie. Back in the day they would have both been useful in a scrap but, you know...

And, of course we don't have Don... or Gerry.'

Ernie Fletcher stands up. As a right back he had a fearsome reputation. During the first five minutes of the match he would spy his chance to slide tackle the other side's left winger, usually crashing through him and propelling him onto the dirt track by the side of the pitch, shaving lumps of skin off his opponent's knees and crunching him into the advertising hoardings. After that, he wouldn't see much of the winger for the rest of the game. He still looks as if he eats raw meat for breakfast.

'These bastards who shot Don. They're the same ones who are after Gerry? And who've got hold of Eileen?'

'Probably.'

'Who are they?'

'Don't know exactly, but they must be working for the folk Don knew.'

More murmuring and nervous glances.

'You know me, Bill. Never walked away from a fight in my life. But guns... that's summat different.'

'Don was close to these guys, set up the deals, handled the money. Obviously, something went wrong.'

'You can say that again.'

'We don't know why they shot him. But this lot, so far as we know, haven't ever mentioned guns.'

'Knives, though,' adds Harry.

'Yes, thanks, Harry.'

'And they threatened to burn their house down. And they wrung that dog's neck.'

'Yes, thanks, Harry.'

'Just saying...'

'The point I'm making, Ernie, is that we've no reason to believe they are carrying guns but, as Harry says, they are dangerous. No getting away from that.'

Frank Goodall, once Ernie's partner in crime on the other wing, puts up his hand. He hadn't had the same talent for intimidation but nothing much got past him back in the day. Solid as a rock.

'How many are we talking about?'

'Not sure. At least three. Maybe four.'

'And they've got Eileen in Don's old house?'

'We think so.'

Frank purses his lips.

'Gerry were always good to me when I needed a hand. So I want to help him and Eileen. That's why I brought my lad, Terry.'

He puts his hand on the outsize shoulder of the man next to him.

'Ex-army. Knows what he's doing. But I dunno. We need to be sure about what we're getting in to.'

Gordon Clifford is next. He didn't make the grade like the others and slipped into non-league football. He went to night school instead, found he had a head for business and ran his own successful double-glazing firm for years. His son and his nephew now run the company and are by his side.

'Frank's right, Bill. Not being funny, but you don't seem to know much about these fellers. Might be three or four. Could be more. Could be armed. Might be hiding out in Don's house. Might not be. Not much to go on, is it?'

'Look – I know. But if it turns out that they're not there then we've not lost anything, have we?'

'No – but Eileen will have.'

He leaves him to wrestle with that thought before carrying on.

'The thing is, like you said, we don't know exactly what Don was up to, but he was in a lot deeper than the rest of us. Must have been coining it. Got a bloody big mansion off the back of it.'

Grumbles of agreement round the room at this.

'And Gerry and Eileen were doing alright as well. New house. Driving a Merc.'

Harry bristles and interrupts him.

'What are you getting at, Gordon?'

'Don must have done something to get himself shot. Double crossed them. Stole from them. I don't know. Maybe Gerry did the same.'

'And that means we shouldn't help him?'

'We were kept in the dark. Don and Gerry were the ones who made all the arrangements. This mess, whatever it is...'

He looks round the room for support.

'... I don't know. Is it our business? Should we be risking our lives and our families to save Gerry – who's buggered off altogether – when we don't know what he might have done to make this happen? I mean... where is he? Why isn't he here helping us save Eileen?'

Bill and Harry have been watching the rest of them while Gordon has been speaking and there is some uneasy shifting in their seats going on.

Stan Roberts has been weighing all this up. There was talk of him playing for England at one time after he made the move to Everton. But a broken leg on a frozen pitch at St James' Park put paid to all that and he had to make do as a kit man for the rest of his career in the beautiful game. Mopping floors, picking up dirty strips, attending to the needs of newly rich kids with more money than sense. And it was Gerry who convinced him he was entitled to more than that.

'Alright. We don't know exactly what Gerry's done and we don't know why he's gone to ground. But we do know Gerry and every one of us owes him. Including you, Gordon.'

He fixes him with a stare until Gordon looks away and studies his knees.

'It's not like we didn't know the money was dirty. But we all took it. Made a big difference to my life. Cleared my debts. Paid off my mortgage. Couldn't have done that without Gerry.'

He looks round the room.

'Same for every man here. And it's no use saying we weren't as closely involved as him and Don. Nobody asked any questions about what was in them bags but we all bloody knew, and we turned a blind eye to it.

Now summat's happened we can't ignore.'

There is silence now as the reality bites. Any of them could walk away, but what would that mean? These friendships, the times they shared when they were young and strong, have lasted a lifetime. At their age there are many more goodbyes than hellos and if they leave now they will be turning their backs on the only men who understand what made them who they are. And it was Gerry, more than anyone else, who reminded them of that, kept them in touch with each other and helped them relive the days when their lives mattered to thousands of people they never knew. Are they really going to leave all that behind?

Bill leans forward on the table in front of him.

'Ever since this whole business started, I've been frightened. Frightened that we'd be found out. Frightened of what they might do to me or my family if I tried to stop. Frightened that when I read of some kid who'd died of an overdose that it was from what I'd brought in.

Let's be honest – frightened of how we'd manage if I didn't have that money coming in.

And I'm frightened now. Of taking these men on.

But I'm sick of living like this. I don't want to be frightened any more. And I reckon the only way that's going to stop is if we bring Eileen back and get out of this mess once and for all.

Dun't matter what Gerry did or didn't do. We never used to ask questions when we played together, did we? Kick one of us and you kick us all. Well, someone's trying to kick the shit out of Gerry and I'm not standing by any longer.

Who else feels the same?'

One by one, like a ragged and random Mexican wave, the hands go up. All of them. Ernie says what is going through their minds.

'Alright. We're in. God help us.

I don't suppose there's a plan is there?'

THIRTY-ONE

1983

When you've been married for twenty-five years it's traditional to give and receive presents made of silver. After twenty-five years at Bolton the only silverware I had to show was a runners-up medal for the Third Division championship in 1975. Not exactly what I dreamed of when I signed up as an apprentice.

That longed-for promotion back to the First Division came after I stopped playing. It was great to be part of something that was successful at last, but I couldn't help thinking – why couldn't we have done this while I was still on the pitch? Jimmy Reed had done a great job in attracting a few top quality players who were on their way down, but still had it, and melding them with the young talent that had come through the ranks.

Being Bolton, it was too good to last. Jimmy got tempted back to manage Villa, the old stars faded away and the slide down the table began again. By 1983 we were back where we started and beginning a second stint in Division Three.

That's when the board turned to me. The job of Reserve team coach had changed a lot since I first took it on. I had assistants to do the dirty work and I could concentrate on bringing the young players on, preparing them to make the move up to the First Team. Not all the lads were going to hold down a place but, in my time,

I'd had half a dozen who'd made the grade at Bolton and many others who'd gone on to have good careers at other clubs. I got a lot of satisfaction from seeing these lads have the success I'd never achieved. It wasn't what I'd hoped for, but I was enjoying my job and the pay got a lot better when we were doing well.

That was all about to change. Ken Baker was manager when we got relegated again and was out the door the next day along with his assistant. Rumours started circulating about who might be in the frame to succeed him, but I'd seen all this before and knew that the only thing to do was to carry on as normal and get my players ready for next season.

A month went by and there was still no word about a new man coming in. I'd heard that the job had been offered to a couple of up and coming managers from our league but that they had decided to stay put. Didn't like the look of what they saw by all accounts.

Then I got the call to go upstairs. Jack Nuttall was the latest in a long line of family members who had been chairman of the board. He ran a chain of former weaving mills that had been converted to storehouses for mail order catalogues. He regarded the football club as an extension of the family firm and liked to treat people that way. I could remember when he was a kid coming to games when his dad was chairman, and I knew he was Bolton through and through.

We'd already been told that there would need to be cutbacks in staff and reductions in pay but I wasn't worried about my own position. The club needed its young players as much as ever and I reckoned my track record would save my job. What I thought the chairman was going to tell me was that I'd be losing my assistants and be back to sluicing down the dressing room myself. Not great, but it could be worse. At least I'd still have a job.

He was pacing round the office when I went in, looking distracted and pulling hard on a cigarette.

'Sad times, Gerry.'

'We've been through worse, Jack. Got some good kids coming through. Just need a bit more time.'

'Sure, but time's not on our side. The lads will be back for pre-season in three weeks, and we still don't have a manager.'

'I can take them through fitness training while you carry on looking. Give you a bit more breathing space.'

He stopped pacing then and stubbed his cigarette out.

'The thing is, I reckon we've been looking in the wrong place. The right man has been in front of our noses all the time.'

He was looking directly at me.

'No. Hang on, Jack.'

He pushed his arm towards me, palm flat out to block any more words.

'Hear me out, Gerry. You've done a great job with the Reserves. You know the club inside out. And the fans love you. You've served your time, mate. Now it's your turn.'

I knew it wasn't right. I could be a good number two, but I'd seen what the job had done to so many others, buckling under the strain of expectancy.

'I'm not sure I'm the man for the job.'

'Trust me. I've seen some other applicants and you're head and shoulders above them. This is your moment, Gerry. Don't let somebody else come in and take it from you. Somebody who might want to bring in his own people. Start with a clean slate.'

I got the message. Take the job on offer or risk losing the one I had. As usual, no choice.

Eileen was delighted when I told her.

'You've worked like a dog for that club. About time they gave you some credit.'

And she liked the extra money. Started looking for a new house in a better part of town. I let her enjoy herself, but I knew from the start it wasn't going to last.

The better players left for bigger clubs and the ones we could afford to bring in weren't as good. The current crop of kids in the Reserves didn't have the same talent as the ones I'd had before. I felt I wasn't playing with a full pack of cards.

And then there was me. I was always good with the players – I knew which ones needed an arm round the shoulder and which needed a kick up the arse – but tactics were never my strong suit. I'd never done my FA coaching badge – thought I knew it all from experience. I soon found out that other managers knew how to change things round at half time, give us a different problem to solve. Me, I'd put all my effort to encouraging the lads, telling them to play better, move the ball quicker, tackle harder. And you needed more than that these days.

It was all over by Christmas. We'd only won four games although we'd had plenty of draws. If only we'd been able to convert some of them into wins maybe it would have been different.

Jack Nuttall didn't tell me to my face. That hurt. I'd known him almost all his life. I suppose he just didn't have the heart to do it himself, so he sent me to a solicitor who was an adviser to the board, Matthew Curtis. Nice bloke. We became good friends later. Mad keen Bolton fan. He met me in his office in town. Had a copy of my contract.

'I don't suppose you had a solicitor look at this before you signed it?'

I shook my head.

'Something wrong?'

'Contracts these days usually last at least three years and if the employer decides to terminate early, they are required to pay out the unexpired term – which would have been two and a half years in your case.'

'But…?'

'But you're on an open-ended monthly contract. So you're only entitled to one month's pay.'

How was I going to explain that to Eileen?

'Is there nowt you can do about that?'

'I'm sorry, Gerry. The board has authorised me to offer you three month's salary as a gesture of goodwill but that's as far as they are willing to go.'

I was shattered. Couldn't speak. Twenty-five years and I was out on my ear. Forty-one years old. No trade. No qualifications. Another twenty-five years before I got my pension. What the hell was I going to do?

'Couldn't I have my old job back? Look after the Reserves?'

He was embarrassed. I could see that.

'The board thinks it's in the best interests of all parties to have a clean break.'

Nothing more to say. I signed some forms, he gave me a cheque and I walked away from the game forever.

Eileen stood by me. I will say that. I thought she'd blame me for trusting the club too much, but she was more furious about the way they'd treated me. I was worried about how we were going to pay the mortgage, but she put on a brave face.

'You've got three months to find a job. We'll be alright.'

I rang round other clubs, went to see old mates who were still in the game, told them I'd consider anything. After a few weeks I'd exhausted all my contacts and no one had come back to me. I started to stay at home all day. I suppose I was depressed. I know I was ashamed.

Then one morning, Denis Green turned up at our house. He were one of the clever ones. Been preparing for retirement years before he stopped playing and now he had his own building firm and was doing alright.

'Got a nice contract to build some new houses up Montserrat, near the golf club.'

'That's great, Denis. I'm glad for you.'

'Going to need to take on some more men.'

I didn't get it at first. Thought we were just chatting. Then the penny dropped.

'Did Eileen ring you?'

Denis didn't bat an eyelid.

'I know you're looking to get back into the game. But I could do with some help. You'd be doing me a favour. Anyroad, it'll tide you over until something turns up.'

He were very good about it. Helped me go to night school to learn the trade. And that's how I became a brickie, building big houses for them as has the money. After a year I had to accept that I was never going to get back into football. That was over and this was my life from now on.

I'd come home at night, worn out, covered in brick dust, aching in every joint. I was still pretty fit but it's back-breaking work when you hit your fifties. Occasionally people passing the site would recognise me. Watch me carrying a hod of bricks up a gangplank and come up to me, not quite sure what to say.

'You don't mind me asking… but didn't you used to be Gerry Bradshaw?'

Eileen was good at managing money. It was always a bit tight at the end of the month, but we managed to keep our head above water at a time when a lot of folk in Bolton were put out of work. So, I really shouldn't have had anything to complain about. But when I saw the wages the players were getting by then – and they went through the roof when the Premier League came in – it started to get to me. I'd come away with nothing after a whole lifetime in the game. That wasn't right. I deserved more than that.

THIRTY-TWO

The Fylde coast, that seventeen-mile stretch between the Ribble estuary to the south and the River Wyre to the north, has been Lancashire's playground for 150 years. Before the arrival of the railways this would have been an unbroken ribbon of sand dunes and wide beaches with the odd fishing village along the way, although Blackpool already had a few hotels for the landed gentry to enjoy the sea air. And then the hoi polloi started turning up in large numbers, rammed into holiday trains as weavers and spinners enjoyed their newly earned Wakes weeks, forcing the Quality to follow their more refined pursuits elsewhere.

Now the A584 hugs the coast and snakes through a chain of resorts from Lytham to Fleetwood with hardly a break in the brick, steel, concrete and tarmac to be seen. The mills that once provided so many revellers have long since closed and working families with a bit more money have followed their betters to the Mediterranean and beyond.

Numbers are still holding up in Blackpool but ask any local and they'll tell you it's not like it was when the sand was impossible to see through the crush of bodies sunning themselves on it. Old guesthouses and hotels down on their luck have new guests who stay for much longer and spend very little at all as they try to eke out their benefits. People used to come for their health and the bracing air. Now many stay on because they're too poor or too sick to move anywhere else.

But go on from Fleetwood and its vanished fishing fleet, cross over the Wyre (by ferry if you're feeling romantic) into Knott End and the landscape changes. Soon the strings of bungalows give way to a coastal path overlooking tussocky marshes and a gently sloping beach that slips gradually into a turbulent grey sea. The funfairs, sticks of rock, fish and chip shops, cafés and pubs are left behind and their memory blown away by the ever blustery winds that whip up the sand and thrash the waves. This is the territory for ramblers, dog walkers, the hardiest and most desperate of courting couples and, possibly, serial killers on their days off.

And this is where they want Sarah to meet them. She gets the call early evening.

'There's a car park near the slipway to the ferry. Be there at nine o'clock. And Gerry best be with you.'

'He will be.'

'And nobody else. We see another car and you won't see Eileen again.'

'It's a car park. There'll be lots of other cars there.'

Sarah feels the exasperation at the other end of the line.

'Fucking amateurs! We're not doing the exchange there. You'll get instructions when we ring. We'll be watching you.'

Seven thirty, and it takes well over an hour to get there. They'd deliberately left no time to prepare. Marcus gets a map of the area up on his laptop.

'They won't want other people around so the meeting must be north of there.'

'Or east,' adds Taylor. 'Doesn't have to be on the coast. Quicker for them to scoot back to Jackie's house if they meet inland.'

'Yeah, but more deserted spots by the beach. No one's going out there at night-time.'

'I dunno, folk might drive out to look at the sun setting over the sea. Could be lots of cars parked up.'

'They won't want to be that near...'

'BOYS!'

Sarah has had enough.

'We don't have time for this. Sort it out in the car. I'll ring you when they tell me where. Just pick a spot north and east of Knott End and keep out of sight until you hear from me.'

Marcus and Taylor pick up their coats and head off leaving Sarah with Jim who is looking mutinous.

'Don't look so worried. It'll be fine.'

'You're not the one who'll be walking towards a gang of homicidal drug dealers expecting someone entirely different. What do you think they're going to do when they find out? Pat me on the back and say, "Well... you certainly had us fooled, you old rascal".'

'We've gone over this. It won't come to that.'

'You hope.'

'Marcus and Taylor will be watching us. When you and Eileen are both halfway across, they'll switch on the headlights and drive towards you making as much racket as possible. They won't have time to think or get hold of either of you. They'll go back to their car and get away to Jackie's place as quick as they can.'

This was Taylor's plan.

'You'll have seen this in loads of films, Jim,' he'd explained. 'Like that one with Tom Hanks. *Bridge of Spies*.'

'I don't go to the pictures.'

'Come on, you must know how it works. The cars park facing each other with the headlights pointed at the space between. Eileen and you walk towards each other and when you get to the middle you stop instead of passing by. And we come roaring in. They'll think we're the police and make a run for it.'

'And what if they decide to shoot us instead? Or get hold of both of us as hostages? What do you do then?'

Taylor felt all their eyes on him as he weighed this up.

'There's a risk. I realise that. But they won't have time to think. You and Eileen crouch down on the ground. Hold tight to each other. They'll see it'll take too long to get hold of you and escape, so they'll get back in the car before it's too late.'

'Hmmm. What happens to Tom Hanks in this film?'

'Nothing. He's not the hostage. He hands Mark Rylance over to the KGB.'

'Not a great example then, is it? You and Sarah walk off scot-free and I end up at the mercy of a group of killers and torturers.'

But now he was stuck with it. Time had slipped away until there was no other option. If he refused there was no Plan B. He munches a few salted cashews for comfort. Sarah hands him his coat and Helen watches from the porch as they drive off into the gathering gloom. She waves bye-bye to the tail-lights as they fade away.

*

Elswick House was not hard to find. There would have been a time when it was the only building of any substance in the area. The brick walls and high hedges give a clear enough message to the scatter of contemporary executive homes that have seeded in the surrounding fields – we accept that you have a right to be here as well as us, but we'd rather not get involved thank you very much. A hefty gate has been slung across the entry to the driveway blocking any view of the house itself and governed by a video door entry system. The owners haven't bothered to hang a "Keep Out" sign on the gate but any casual caller would get the gist.

Bill and Harry can see all this from their car, parked out of sight under a horse-chestnut tree fifty yards down the lane. They've been there since mid-afternoon, watching to see if anyone comes or goes. Three other cars have been stationed in and around the neighbourhood in shifts since early morning, carefully located so as not to attract the attention of local curtain-twitchers neurotic about burglary rates. Gerry's teammates are on the bench and ready to get stuck in when called.

They can see the top storey above the hedges and the lights were on first thing. Someone is in there but since then nothing else to report. They get the call from Helen to say the first rendezvous is at nine o'clock but it's now almost eight and there is still no sign of movement. Harry is getting twitchy.

'What if we're wrong and it's not them?'

'Let's see what Frank's lad comes up with.'

Terry has taken a walk round the outside of the house, along the lane and in the fields behind. He's brought his Alsatian, Oscar, with him so as not to attract attention. He rings them when he gets back from his stroll.

'Two storeys. Probably a basement. She could be anywhere in the house.'

Terry used to be in the Queen's Lancashire Regiment until it disbanded in 2006. It didn't break his heart. This wasn't a regiment with a long and glorious history going back to Waterloo. It had only been going since the 1970s when two other regiments were combined. Another restructure and a series of cuts had seen it amalgamated in turn with two other redundant regiments. But not before Terry had done a tour of duty in Bosnia ('Fucking nightmare') and a civil order mission in Basra ('Lovely people; very polite. Can't understand why.').

This little outing wasn't causing him to break sweat.

'Getting over the walls wouldn't be too tricky but hard to get close to the house without being seen. The garden at the back seems well tended so not much cover there. 'Course, it's a different matter now it's getting dark. Unless there's a lot of them in there they'll have trouble keeping eyes on all the perimeter. Best bet might be to go over in several places at once. Distract them.'

Bill and Harry try to imagine heaving themselves over a high wall and dashing for cover as bullets start flying. They don't get very far.

'Err...'

'Wouldn't recommend that, though.'

Thank God for that.

'Haven't got the personnel or the equipment for a move like that while there's daylight. Something to think about though if there's no change by tonight. They'll be getting restless by then.'

'What if it isn't them, though? Maybe it's someone else in the house.'

'There's some oak trees in the lane at the back. Managed to shin up one while Oscar stood guard. Gave me a good view over the wall.

What was the colour of that van they tried to get Matthew's lass into?'

'Black.'

'There's a black transit parked by the side. Couldn't see the registration. Someone's conveniently smeared mud all over the number plate.'

'Right then. What do we do next?'

On cue, the gates shudder open and a dark green Audi glides over the private gravel and onto the road. Two figures in front, one smaller one in the back. The black van follows close behind and the gate shuts again as they disappear into the dusk. Bill feels massive relief and gut-gurgling anxiety in equal measure.

'OK, Terry. We're on.'

*

They get there with less than five minutes to spare. The chippie that greets day-trippers as they get off the ferry from Fleetwood has been closed since teatime and the nearest pub is a couple of hundred yards away, so the car park is almost empty. Jim is hunched in the back seat with his collar turned up and a cap on his head. Just an indistinct silhouette in the remaining light of evening.

Sarah switches off the engine and casts her eye over the area. Everyone in Knott End must be safely tucked up in bed because there is no sign of life at all except for a few gulls sifting through the bin bags by the toilet block. They squawk in disappointment. Thin pickings these days.

There is a rusting, sky-blue Fiesta near the entrance that looks as if it has had a little too much sea air, a small white van next to the café with Fylde Marine Services written on its side and some sort of people-carrier in the far corner that has at least one flat tyre. And that's it. None of these looks like the getaway car of choice for any self-respecting hoodlum.

But someone, somewhere is watching. Her phone rings.

'Well done. Made it on time. There'd better not be anyone following you.'

'No. Just me and Gerry. What now?'

'Drive down the Esplanade and follow Sandy Lane out of town for a couple of miles till you come to the junction of Burned House Lane and Cemetery Road.'

'Really?'

'Just listen. You haven't got time to piss about. You can park on the grass verge there. Should take you about ten minutes.'

'Right.'

Sarah starts up the engine.

'Hang on, hang on. I haven't finished yet. I want you to take your phone and Gerry's and put them in that bin by the café. Go on. I'm watching.'

Sarah freezes.

'But... if I do that...how are you going to contact me?'

'Just do it. Clock's ticking. If you're not at the next rendezvous in ten minutes we're calling this off.'

Sarah takes a deep breath, grabs Jim's phone and runs over to the bin stores. The gulls rise up in protest around her. There may not be much here but it's all theirs and they don't like to be interrupted when they're on a scavenge. She raises the two phones ostentatiously above her head, chucks them in a bin and rushes back to the car.

*

Marcus has got his foot down and even though they have left the M6 for a narrow country road they are still hurtling along at over seventy miles an hour, hedgerows streaming past either side in a blur, their branches occasionally scraping the electric-blue paintwork. In a film this would be the exciting car chase section, as obligatory in thrillers as the extended drum solo used to be in Prog Rock. Taylor's mind flashes over famous examples from James Bond to Jason Bourne but the thought is not diverting. In his mind he sees only the sickening denouement where a vehicle cartwheels several times off the tarmac, usually careering down a steep ravine, before landing on its roof, rocking and groaning for a few seconds and then exploding in a ball of flame. Always great fun to watch in the cinema but not so entertaining if you are actually inside the car.

Taylor has fully extended his legs and is pressing hard on a phantom brake pedal every time they reach a bend. He read somewhere that the front passenger seat is the most dangerous spot in a car because the driver, at the moment they realise they've lost control and that a crash is inevitable, instinctively turns away from the point of impact giving them a higher chance of survival and leaving their passenger to be crushed into mincemeat.

He gives a glance at Marcus who is gripping the steering wheel tightly, his whole body tensed, head angled forward, eyes fixed on the road ahead. Taylor doesn't want to distract him, so he adopts what he hopes is a light, enquiring tone.

'Ermm... what do you think the speed limit is on this road?'

No response from Marcus; not a flicker of acknowledgement that he has heard anything.

'Only the last thing we need is a speeding ticket from some copper with nothing better to do.'

The car lurches to the left as they slew round a tight corner, banging Taylor up against the side window.

'You know that old joke?'

Still nothing from Marcus.

'You know, what do you call a black man driving a BMW?'

Marcus does not turn his head but gives a grudging response.

'I've heard it.'

'A target.'

'Yeah, I said I've heard it.'

'So, no point in giving them an excuse, cos I know from my time in the police that racism is, you know, in some of them, embedded...'

Another sharp corner, this time to the right, and Taylor's head rocks over towards the gear stick.

'Taylor?'

'Yes.'

'I'm trying to concentrate.'

'Yes.'

'So do you think you could manage to shut the fuck up?'

'OK.'

They are heading for an area near the village of Pilling, picked out at random from the map, roughly equidistant from Garstang and Knott End. Marcus reckons that from there he can get to wherever they are likely to make the exchange within less than ten minutes. All they need to do is get the call from Sarah.

And arrive in one piece. Taylor decides to close his eyes and hope for the best.

*

Burned House Lane is at a non-descript junction of three roads with a triangle of scrubby grass in the middle. Sarah pulls over onto the grass verge. They can't see the dramatic ruins of whatever accident gave the place its name, just a few run-of-the-mill bungalows, some with a caravan pulled onto the driveway, dotted in each direction. Just ahead, on the right-hand side, there is a small garage with several cars parked in the forecourt. If someone is watching that would be the obvious spot but it's too far away to pick anyone out and anyway the light is fading now.

Nothing much else to see. Flat fields of untended grass. A few isolated trees buffeted by the wind. And a phone box. Which is ringing. Sarah dashes over to pick up the receiver.

'Gerry holding up alright? Not car-sick, is he?'

'He's fine. Where to now?'

'Turn left at the junction until you come to Dyke Way. Follow that and go second left on to Black Dick's Lane which will take you all the way back to the coast.'

'Are you picking these road names deliberately?'

'Shut up and listen. There's a little sewage outlet by the beach. Pull in there and wait.'

'Lovely.'

'And don't think of making a call from here or stopping off on the way. We spot anyone else nearby and the deal's off.'

'But then you don't get Gerry – whatever you want him for.'

'You've got five minutes to be there.'

Sarah runs back to the car and pulls away from the verge at top speed, the rear wheels scarring deep ruts in the turf as they get back on the road. She glances in the rear-view mirror and sees something in Jim's eyes she's never noticed before. The old feller is frightened.

'Well?' he asks.

'They're taking us back to the sea. Some lonely spot where there aren't any houses I'm guessing. It'll be dark by the time we get there. This could be it.'

'And there's no way we can let Marcus and Taylor know?'

'I daren't stop. They could be watching us. Anyway, I doubt we'll pass another phone box now.'

Jim goes quiet for a while.

'I've had it then, haven't I?'

Sarah can't think of anything to say in reply as she swings the car left onto the single track road that leads to the beach.

'What am I supposed to do when I walk towards them?'

'I don't know, Jim. I'm thinking.'

'Eileen and I can't run for it. We're too old.'

'It won't come to that.'

'You've done for both of us, haven't you? All because you wanted to prove yourself as good as your father.'

They can hear the waves murmuring ahead of them and see a small brick building on the left-hand side that has a bulky pipe slinking down onto the beach. They've run out of road now, so Sarah pulls in by the sewage station and switches the engine off.

It is pitch black, only a few isolated house lights glinting on the waves in the far distance.

'Dead end,' says Jim.

*

A scooter has pulled up by the side of the road, close to where Bill and Harry are parked. The rider has slipped off his helmet and is running his finger up and down the screen on his phone and looking round about him for a landmark. There is a large wooden box mounted behind him, where a passenger might sit, with a multi-coloured sticker on it that says, *"Grub's Up – You **can** always get what you want"*.

'Here's our chance,' says Harry.

Before Bill can ask what the hell he is talking about, Harry is out of the car and signalling to the young man on the scooter.

'Found it all right then?'

The delivery lad looks a bit confused, but Harry strolls up to him full of confidence, as if he were still Mine Host at the Cotton Tree Inn.

'Elswick House?'

The delivery lad nods.

'Good timing. Just got back meself. Now, what do we owe you?'

'Err...' checks his phone, '£63.20, mate.'

Harry peels a few notes from his wallet.

'Call it seventy, shall we?'

Big grin. He hands over a couple of large paper bags.

'Cheers.'

Slips his helmet back on and is away.

Harry walks back to the car, puts the bags on the rear seat and settles in beside Bill.

'Give Terry a ring. I reckon we've got a key to the door.'

He hands Bill the docket for the food order.

'And have a look at the name on that.'

*

Sensing that hanging around Pilling they'd be as inconspicuous as a Russian tourist asking the way to GCHQ, Marcus drives through the village and back into the open countryside. Once he switches off the engine an unnerving silence washes in from the deserted fields surrounding them.

'She should have called by now.'

'Could have been a hitch.'

'It's well past nine. She'd have told us if there was a problem.'

'Yeah, but she won't want to use her phone in case they ring her.'

'Jim's got a phone.'

'But that's going to look really suspicious if they're watching them.'

Marcus grunts. He is not convinced. Taylor feels the need to fill the silence with some consolation.

'Could just be a test.'

'Huh?'

'You know – to be sure that no one else is around. Leave them sweating and see what they do.'

'Maybe.'

'So she'd just have to sit tight and wait.'

Marcus's mouth is bone dry. He licks his lips and swallows deeply. Should have thought to bring some water.

'Give it a bit longer then.'

'Yeah.'

The road stretches straight ahead of them, a dusty brown track that has unspooled itself over the uniform and unvarying landscape. Taylor gazes at the fields on either side of the road. No one seems to have any use for the land here. No sheep or cows. No swaying waves of barley or golden heads of wheat. It isn't wild and it isn't farmed. More like some vast abandoned set of lawns that have been allowed to go their own way because nobody could be bothered to tend them any more.

'You know that bit in *North by Northwest*?'

'What?'

'You know, where Cary Grant gets lured into the countryside and is left standing on a deserted highway?'

'What the hell are you talking about?'

'Reminds me of that.'

'There's something wrong with you, mate.'

Taylor looks over to the far distance in search of a biplane dusting crops where no crops have been.

*

Sarah checks her watch again. It's now ten minutes past the appointed time for the exchange. Jim turns his head to look back down the road they came on. Nothing. He allows himself to hope. Perhaps they've been scared off. Maybe he won't have to go through with it.

'You think they've had second thoughts?'

'Maybe. More likely they're waiting to see if someone's been following us.'

'Which they haven't.'

So they'll still come. Jim can't see any way out. He can't just sit in the car and refuse to get out. Either they'll drive off with

Eileen or simply come and drag him out of his seat. Then they'd have both of them. Sarah is watching him through the rear-view mirror.

'It's up to you. Your choice.'

'I know.'

She can see him going through the options in his head, weighing the risks, calculating the odds. They aren't good.

'What do you think they'll do when they realise I'm not Gerry?'

'I don't know,' her words dying away, 'I'm sorry.'

And this is what it's come to, he thinks. All those years of plotting the angles carefully, making sure he had covered all eventualities before taking any action, this is what it's boiled down to. Sitting by a dark shore waiting to be taken hostage and all he is relying on for back-up is what Sarah and Taylor have learnt from watching cop shows on the telly.

He tries to picture Marion's face. It takes an effort not to see her frozen expression as she lay in the coffin at the undertakers, lifeless and unblemished like a waxwork. He tries to summon up different images. Marion in her wedding dress, blushing at all the attention and blinking as the flash bulbs crackled around her. Marion in a floral frock on the beach at Morecambe. Just up the road. Marion kneeling in the garden, planting spring bulbs. She loved those tiny daffodils, the miniature ones that come out early in little clumps, telling you that winter is over.

Marion looking ashen-faced as they drove back from the hospital after seeing the specialist.

Which Marion would he see if it all ended tonight? Would she be in the prime of life, the perky lass he'd met at that dance he hadn't really wanted to go to? Seeing him too shy to ask her so taking charge and dragging him onto the dance floor. Or would it be the elderly lady, coughing incessantly, spittle filling her handkerchief, too weak to get up from the chair without his help?

Or none of these. Gone and that's it. No reunion. Joining her only in his absence from life.

Headlights suddenly stretch out on the path in front of them. A car is bouncing over the terrain towards them. Not from behind as they expected but following the bridle path that hugs the seashore.

It pulls up about twenty yards away, the car engine idling. Sarah turns on their headlights and the patch of ground between them is lit up like a football pitch.

The passenger door in the other vehicle opens and a tall man steps out and slaps the car roof hard.

Make your mind up time.

*

Nine twenty-five and still no call from Sarah. Marcus has pressed the palm of his hand up against his left leg to stop it from twitching.

'Something's gone wrong.'

Taylor looks straight ahead, not wanting to look into Marcus's eyes.

'Yeah. Looks like it.'

Marcus slams his fists into the steering wheel. The car rocks with the force of each blow.

'Fuck, fuck, fuck, fuck, fuck!'

Taylor speaks as quietly as he can. Need to bring this down, take some of the heat out.

'What do you want to do?'

'How the fuck should I know?'

Without warning Marcus punches Taylor in the shoulder, not so hard as to do any lasting damage but enough to send him sprawling against the side window.

'This is your fault. You wanting to play at detectives. She'd have never gone for this if you hadn't persuaded her.'

He grabs Taylor by the neck, squeezing his Adam's apple, blocking the air flow.

'All along, you've been the one telling her to take these guys on. And now she's out there and we can't find her.'

Taylor tries to push his fingers under Marcus's hand, but the grip is too strong. He splutters and gasps for breath.

'And what are you going to do about it? Eh?'

Taylor feels the pressure moving up to his eyes, pushing them against their sockets. If he doesn't break free soon it will be too late.

'Come on, smart arse. What are we going to do now?'

Just as he is about pass out, the pressure starts to ease and Marcus's hand falls from his throat. He is almost sobbing now.

'What am I going to do?'

Taylor sits back gasping, rubbing his neck where Marcus's fingers have left red tracks in the skin. It takes a while for him to croak out a few words.

'We're going to have to gamble.'

Marcus peers at him suspiciously as he starts to wipe under his eyes with the back of his hand. Taylor shrugs.

'Coast or country?'

'This isn't a game. I'm not just tossing a coin.'

'No, I know. But it's stick or twist. And I say twist.'

Marcus is breathing heavily, and Taylor is watching for any sudden movements.

'Like we said when we set off. They'll either go for a deserted place on the coast or some out-of-the-way spot in the countryside where they can get away quickly.'

There is a look of undiluted hatred boring into him from Marcus. Suddenly he bellows in Taylor's face like a stricken animal brought down by a hunter's gun. The yell erupts from deep within his belly, some primal source of anguish beyond words, making the car resonate and leaving Taylor shaking with fear at what Marcus will do next.

Without warning he is rocked back into his seat as they scream away down the empty road.

*

Terry and Ernie Fletcher's lad, Carl, have hauled themselves over a corner of the wall at the rear of the garden. Gordon Clifford's son and nephew have clambered over the opposite corner. There are deep flower beds along the perimeters that provide enough cover in the darkness to crouch low and make their way closer to the house. Terry gives the signal and both pairs move forward in single file. They can see a paved terrace that runs the width of the building and beyond that there are floor to ceiling French windows overlooking the garden. Some of the windows are boarded over with plywood.

A cat picks its way across the patio and suddenly the whole area is flooded with light. Terry texts Bill.

In position. Security lights in operation. Will wait for your call.

Stan Roberts's son, Chris, has joined Bill and Harry in the car. He works in telephone sales for an insurance firm. Wouldn't be much use in a bust-up, bit weedy in fact, but he has a baby face and a lovely speaking voice. Just what is needed. He picks up the food bags, walks over to the electronic gates and presses the intercom.

Bill and Harry position themselves either side of the gate.

A voice crackles in reply.

'What do you want?'

'Grub's Up. Got your order.'

''Bout bloody time.'

'Yeah, sorry. Trouble finding the place. Shall I come up to the house?'

'Stay where you are. I'll come and get it.'

They hear footsteps crunching down the gravel and then the door starts to swing open. Bill presses send on his phone.

NOW!

At the rear of the house, Terry flashes his torch and both pairs of men rush onto the terrace, bathed immediately in the floodlights. He and Carl pick up a large wooden bench and charge at the boarded-up section of the French windows, using it as a battering ram. The plywood splinters and breaks as they crash through into the living room. Terry and Carl both dive to the floor and start crawling towards the cover of a high-backed corner sofa, expecting a shot to come at them any moment.

Meantime, Gordon's contingent have picked up a patio chair and chucked it through one of the glass doors. The noise is deafening as shattered glass cascades across the parquet floor and Terry sees his chance to break cover and make for the far end of the room. He is ready to smash his way through anyone who gets in his way but reaches the double door at the back of the room without any interference.

He looks back towards the garden. Carl is peering round the edge of the sofa and Gordon's lads have crouched behind an extended dining table. He pushes both arms down in a signal, palms flat out in parallel with the floor. They wait and listen. No sound of anyone calling out instructions, moving towards them or making a break for it. Nothing but the sound of the four of them catching their breath.

Back at the front, an arm is being extended with a roll of cash. Chris hands over the bags and as they are taken, Bill and Harry rush forward, grab the arm and pull hard. They are expecting some bruiser to come crashing out and are poised to put the boot in, but they feel very little resistance and instead an elderly woman in a red cagoule topples onto the pavement.

The three of them start to fuss over her and check she is alright. They dust her down gently and help her to her feet. No harm done it seems.

'Long time no see,' says Bill. 'How are you doing, Jackie?'

*

The headlights in the Audi flash on and off a few times. Are we doing this or not?

Sarah looks over her shoulder at Jim. His eyes are unfocused as if he were looking into himself rather than at her. Without a word he hitches up the collar of his coat, pulls his hat down over one side of his face, opens the door and steps out into the blinding glare.

He waits until the man facing him slaps the car roof again. The rear passenger door opens, and a small figure emerges from the darkness. The man holds out his arm as Eileen starts to move forward, blocking her way.

Sarah moves to open her door but Jim pushes back.

'Stay in the car. And be ready to switch the engine on.'

The man is saying something to Eileen and then he cups his hands to his mouth.

'Walk towards us. Slowly.'

'That's the only way I can walk,' mutters Jim.

The man nods to Eileen and she also sets off, tentative and stiff in her movements. He waves Jim to come to them, beckoning him with the back of his hand. The wind is getting up and spray is spin-drifting over the sand and into their faces. Eileen turns her head away and almost stumbles. In the distance they can hear a rumbling noise inland. Sounds like bad weather on the way.

They are close to the halfway point. If they cross it Jim knows there is no way back for him; still, he lowers his head into the wind and keeps on coming. But Eileen is slowing down and is almost at a standstill, her eyes fixed on Jim. She turns back to the man by the car and Sarah sees her shake her head.

'Shit! What's she doing?'

Jim is stuck in No Man's Land. Too far to get back to Sarah and not quite close enough to grab Eileen, who is starting to back away. He puts out his hand to her as if he were trying to drag her to safety.

'Keep coming. You're almost there.'

The lights in the Audi flicker momentarily as the driver switches on the ignition and revs the engine. The other man starts running towards Eileen who turns back but is caught by a sudden gust and loses her footing. Jim stumbles forward and throws himself on top of her. He wraps his arm round her trim little waist and grips tight.

The rumbling from inland has been growing louder until it turns into a crashing, scraping racket, the screeching of metal on metal and then the whine of an engine under severe pressure as a car breaks through onto the road, no headlights showing, and shooting straight towards Jim and Eileen.

At the last moment, the driver sees the bundle of bodies crouched between the other cars' headlights and slams on the brakes. The car slews to one side as the tyres grip on the last section of road, the back end swinging round, out of control. It isn't stopping and carries on sliding ever nearer to them over the sandy turf. Sarah sees Jim brace himself and arch his body to cover Eileen, waiting for the impact. There is a shower of sand as the edge of the boot sweeps past their bodies followed by a sickening crunch as the car smashes into the sewage pipe and settles into the sludgy mess beneath. A sickly, foul stink spreads rapidly across the beach and stops everyone in their tracks. Whatever muck the people of Knott End have been eating lately, this is where it has ended up.

No one is moving in the smashed-up car, but it has come to rest between the other two, cutting Jim and Eileen off from Sarah who can't see much for all the sand and spray in the air. When she hears the Audi reversing at high speed back along the bridle path she gets out of the car and stumbles towards the crash. She pulls on the crumpled car door and Marcus lolls forward out of the driving seat, his head bouncing against the airbag.

'Oh my god! Are you alright?'

He is gasping for air but almost gagging as he takes in the sewage stench. He nods weakly.

'Have you got her?'

Sarah looks over the car roof and can see the Audi's red tail-lights in the distance. She leans down to help Marcus out of his seat belt.

'They've gone. Taken Eileen with them. Jim as well by the look of it. What a fucking mess.'

Marcus collapses onto the sand and Sarah slides round to the passenger side to check on Taylor. His head is lying to one side, staring directly at her when she prises the door open.

'I think I'll stick to the bus in future.'

She helps him out of the car, leaving him propped against the side, gingerly rubbing his neck.

'Jim?' he asks.

She shakes her head. They gaze at each other, knowing that they made this happen. No one else. Them. And it really is a car crash.

'I'm over here, you gobshite.'

One of the little dunes ahead of them shifts and Jim's head shakes free, wet sand clogging his hair.

'Don't just stand there. Get me out of this.'

Sarah scrambles over the beach and starts digging Jim out with her hands.

'Thank God.'

'Might as well.'

'What about Eileen?'

Jim flicks his head in the direction of the Audi, which has now disappeared from view.

*

Bill and Harry are making themselves comfortable in the kitchen. The takeaway curries have been distributed to the lads, who were all peckish after a day in the field. Now Ernie and Frank have taken guard at the front of the house with Gordon's lads while Terry and the others have positioned themselves at the back and by the gates.

Jackie is also at the kitchen table, looking nervous and furious in equal measure. Mouth drawn tightly shut. Cheeks sucked in and taut. Harry mops his plate with the remains of a chapati, sits back and licks his fingers appreciatively.

'Expecting company, were you?'

Jackie responds with a look of haughty disdain, the sort she reserves for cold callers selling dishcloths and dusters from a duffle bag.

'I suppose you can always give 'em beans on toast.'

She turns away in disgust, not wishing to dignify anything Harry says with a reply.

Bill pushes his plate away and wipes his mouth with a serviette.

'What time are they due back?'

A flicker of interest from Jackie.

'Who?'

'Come on, Jackie. We don't want any more trouble. Just tell us what you know.'

'I know that you've broken into my house, smashed up my living room and now you're holding me prisoner in my own home.'

Harry chuckles.

'You're right. That's terrible. I'd call the police if I were you.'

She abandons righteous anger and starts fiddling with a large diamond ring on her finger. Bill waits a few moments.

'I see a couple of them windows were boarded up. Is that where they shot Don?'

She takes a deep breath, and he sees her face soften a little. Bill tries again.

'What was it? They came back? Threatened you if you didn't help them? Is that how it were?'

She starts to sob. Harry offers a serviette, realises it is spotted with tandoori sauce and swiftly gives her a clean one instead.

'I didn't have a choice. They said they'd kill me as well if I didn't cooperate.'

Bill has been watching her face as she dabs her eyes, his head slightly to one side.

'What's supposed to happen when they come back?'

Jackie begins rubbing her diamond ring again.

'I don't know. I suppose they'll have Gerry. Maybe there'd be no need to come back here.'

'So why did you order all that food?'

'I didn't. They must have done that.'

'But you were happy to pay for it. Very good of you.'

He can see she's rattled, desperately trying to get her story straight. More tears now.

'You don't know what it's been like. With Don gone. I'm all on my own.'

'Jackie...'

Terry bursts into the kitchen.

'Stan's rung. The Audi and the van have just passed him on the road. Be here in a couple of minutes.'

'Could he see who was in the car?'

'Going too fast. But he said the van looks like it's been in an accident.'

'Right. Now, Jackie. You need to do exactly what we tell you.'

*

Sarah and Taylor have put an arm under each shoulder and helped Jim hobble back to the car. Sarah gets down on her haunches and brushes more dirt off his coat with her hand. He pushes it away impatiently.

'I'm alright.'

'You've had a shock.'

Jim seems frail and uncertain in her eyes now, the years suddenly catching up on him.

'I couldn't stop 'em.'

Taylor leans down from outside the car.

'You did everything you could.'

Things aren't so bad that Jim needs Taylor's sympathy so he ignores him and focuses on Sarah.

'I had hold of her but after the car crashed she must have rolled free.'

'It's not your fault.'

A spasm of anger from Jim.

'I know that. But I wanted to make it right anyway.'

Sarah is embarrassed, jiggling her legs nervously as she crouches by his side.

'You're sure you're OK? Do I need to get you to a doctor?'

'Just let me get my breath back.'

She and Taylor walk over to Marcus who is sitting on the sand, looking at the remains of the BMW. Sarah rubs his shoulder and he puts his hand on hers.

'How did you know we were here?'

'I didn't. It was a guess. I always thought the coast was most likely, so I headed for the nearest place that had a road to it but no houses nearby.

I thought I'd cocked up but then we saw the van blocking the road. Then we knew we were on the right track.'

'How did you get by if they were in the way?'

Taylor wanders in front of Marcus, holding his hand over his nose as the breeze catches the dribbling ooze of sewage seeping under the car and shifts the aroma their way.

'Yeah, well… Marcus isn't like most other drivers. If there's no road he just drives through a hedge and goes via the field instead.'

Sarah sees Marcus give Taylor a sly grin. Her boys bonding a little.

'I swerved to avoid the van but clipped the side and bounced off into the hedge. Just kept going until we got back onto the road through a gate further down.

Must have smashed the headlights so we were driving blind. Didn't see Jim and Eileen until we were nearly on them.'

He goes quiet and hunches forward.

'Got lucky.'

Sarah kisses the top of his head and all three of them stare at what's left of the hire car. One side has been staved in where they hit the van; the headlights are hanging out of their sockets; one of the tyres has been torn to shreds; the once gleaming electric blue finish has been scratched, gouged and smeared with mud, leaves, sand and pureed excrement.

Taylor turns his back and moves away.

'I hope you took out the extra insurance.'

Suddenly Sarah jumps up.

'Shit! I need to ring Bill. Tell him what's happened. I need your phone, Marcus.'

He reaches into his back pocket and looks at the shattered screen. He taps a couple of times but it's no good.

'Dead.'

'Taylor. Your phone!'

Taylor pats his pockets. He furrows his brow as the penny drops.

'No. You haven't?'

'I was charging it at Helen's.'

'Brilliant!'

She belts Marcus on the back and gives him a hand up.

'Come on. We need to get to the house. I'm driving.'

*

The gates slowly swing open as the remote control is triggered from the road. The Audi scrunches to a halt by the front of the house while the van continues round to the side.

Two men, both hefty and wearing dark clothes, get out. One of them fetches Eileen from the back and shepherds her to the front door. They can see the kitchen light on and head straight for it, finding Jackie waiting for them, sitting stiffly by the table.

'Where's Gerry?' she asks.

The taller of the two men throws himself down in the nearest chair.

'Bastards tried to pull a fast one.'

Eileen lowers herself gingerly into a seat.

'It was Jim. I couldn't see at first. The headlights were too bright. But when he got close...'

She waves her hand helplessly. The other man is pacing round the room looking as if he is about to blow up.

'You told us they'd find him. You said he'd come back once he knew you were in trouble.'

Eileen looks at him defiantly.

'Kelly told you they had 'im. That's where it's gone wrong. You said you had her under control.'

He pauses in his tracks and gives a reluctant nod of acknowledgement.

'Alright, alright. We'll deal with her later,' turning to the man seated at the table. 'What now?'

He pushes some tablemats around while he thinks before stacking them neatly in a pile.

'I'm calling it in.'

Eileen looks at him in disbelief.

'What?'

'They're on to us. It's only a matter of time before someone checks this place out.'

'No one knows you're here.'

'Not yet. But the police will get called to the accident on the beach. They'll tell them about the van. You know what people are like round here. Somebody's bound to have seen a banged-up van going in the gate.'

The other man has stopped pacing about and is leaning forwards on the table.

'Best get going then.'

'Soon as Gary comes in, we'll pack up.'

Eileen sniffs in disgust.

'Is that it, then? You're giving up?'

'Shut it, Eileen.'

'Your bosses aren't going to be too impressed, are they?'

He moves his face close to hers.

'No wonder your husband left. Can't keep your mouth closed, can you?'

Eileen turns to the other man.

'Without me you don't get anything. And I want my share. I've not gone through all this for nothing.'

But the man is not paying any attention to her. He is watching Jackie who has been sitting frozen and motionless throughout. He flicks one of the tablemats in her direction.

'You're very quiet, Jackie.'

Something in her expression makes his stomach heave.

'Where's that food you ordered?'

Two men appear from behind cupboards by the window. He hears the door click behind him as three others enter the room.

'Sorry about that,' says Terry, 'but we hadn't had a bite to eat all day.'

The man shifts his chair back and crashes into Terry's belly, knocking the wind out of him and bending him double. He picks up the chair and swings it at the next man he can see, catching him full on the shoulder and sending him flying against the wall. Before Carl can react, he charges him head on and butts him in the chest. He falls to the floor and the man puts the boot in just in case and heads for the door.

'Stop him,' croaks Terry.

The other villain has not been so quick off the mark. One of Gordon's lads has pinned his arms behind his back and the other is wrapping duct tape round his ankles as they wrestle him to the ground.

But the other is away down the corridor to the front door which is invitingly open. He can see the Audi waiting for him on the drive and pats his pocket to check he has the keys. He allows himself a half smile as he makes a final spurt for freedom bursting into the night only to trip over an outstretched leg and go tumbling down the stone steps. Two men pounce, pin him to the deck and tie his hands behind his back. When they turn him over his nose is flattened and blood is streaming down his face.

Ernie and Frank stroll down the steps from where they'd been standing like two guardian statues, one either side of the front door. They look at the trussed-up gangster squirming in fury on the gravel and shake hands.

'Just like what you did to George Best in '67,' remarks Frank.

Ernie acknowledges the tribute.

'It's all about timing, in't it? You never lose it.'

Bill and Harry approach from the side of the house and nod appreciatively.

'That's the lot then. T'other one's roped up and locked in the back of the van.'

The four of them saunter back into the house and make way as Gordon's lads drag the third man out of the kitchen. Terry and Carl are sitting on the hall stairs, grimacing as they rub the bruises on their bodies, but they signal that no serious damage has been done. The old stagers press on and find Eileen and Jackie sitting at the table, surrounded by bits of broken chairs and smashed crockery.

Eileen struggles to her feet as they come in with a grateful smile on her face.

'Oh, it's you, Bill. And Harry. Thank God. I thought they'd kill me after Gerry didn't turn up.'

Bill puts his hand on her shoulder and gives her a peck on the cheek.

'Good to see you in one piece, love.'

'How did you find us? We'd given up hope, hadn't we, Jackie?'

She turns to Jackie for support but only gets an impassive stare in response.

'I should have known Gerry's pals wouldn't desert us.'

Her smile freezes when she sees that Bill's face is full of regret and disappointment.

'Why did you do it?'

'Do what?'

Bill closes his eyes, rubs the bridge of his nose and sighs.

'We were listening. When you came back.'

Eileen lowers herself into her chair, takes out a handkerchief and starts winding it round her finger.

'I didn't want to. Jackie made me.'

A dinner mat flies across the table and narrowly misses Eileen's head.

'You lying bitch!'

Harry puts a restraining hand on Jackie's arm and confiscates the remaining mats.

'No need for that. We've called the police. You can explain it all to them. Meantime… who'd like a nice cup of tea?'

Thirty-Three

Burnden Park, where Gerry and his pals used to toil, sweat and occasionally triumph did not survive the twentieth century. Sarah's father, Matthew, had been inconsolable after the last match in 1997, a rousing victory that secured promotion to the opulent paradise that is the Premier League. Sarah remembers waiting up for him that night, her sitting with a cup of hot chocolate, him cradling a brandy, while he tried to explain how he felt. Helen had left them to it, so they sat together on the settee, Sarah in her pyjamas with her knees up to her chin and Matthew leaning forward into a pool of light from a table lamp.

'That's the first time I was ever on the pitch. Last time ever as well. Everyone else seemed to be doing it so I thought – why not? Won't have the chance again.

People were singing, dancing, chanting. Going mad. We'd won the match, won the league. Not like us. And you don't want a moment like that to end. You want to savour it. Like a good drink. Let it linger.'

He took a sip of his brandy and let the warmth slither into his chest.

'When they're doing well, so are you. You feel bigger. Better. More sure of yourself. So none of us wanted to go home because we knew we couldn't take that feeling with us. And we knew that once we left, we could never come back. No more nights like this.'

He craned his head round to check he still had her attention and Sarah smiled encouragingly. Go on, Dad, it's alright.

'But then we started to feel awkward. Like we didn't belong. The players had gone in. We'd stopped jumping up and down and shouting and were just kind of… stood there. What were we supposed to do next?

People started drifting away. Wandering round, taking a last look, hanging about by the exits. Not wanting to go but not having any reason to stay. What do you do when something's over?'

He took another drink and stared at the display cabinet against the far wall, where he kept some old family photographs in frames.

'You never knew your grandad, but he was a big fan as well. As I stood there on the pitch, I started thinking about him. He was on the Embankment that day in March, the year after the war, when a load of men got trampled to death after the barriers broke. Bodies laid out along the touchline. His mate said to him – "Hey, there's some people fainted" – but Grandad knew. He'd seen dead men before. He wasn't the only one. A lot of demobbed soldiers would have been there.

We were living in Tonge Moor then and I remember standing with Grandma outside the house. Waiting. Men with slumped shoulders dragging themselves home. No, they hadn't seen him. Not sure how many were killed, but it's bad.

So we waited. It was dark now. Grandma pulled me tight against her legs, pressing my body so hard I couldn't breathe properly. How could that happen, we thought? Just set off to the match and never return.

Then we saw two men down the bottom of the street, one hopping, his arm slung round the other. "I'm alright. I'm alright," he shouted. "Just a sprain.".

Grandma hugged him as if she'd never let him out of her sight again. Like when he'd turned up on the doorstep, still in his uniform, back home for good. Alive. All in one piece.

A deliverance. That's what Grandma called it. Grandad called it luck.'

Sarah rubbed his back, and he patted her feet in return.

'As I walked away, I wondered what Grandad would have made of all this. Or his dad for that matter. He might have been at the first ever match at Burnden Park. I was at the last. And now that line is broken.

And we can never go there again.'

All this comes into Sarah's mind as she approaches the site of what used to be the old football ground but is now a hypermarket, and next to that is the new police station. The truth being that you can go back but you can't always find what you are looking for.

Assistant Chief Constable Alec Timpson is waiting for her in the foyer which, for a reason very difficult to fathom, is shaped like a small aircraft hangar with a miniature minaret on top. Perhaps the architect was making a deferential nod in the direction of the growing Muslim population locally or perhaps they simply got bored with the otherwise functional and dreary design and what began as a doodle became a reality.

'A word,' he says opening a door into an interview room and inviting her in.

Sarah is about to sit down but notices that Alec is standing ramrod straight, so she decides against it.

'Why didn't you tell me what was really going on when you came to see me?'

'I didn't know then.'

He gives her the contemptuous half smile that criminals become accustomed to from arresting officers. Tell me another one.

'You never mentioned that this gang had tried to kidnap you. Slipped your mind, did it?'

As this sounds like the start of a series of rhetorical questions Sarah opts to look sheepish and not interrupt the flow of Alec's rebuke.

'And then they lift the old lady. Didn't it occur to you to call us in then?'

Sarah waits. There's more.

'I mean, what the fuck were you thinking?'

Actually, that is a good question.

'You could have got yourself killed – not to mention Jim and Gerry's missus. How did you think you were going to save them?'

And still they come.

'And whose brilliant idea was it to rope in a load of pensioners to take on a gang of professional criminals?'

Taylor's, but best not to drag him into it at this stage.

He seems to have paused, but not necessarily finished, so Sarah takes her chance to put the case for the defence.

'I know, Alec. It was stupid. I should have come back to you.'

'You think?'

'But it worked out alright in the end, didn't it?'

Alec finally sits down.

'You could say that. Apart from the fact that I've got two old ladies in custody that I don't know what to do with; three villains who refuse to tell me who hired them or why; some old footballers who knocked seven shades of shit out of them; not to mention another half-dozen family members who aided and abetted. And I haven't even got round to your boyfriend, who seems to have broken every regulation in the Highway Code. And you.

Apart from that – yes – all tied up nicely with a bow.'

Sarah is about to come back but Alec hasn't finished.

'And you still don't know where Gerry Bradshaw is. Which was the whole damn point of this, wasn't it?'

Time for her to sit down as well.

'Are you going to charge Bill and Harry and the others?'

'What do you think? They've all admitted to smuggling drugs into the country for the last five years. And if that wasn't enough, they've added assault, criminal damage, breaking and entering, holding someone against their will, fraud and a litany of other offences I won't bore you with.

By the time they come out of jail they'll go straight to a nursing home. If they live that long.'

'You're going to throw the book at them? After what they did?'

'The police don't decide on whether someone is prosecuted. That's up to the CPS.'

'Oh come on, Alec, don't give me the party line. You're telling me that you don't have any influence?'

She catches a slightly shifty movement in Alec as he eases his shoulders.

'Actually, why are you here, anyway? Bit below your pay grade, isn't it?'

He runs his tongue over his teeth. Nasty habit but he can't seem to help it. He gives a low growl in acknowledgement of her question.

'You can be very annoying, but I suppose you know that.'

'No one's ever mentioned it before.'

'As it happens, there are some… sensitivities about this case. People have long memories in this town. Putting local heroes on trial won't go down too well.'

'Especially as they've broken up a drugs gang and brought them to justice.'

'Having first profited from the trade for years. And let's not get carried away with them being the sword of justice. All we've got are the hired hands. The real villains are still out there.'

Sarah takes a moment to absorb this.

'But now you've got the men who shot Don Bradley. That's got to be worth some credit.'

'They deny it.'

'Naturally. They would.'

'Yes… but we're not convinced. They've got muscle but not many brains. We think their bosses brought someone in to get rid of Don. A specialist.'

'I see.'

She starts to rub absentmindedly at an ink spot on the table.

'Any other reason you might not prosecute them?'

'Such as…?'

She examines the mucky tip of her finger with surprise.

'Just wondering. Doesn't look great that the police have had a bunch of old men bringing drugs into the country for years and no one has spotted it.'

'Border control isn't our responsibility. Neither are custom checks.'

'No. They're Home Office, aren't they?'

She is about to suck the ink off her finger, but remembers in time where she is, gets out a hankie instead, licks that and starts wiping away the smudge.

'Someone at the top been on the phone to your boss? Local MP is a junior minister, isn't he? Rather not see the headlines about our borders having more holes than a string vest?'

Alec gives her what he hopes is his most unnerving hard stare, but Sarah seems unabashed.

'No comment.'

'Thanks, Alec. Can I see my client now?'

'Now that's another thing. I can't believe you're proposing to represent Eileen Bradshaw.'

Sarah flips open her briefcase and hands Alec a sheaf of papers.

'My dad was her solicitor and I've inherited his business. And she's asked for me.'

Alec flicks through the papers and hands them back.

'Just because she asked doesn't mean you have to do it. For God's sake! I'd have thought you wanted to get out from under this case, not burrow more deeply into it.'

Sarah stashes her instructions away and stands up. She puts on her best, officious voice.

'Too many loose ends. As a copper I thought you'd understand that. Now… could someone take me to her?'

*

A week ago, Eileen toddled into the offices of Curtis and Curtis and turned Sarah's world upside down. Now it feels like the pair of them have come full circle; back in an interview room again with Eileen trying to find the words to explain what has been going on. She is looking very weary. A couple of nights in custody have rumpled her neat and tidy demeanour and without make-up her face looks almost obscenely naked, like an old doll scrubbed clean of rouge and lipstick, left with nothing to hide behind.

But there is a defiance there that Sarah had failed to notice before. She could have tried the "I'm just a little old lady who got caught up in something I didn't understand" routine, and perhaps she might still fall back on that. For the moment, she is all business – more of a "What can you do to get me out of this hole?" look about her.

Sarah takes the notes from her briefcase, opens her laptop, and goes to work.

'First things first, Eileen. Are you sure you want me to represent you?'

'Gerry trusted your father. He always went to him with any problems.'

'Yes, I understand but, you see, I'm not a criminal lawyer. You might be better with…'

Eileen cuts across her.

'Matthew was our solicitor,' looking meaningfully at Sarah, 'and our friend.'

'OK. I needed to check. Speaking of Gerry, do you have any idea where he is?'

A polite, controlled snort from Eileen.

'Well, I'd have hardly gone through all this palaver if I knew that, would I?'

'Alright. If you're sure. But I can't help you unless you tell me the truth.'

'I know.'

'Only, you haven't told me much of that up to now.'

'I did what I thought was best.'

Sarah starts to type a few preparatory notes and then turns the palms of her hands outwards, inviting Eileen to begin.

'Let's go back a bit. How much did you know about what Gerry was up to?'

Eileen sucks up a little of the tea sitting in a flimsy brown plastic cup in front of her and immediately wishes she hadn't bothered.

'Nothing, at first. 'Course I noticed he had a bit more cash, but it wasn't like he was splashing out. He told me he was getting a few little jobs helping out at the club and I didn't think any more about it. He wasn't fretting about money any more and that was a nice change so I didn't bother to question it.

Then one day he comes home in a new car. A Mercedes. He cracked on that one of his mates knew one of these young players who has more money than he knows what to do with. Said he'd offered it to his mate as a long-term loan because he had three other cars to choose from. And he'd passed it to Gerry as a favour.'

'And did you believe him?'

Eileen curls her lips.

'Let's say I didn't quiz him too much about it.'

'Go on.'

'Well, we were going along quite nicely. Gerry had treated me to some new clothes and took me out more than before. Nothing to complain about.'

'But…?'

'He was getting more distracted. A bit stressed. And he was out more at night and wouldn't say where he'd been. So, naturally I smelled a rat. Asked him straight out. Had he got some piece on the side?'

'And had he?'

Prolonged giggle from Eileen as she remembers the shock on Gerry's face when she confronted him.

'Very offended he was. Said he wasn't that kind of man.'

The laughter subsides.

'And I believed him. He wasn't.'

Sarah looks up from her laptop.

'Wasn't?'

'Isn't, I mean. Isn't that kind of man.'

Sarah decides to let that go, for now.

'And then what?'

'We got invited to Don and Jackie's place.'

'Elswick House.'

'That's right. I knew Don had been doing alright since he gave up playing, had his own business and everything, but I had no idea…

I'd never been anywhere so posh – except, you know – a stately home or something – and there's Don like the lord of the manor and Jackie giving it all that with her aperitifs and her canapés. I remember when she lived above a chip shop in Halliwell.

But she had it nice. I'll give her that. Lots of antiques and lovely old furniture. Not my sort of thing but classy – like your dad used to have. Only genuine.'

'And that's when you found out?'

'Don explained it to me over dinner. Except he didn't really. He had this way of talking so that you were never quite sure what he meant. It was all about contacts, business partners, market forces, supply and demand – that sort of thing. Never came right out with it. He wasn't saying it was legal but he sort of suggested it was, you know, nothing to worry about. Bending the law a bit. Like fiddling your taxes. Lots of people do it. Just need to keep it between ourselves.'

'And you accepted that, did you?'

'I had it out with Gerry when we got home. Asked him what was really going on. Did he know what he was getting into?'

She pauses, her mind cast back to that evening. Sarah is waiting, her fingers suspended above the keys on her laptop.

'Yes…?'

'Gerry was always very good to me. Not like one or two of the others he played with. The way they treated their wives. Handy with their fists when they'd had a few then all tearful the next morning. But I saw a different side of him that night. Ranting, shouting at the top of his voice. Telling me not to stick my nose in where it wasn't needed. That I was doing alright out of it wasn't I so I should keep my mouth shut and let him handle it. I thought he was going to go for me at one point, so I just kept quiet, didn't look him in the eyes, waited for it to blow over.

When he started to calm down I could see he was shaking. Came and sat down by me and put his hand on my cheek. I must have froze because he looked at me so sad. He knew he'd let himself down.

"I would never," he said to me. And he put his head on my shoulder and I cradled him like a baby.

You see, I hadn't realised until that night. How frightened he was.'

Eileen looks at the plastic cup of tea which seems to have congealed and Sarah fetches a jug of water from the table behind and pours her a glass.

'Thanks. After that I didn't ask any more questions. A few months later he took me out for a drive to see this new house over by the golf course. "How would you fancy living here?"

And then it gets too late to ask how can we afford it? We'd never been so well off. And you get used to it and you don't want to go back to how it was before, counting the pennies.'

'So you're telling me that you never suspected anything about drugs? The police are going to find that hard to believe after what you've done.'

'Why? It's the truth.'

Sarah sits back. No need to keep a record of this part of the interview.

'You might have been able to persuade them you're an innocent beneficiary in all this, someone not fully acquainted with the world around them. An old-fashioned housewife who relied on her husband to make the decisions and handle the money side of things.

But they're going to have some difficulty reconciling that with the woman who organised her own kidnapping.'

Eileen considers this as she sips some water. Sarah tries to imagine her in the witness box. Would she come across as an elderly lady hopelessly out of her depth or a calculating old witch? The first one might get a light sentence, partially suspended but the other is looking at a long stretch.

'I've already told you I knew something not exactly legal was going on. But I didn't know any details. What do I know about drugs? Anyway, after that night I didn't ask any more questions and Gerry never mentioned it. Not until…'

'… until Don was shot.'

Eileen pushes her glasses up on to her forehead and rubs her eyes as if trying to focus them more clearly.

'Jackie rang him. She was in bits. I could hear her screaming down the phone. She'd been out to lunch and found him lying in the conservatory with his brains blown out. Police were on their way.

Can't say I've ever liked her that much. Always looked down her nose at me. But… how do you ever get over that?'

They decide to take a break. Asif comes over from the office with some sandwiches and persuades the officer in charge to allow him in with two coffees. Sarah watches Eileen pick at her food, peeling back the bread and daintily lifting the ham salad to her lips. Still keeping an eye on her figure. But she knocks back the coffee, glad of the caffeine boost that brings a lustre to her tired eyes.

'What did Gerry say after he got the call?'

'He was in shock. We both were. It all came out then. How Don had met these "contacts" as he called them, who had come up with the idea of bringing drugs into the country in footballers' kit bags. Apparently, some of them were keen fans and they went to these games abroad and it dawned on them how easy it would be to get through customs on the way back.'

'Just to be clear… Gerry told you it was illegal drugs.'

'Cocaine. I swear that was the first time he ever mentioned it to me.'

'It's alright, Eileen. You're not on oath here.'

She looks imploringly at Sarah.

'You believe me, don't you?'

Sarah resumes typing.

'What did you say when he told you?'

'I couldn't take it in all at once. Jackie said she'd already had a call from Don's "associates" who'd warned her about talking to the police, so she wasn't going to say anything about the smuggling. She asked Gerry to tell the others and for everybody to keep quiet.

We thought about running away. But where could we go? And they'd find us anyway.'

'So you did nothing?'

'Gerry thought that was the best thing. The football season was nearly over so there wouldn't be many more runs and then there'd be two or three months before it started up again.

We thought maybe they might decide to pack it in. Gerry thought we should wait and see.'

'Did he know why they'd shot Don?'

'No. I don't think so. He was as shocked as me when Jackie rang. He reckoned Don must have been pulling a fast one and got caught out. That would be just like him. Too greedy.'

'And then the phone calls started?'

Eileen lifts back the wilting bread of her sandwich and levers out a slice of tomato she'd missed the first time round.

'About a month ago. They'd been trying to get some money out of Jackie that Don owed them… or had stolen from them, I don't know, but he'd squirrelled it away somewhere and she didn't have the details. Then they thought they could get it back from Gerry, thought he might know where Don kept his money.'

'Did he?'

'No, of course not. Whatever Don was raking in, that was his.

But he'd advised Gerry to do the same as him. Move the money around a lot until it found its way into some bank account abroad.

But they didn't believe that. Thought Gerry was in cahoots with Don and could get his hands on the money.

Then they changed tack. Told Gerry that unless he could get the money Don owed them then they'd take it from him.'

'And how much did Gerry have in this bank account?'

'A lot less than they were after from Don.'

'How much, Eileen?'

She fiddles with the remnants of her sandwich again but only the carbohydrates remain, so she pushes the plate away.

'I'm not sure.'

'You must have some idea.' She waits and then adds 'You're telling me, not the police.'

Eileen taps the table top lightly with her fingertips.

'Just over a million… might be nearer 1.2.'

Sarah tries not to look surprised and receives the information without registering any emotion.

'And they wanted the lot?'

Eileen nods.

'And Gerry wouldn't give it to them?'

Eileen runs her tongue over her lips and hesitates. I hope she's not going to start wringing her handkerchief again, thinks Sarah. Then suddenly it dawns on her.

'Oh. I see. He did want to give it back – but you wouldn't let him.'

Eileen reaches out across the table and puts her hand on Sarah's. Holds it there while she makes her case.

'What Don had done, that wasn't anything to do with us. Jackie's probably sitting on three or four million so why should we have to lose all our money when we'd done nothing wrong?'

'Done nothing wrong?'

'To them, I mean. But Gerry didn't see it that way. Said we'd never be free of them unless we handed it all over.

Then, when they said they'd burn the house down – that's what did it. We fell out. I tried to get him to calm down. Told him they wouldn't really do it, or they'd never get anything. They needed to put more pressure on Jackie. Sweat it out of her.

You see, he thought he could get shut of the whole thing if he paid them off. Be done with it for good. But I said to him, what if they take the money and then force you to carry on? We'd have given away all we had and be no better off.

That made him think. We agreed to leave it to the morning. Decide then.

When I woke up, he'd gone. No note. Nothing.'

She presses down harder on Sarah's hand.

'He shouldn't have done that, should he? Leaving me on my own, knowing what they were like.'

Sarah tries to put herself in Eileen's shoes. She'd turned a blind eye to what Gerry and Don were up to. Allowed herself to be convinced it was some sort of tax dodge, a victimless crime. That somehow they were entitled to a bit of money in their old age. If everyone else was at it they'd be stupid not to take some for themselves. And then the real world came crashing in. Don's brains had been splattered all over his conservatory floor and now they were turning their attention on them. What would she have done in her place?

Gerry thought he could buy them off by handing over their share. But what if they took that and still wanted more? The house. The car. And would they really have let him walk away?

So maybe Eileen wasn't so wrong to try and talk him round. Maybe it would have been better to work with them to put the squeeze on Jackie and leave them be. That probably wouldn't have worked either but at least they would have been facing it together.

Anyway, Eileen is right. Gerry shouldn't have walked out on her like he did.

'Makes you think what your marriage is all about when that happens. I thought he loved me. He always said he did. But... I don't know now.

Sometimes I wonder whether he loved that damn dog more than me. Fussing over him. I can see him now, tickling his ears. "How's Treacle? Are you alright, boy?" Checking to see his basket was comfy. You'd think it was our bed the way he kept tidying it and changing the blankets.

That's the last thing he did that night before he left. Went downstairs and checked Treacle's basket. Made sure he was safe.

More than he did for me.'

Eileen is still holding onto Sarah's hand. She gently prises it free and starts typing again.

'And that's when you came to me?'

'Well, I could hardly go to the police, could I?'

'OK – but what did you think I could do?'

Eileen looks disappointed in her.

'I didn't have any details about the bank account. Gerry thought it was more secure if I didn't know, but him and your dad were drinking buddies. He was always round his house talking about football. I was sick of hearing about it, but your dad couldn't get enough. And I knew Gerry relied on Matthew for advice. So I thought he might have left the account details with him – for safe keeping.

That's all I was after. But you got carried away. Started thinking you could find him and bring him back. It all got out of hand.'

Sarah slumps forward in her chair and sighs.

'But you were never after Gerry. You just wanted the money.'

'He walked out on me, Sarah. Left me in the lurch. I had to look after myself.'

'We could have kept you safe.'

'Now, don't be daft. I couldn't stay in that poky little house forever. I'd have to go home sometime.

Anyway, they found me soon enough, thanks to Kelly.

So, I made a deal with them. If I could give them Gerry we'd split the proceeds – seventy-five per cent for them and the rest for me. And I'd keep the house and the car.

Not great but better than nothing.'

Sarah can't help herself this time. The look of shock is written all over her face.

'You'd have handed Gerry over to them? Knowing what they'd do to him?'

'Well, he wasn't bothered what happened to me, was he? Not a word since he left. And he's got all that money to himself.'

Sarah is watching Eileen's face. The colour is returning to her cheeks as she fires herself up with righteous indignation.

'But I didn't think he was such a bastard that he'd stand by and not help me when I'd been kidnapped. Be our diamond wedding anniversary next year and that's all he thinks of me.'

'Was that your idea as well? Faking the abduction?'

'I thought he'd be sure to contact you when he heard from one of his cronies. We'd do the swap and I'd go back home.'

'And you weren't worried about them killing Gerry?'

'All he had to do was be sensible and tell them what they wanted to know. They only shot Don because he wouldn't cooperate.'

Sarah closes the laptop lid. Eileen looks confused.

'Are we finished, love? I thought you'd have a lot more to ask me.'

'That's enough for now.'

Eileen raises her wispy eyebrows in enquiry.

'Well?'

'Well, what?'

'What do you think of my chances? Can we come to some sort of arrangement with the police?'

There is an eager expectancy in Eileen's face, like a child who is waiting to be rewarded for finally doing the right thing. Sarah can imagine her as a little girl. Fussy, needing attention, keen for praise but also wilful and strong-minded. Not beyond throwing a tantrum if she didn't get what she wanted or what she thought she deserved. And this little girl was still there inside her, telling her that what happened to her wasn't fair and that Gerry had only himself to blame if he didn't do what she'd asked him to.

Sarah crams her papers back into her briefcase and slings it over her shoulder.

'I'll see what I can do.'

*

A constable stops her on her way out and escorts her to an office on the first floor where Alec has taken up temporary residence. He slaps down a hefty file on the desk as she enters.

'Whatever you have to say to me it's got to be better than reading a feasibility study on the options for installing air source heat pumps into our offices.'

He motions her to take a seat.

'What's her story then?'

'You know I can't tell you that. You haven't even charged her yet.'

'Alright, let's put it another way. What is she looking for?'

Sarah can't tell whether Alec is fishing for information or seriously considering a deal but after that performance by Eileen she is not keen to put her before a jury if she can help it. Worth risking a bit of barter.

'Could we just review where you are on the case... as a whole?'

Alec leans back on his executive chair, swaying it slightly from side to side, apparently relaxed, hands clasped across his belly.

'Go for it. Let's see how far we get.'

'You've got the three men who threatened Eileen and Gerry, staged her kidnap and tried to do the hostage exchange.'

Alec nods.

'I'm not sure I can positively identify the two who tried to snatch me. They were wearing balaclavas and it was getting dark.'

'Don't worry about that. They've been on their best behaviour. You know where you stand with career criminals. They know the best they can do is get a few years knocked off by pleading guilty, so they've been cooperative. Up to a point.

They won't tell us who they've been working for, and they definitely won't cop for the shooting.

We'll probably have to settle for that.'

'Then you've got Gerry's friends and their families.'

Alec swings his chair more expansively and rubs his hands together.

'Ah yes. The Dirty Dozen.'

'Not so straightforward.'

'The old bastards are the problem. Sons, nephews whatever... we can settle on a suspended sentence and community service. They were only trying to help out. But the others...'

'So were they. If it hadn't been for them, you'd never have got those three criminals.'

Alec stops swinging from side to side in his chair.

'We would have got them if you'd told us the whole story instead of acting like the fucking Famous Five.'

'Oh come on, Alec. I told you Eileen was being threatened by criminals and that Gerry had disappeared and you said it was nothing to worry about. Sent me away like a kid who'd been told to go home and play with her dollies. You don't want me saying that in court, do you?'

'Don't push your luck.'

'I'm only saying... they did the right thing in the end. You've got to give them some credit for that.'

Alec is beginning to enjoy this now, much more diverting than workforce planning, but he doesn't want to let Sarah see it, so he composes his face into an impassive mask and narrows his eyes.

'Alright. Let's say we don't bring charges for the breaking and entering, criminal damage etcetera. Rap on the knuckles. Shouldn't have done it but all in a good cause. OK. But what about the drugs? We can't get round that.'

'It's not like they made a lot of money out of it. Bill said they only got five hundred pounds per trip.'

'Mounts up over five years.'

'Come on, Alec. Probably about ten grand a year if they're lucky. They're hardly drug barons.'

'Can't say that about Gerry and Eileen though, can you? Or Jackie, for that matter? Big money for them, wasn't it?'

'I can't speak for Jackie, but she's paid the price, hasn't she? Christ, her husband was executed. And we've no idea where Gerry is, so he's out of the picture for now.'

'Exactly. So that leaves us with Eileen.'

'A seventy-nine-year-old woman with a bad hip.'

'Has she?'

'Dunno, she might have. But you take my point. She's the only person who ends up in the dock? That can't be right.'

'Somebody's got to pay the price.'

Sarah sees a narrow ledge she might be able to clamber onto if she can only reach out and get a firm grip.

'Right. The money.'

'What about it?'

'The Criminal Proceeds (Recovery) Act 2009. Allows police to seize cash and assets that have been obtained directly or indirectly from the proceeds of crime.'

Alec starts swaying again in the chair.

'Go on, I'm listening.'

'You've got Jackie's house. That's a no-brainer. Must be worth a couple of million – maybe more. Lots of money for good causes. The crime commissioner's going to love that.'

'Fine. We'll take it. But that doesn't help Eileen.'

'OK – but what if we were to recover the money Gerry has? Or find him? That would be another million or so.'

'IF! Are you telling me you think you can get hold of that account? Because if you have that information you need to hand it over.'

Sarah hesitates. Shit! I've over-promised again. Too late now.

'We're working on it.'

Alec cocks his head to one side and gives her a quizzical look.

'Cards on the table. I think you've as much chance of finding Gerry or that money as I have of being cast as the next James Bond. But we're going to have to let her out on bail when we've charged her so there's no immediate rush. Courts are backed up, anyway.'

'So it's a deal then!'

Alec puts out his hand as if he were fending off unwanted attention.

'I didn't say that. She's going to have to serve some time. But if we were to recover that money then I'd recommend a lighter sentence.'

'Maybe a suspended sentence on compassionate grounds?'

'I don't have any compassion for her. Can't understand why you have. No. Best I can do. Take it or leave it.'

Sarah decides to quit while she's ahead.

'How long have we got?'

'Let's see… a week?'

'No, no. We need more time than that.'

'Think of all you've achieved in the last seven days. This should be a piece of cake.'

He stands up. Interview over. Sarah slowly collects her bags and moves to the door.

'Sarah?'

'What?'

'Why are you doing this? I bet you don't even like the old bag.'
'I'm not sure.'

Alec gives her a wry smile.

'It's your dad, isn't it? This is you trying to make things right with him in some sort of way.'

And you're more perceptive than you look, aren't you, Mr Policeman, thinks Sarah as she turns her back and leaves Alec to his spreadsheets.

THIRTY-FOUR

If Helen had visited Jim's house before today, she has no memory of it. Their relationship, if you could call it that, was always brokered through Matthew. When she met Jim, it was always something to do with business – papers to sign, accounts to agree, staffing problems to resolve, and the like. Occasionally he would come to the house and he and Matthew would retire to his study and she'd only know that he'd left when she heard the front door pulled to behind him.

Consequently, she knew very little of his home life with Marion. They'd been together since they were teenagers although it was hard to imagine Jim ever being anything other than middle-aged. They had never had children but, if Matthew knew why that was, he never mentioned it to her, and Jim was not the sort to let others share in any private regrets. She remembered that they were both keen gardeners and Matthew would occasionally bring home out-sized courgettes or cabbages that Jim had nurtured, but in terms of his life outside the office that was about it. His married life had been a closed book to her.

Jim was never the most animated or engaging of conversationalists. Small talk was not his forte. If you have something that needs saying, then say it. Otherwise keep quiet. That appeared to be his maxim for productive social intercourse.

But while Marion was alive there was a faintly detectable core of suppressed joy within him. It seemed to Helen that whatever their marriage was based on it gave him the security to function successfully in the world outside their home. He loved and he knew himself to be loved. That was how she interpreted it. She envied him that.

When Marion died – a long drawn-out nightmare of a death – that spark went out. Helen saw other aspects of his character take over and form a protective shell around him. He became more dismissive of other people's opinions, more morose and even less talkative. Work became the sole focus of this life and turned into a grinding, unflinching obsession. Finding him tetchy, impatient and liable to fly off the handle if others fell below the standards he set for himself, members of staff kept out of his way as much as possible. He was isolated, cut off from other people but it didn't appear to bother him. He had his work and his vegetable patch and the rest of the world could go hang.

With one exception. In Helen's opinion, love has to go somewhere. With Marion gone, Jim became devoted to Matthew. He had always been loyal but now that turned into a deep-seated affection. He would hear no criticism of Matthew and could swiftly morph into an attack dog, savaging anyone who tried to move against him. This was bad news all round in Helen's view although Matthew lapped it up and took pride in Jim's loyalty. But she could see it was more than that. Jim had placed her husband on some sort of pedestal, a noble figure fighting for traditional values in a profession that had sold its soul and lost its integrity.

This wasn't healthy for Matthew who had become increasingly at odds with the contemporary world in which he was forced to live, and it certainly wasn't healthy for their marriage. Helen wouldn't go so far as to say that Jim was a co-respondent in their divorce, but she regarded him as a contributory factor. With Jim's admiration to fall back on, Matthew needed her support less and less and, finally, not at all. And when it came to the divorce settlement Jim had been let off the leash and made life as uncomfortable as he could for her, using a combination of threats ('you'll end up with next to nothing if you ask for too much') and guilt trips ('and you'd take him for every penny after all he's done for you and Sarah?').

Consequently, there has never been much, if any, love lost between the two of them. Even so, here she is now, being shepherded by Jim into his immaculately maintained semi-detached in Bromley Cross. She stands in the hallway, unsure of which way to go, and holds out a casserole dish.

'Vegetarian lasagne. Needs about twenty-five minutes at 180 degrees.'

Jim is nonplussed for a moment, caught off guard. He takes the dish and looks around uncertainly, as if he'd like to hand it on to someone else to look after it. In the end he places it on a small table by the door.

'Thanks. That's very good of you.'

He holds his hand out to the living room door and ushers Helen in.

'Tea alright?'

Helen nods and is left alone while he shuffles off to the kitchen, giving her time to get some sense of what the out-of-office Jim is like. At first glance the furnishings are on trend, which surprises her. Mid-century retro is still in vogue and there are plenty of good examples around her – high-backed chairs with walnut frames and rust-coloured upholstery; a low-lying sideboard with rounded wooden handles; occasional tables with ovoid tops, also in walnut; tall standard lamps with orange and yellow shades. Not like Jim to be fashionable she thinks, but on closer inspection she can spot signs of wear and tear on the fabrics and woodwork. These are the real thing. Bought in the sixties and seventies, well cared for and preserved into the present.

On the mantelpiece surrounding a gas fire there is a menagerie of woodland animals carved in a variety of materials – ceramic, wood, glass and metal. As Helen looks around the room, she sees that every surface has a throng of creatures crowded together. They're all here – squirrels (red and grey), badgers, foxes, moles, rabbits, mice and hares representing the mammals and owls, robins, thrushes, blackbirds, wrens and tits for the birds. As Jim returns with a tray, he finds her examining what she presumes to be a pottery stoat (or could it be a weasel or pine marten?) in close detail.

'Marion,' he explains pouring out the tea and passing her a plate of ginger nuts.

'She was very sentimental about little creatures. Never much cared for knick-knacks myself but I got into the habit of buying her one every birthday and Christmas. Mounts up.'

He sips his tea, dips in a ginger nut and bites off the soggy half.

'Started to pack 'em away after she died but...'

His voice tails off and he crunches the remainder of the biscuit into his mouth. Helen knows she has to be careful. Any sign that she feels sorry for Jim and he's likely to shut up shop.

'What did the doctors say?'

He had been kept in overnight for observation after what he refers to as "the cock-up" at Knott End.

'Nothing broken. Upped the dosage on the statins and told me to rest.'

'And how are you feeling?'

Jim submerges another ginger nut, stuffs the whole biscuit into his mouth and washes it down with a swill of tea.

'Like a spare part at a Zeppelin factory.' Pause for dramatic effect. 'Not likely to be needed any more.'

'Has Sarah spoken to you?'

'Rang me to see if I'd got home alright but then she was off to see Eileen.'

He slams his teacup down with some force on the table.

'She's offered to represent her. Can you credit that?'

'She told me, yeah.'

'I nearly died trying to save her and now we find she was behind the whole thing. And Sarah's rushing to help her out.'

'I know.'

'I didn't have to go that night, you know that, but I did it anyway. Out of loyalty to Matthew. I couldn't care less about Eileen, but he loved Gerry and it's what he would have wanted me to do.'

Helen can see he is getting more and more agitated – which can't be good for him after the shock he's had – but she judges it best to let the storm blow itself out.

'It's not right, is it? Us defending someone like that. There's plenty of others out there who'd take on her case. Why are we getting involved?'

Only you're not involved, are you, thinks Helen, and that's what is really bothering you.

Jim is panting heavily, rubbing his hand across his mouth and she can see that he is making a strenuous effort to bring himself back under control. She waits as his breathing slows down and he reaches out and pours himself another cup of tea. There is a bit of a shake in his hand as he offers to top her up as well but nothing too serious.

'Has Sarah said anything to you about the business?'

Now we come to it, thinks Helen.

'Not to me.'

This isn't very useful to Jim so he tries another tack.

'That Marcus… seems like a good lad.'

'I'd say so. Treats her well so far as I can see.'

'Can't see him settling in Bolton, though. I suppose she'll want to get back to London with him once this is done with.'

'She hasn't said.'

Fishing, but no bite as yet. Jim gives it one more cast.

'When she first came back, I think she was angry with Matthew, but I know she still loves him. I don't think she would have pushed things that far otherwise. Seems to me she felt she owed it to Matthew to help Gerry. I wonder if that means she's changed her mind about the business?'

'It's complicated, Jim. They hadn't really spoken much these last few years.'

He hunches over the coffee table and pushes his teacup to one side. Helen is irritated to realise that she is feeling a bit sorry for him now. Be careful what you wish for, she thinks. At this rate I'll end up mothering everyone I know.

'What will you do now, Jim?'

'Depends on Sarah, doesn't it?'

'You could afford to retire though… if you have to.'

'That's not what I want.' He stares out of the window at the range of beans, brassicas, roots and fruits set out in neat rows and plots in the garden.

'There's only so much pottering you can do in a day. When Marion was here, we'd be out there together you see, but on your own… it's not the same.'

He looks up and she can see the desperation behind his eyes.

'I need my job. Would you tell her that for me, Helen?'

He escorts her to the front door where the cold lasagne is still sitting on the hall table.

'Thanks again.'

As Helen drives back home it occurs to her that Jim has been widowed twice. First when Marion died and then again with Matthew.

THIRTY-FIVE

When Sarah gets back home from the police station, she finds Marcus crouched over his laptop in the kitchen. She drapes her arms round him from behind and nuzzles his neck. That feels so good after a full day trying to make sense of Eileen Bradshaw.

'Mum's not here, is she?' she murmurs.

'Tending to Jim as far as I know.'

She makes a low, contented purring sound. A quiet night in. Just the two of them. She pecks Marcus on the cheek and is about to ask what's for dinner when she sees what he's been looking at on his laptop.

'Are you buying a new car?'

He shakes his head.

'No.'

There are photos of BMWs for sale looking back at her. She unwraps herself from Marcus and takes a step back.

'Oh my god! I've just spent the day at the cop shop. Kelly's had some sort of breakdown. Jim's probably being spoon-fed broth by my mother. We still haven't found Gerry. And you're looking at cars!'

'You don't think much of me, do you?'

'I expected more of you than that.'

Marcus picks up a letter and waves it at her.

'Car hire company. Surprisingly, driving down an unmarked road, through a ploughed field and on to the beach at sixty miles per hour and crashing into a sewerage pipe is not covered by my insurance. They want me to pay for a new car.'

'Oh.'

'They're talking about thirty-five grand, but that's bollocks. I was just checking out used-car prices.'

She embraces him again but feels him stiffen this time rather than melt into her.

'I'm sorry.'

'Still could be looking at over twenty thousand.'

'I could write to them. As your solicitor. Explain the special circumstances. Knock 'em down a bit?'

'Maybe.'

Marcus closes the laptop lid, pulls a bottle of red wine from under the counter and starts unscrewing the top.

'How did it go today?'

Sarah fills him in on all the details and the "deal" she'd come to with Alec. Not much of the bottle is left after that. She plonks her empty glass down on the counter.

'Anything for dinner?'

A voice behind them pipes up before Marcus can answer.

'Hope so. I'm starving.'

Taylor is sitting on the stairs, towelling his hair, a big grin on his face. Sarah turns on Marcus.

'I thought you said we were on our own tonight.'

'Errm… no, I errr… I said your mum wasn't here.'

Taylor has sauntered over to them, dropping the towel on the floor on his way, and is emptying what's left of the wine into a large glass.

'Thanks for offering to put me up for a few days.'

Sarah scowls at Marcus who shrugs helplessly in reply.

'Only my mate Eddie – he's been great – but his girlfriend – well, I was in a bit of a state after the crash – when she heard what had happened, she sort of threw a wobbly and got worried that some hitman was going to come round and finish me off. She refused to stay at his place any more... and, you know, Eddie is very keen on her and he doesn't want to... you know, miss out on...'

Sarah holds the palm of her hand out.

'Yes – alright – I get the picture.'

'Thanks, Sarah. Marcus said you'd be fine with it.'

He spreads himself out on the sofa, dripping water on to the cushions.

'Is there anything nice for dinner?'

*

The plates have been stacked in the dishwasher and the third bottle of wine has been opened. Sarah has calmed down and decided to go with the flow for once. Being angry with Taylor for making a mess is a bit like shouting at a stray dog for treading mud all over the carpet and then showering you with dirt as it shakes its coat dry. Makes no difference as neither can understand what all the fuss is about.

At least he is clean now and the persistent body odour has been temporarily masked by shower gel. And he is trying to be helpful.

'So you reckon the cops won't charge Bill, Harry and the others?'

'Doesn't look that way.'

'That's good. I've got quite fond of them. Still see Gerry as their skipper after all those years.'

Sarah drags her hair back tightly and ties it behind her head with a band.

'But none of them has heard from him?'

'Sorry. They've rung the other surviving members of the team, the ones that don't live locally... but... nothing.'

Sarah rubs her eyes. It's been a long day.

'I know Eileen's in the wrong...'

Marcus snorts.

'You can say that again! She could have got us all killed.'

'Don't exaggerate. The point I'm making is that Gerry did desert her when she needed him most. And like she said to me, even when she was kidnapped, he still didn't come to help her. Left his mates to do it.'

Taylor is swishing the red wine round his glass. Getting more oxygen in. Improves the flavour. Must have read that somewhere.

'Yeah, fair enough, Sarah. Two points though in Gerry's favour. One. She was never actually kidnapped. Two. He didn't know she was a hostage. Who would have told him?'

Sarah palms that away.

'Alright, but the fact remains he left her to face that gang on her own. She wasn't the one who did the drug smuggling so it's not right that she's the only one going to prison.'

'And the Three Stooges. The ones who tried to get you... until I came to your rescue.'

'Yes – OK – I haven't forgotten. But it's still not right. Gerry's the one responsible.'

'Well, if we can't find the man, perhaps we can find the money.'

He nods encouragingly at Marcus who flips open his laptop.

'We were having a brainstorm about this while you were out, weren't we, mate?'

Mate! Sarah looks at Marcus who is dutifully tapping away at his keyboard rather than demanding that Taylor tells him who he thinks he's calling "mate". Oh no, she realises. This is Taylor all over. He'll be treating this like some kind of buddy movie with the two of them cast as Paul Newman and Robert Redford in *The Sting*, socking it to the bad guys. But it's much more likely to turn out as Mel Gibson and Danny Glover in that unending series of *Lethal Weapon* films where they simply wreak havoc wherever they go.

Marcus turns the laptop towards Sarah, showing her a very busy diagram with lots of arrows going to and from boxes with tiny writing inside them.

'I've captured this as a flow chart, so I'll need to take you through it briefly.'

She turns the laptop back to face him.

'Please. No presentation. Just tell me what it says. In plain English. No accountantese.'

Marcus suppresses the desire to sulk and take his laptop home as he's keen to show Sarah that he's on the ball with this.

'It won't be as clear without the slides… but here goes.

We don't know how Don Bradley hid the money, but you can't have large amounts of cash coming into your bank account regularly without someone asking questions eventually.'

Sarah butts in before he can develop the point.

'How much money are we talking about?'

Marcus tries hard to keep his cool.

'It'll be easier if you could keep your questions until the end.'

'Oh, come on. You're not delivering a paper at some boozy symposium. How much do you reckon they were raking in?'

He scrolls through the pages on the laptop, grumbling as he does so.

'If you could be bothered to see the presentation, I cover this later on in some detail. Right. OK. Here it is.

According to news reports of recent drug hauls by the police I calculate that the street value of a kilo of cocaine is about £100,000 at present.'

A small whistle of appreciation from Sarah.

'If I estimate the number of international football matches involving English teams and multiply them over five years that comes to well over 200. According to what they told Taylor, each consignment was four bags.

Over a five-year period that's about 850 kilos of cocaine that have been smuggled in mixed up with footballers' dirty kit. A street value of around £85 million.'

He pauses for dramatic effect and is gratified to see that Sarah is stunned and speechless.

'Now obviously there are overheads and disbursements to be taken into account...'

Sarah is beaming at him.

'I love it when you talk dirty...'

Marcus ploughs on.

'... but I'm assuming that Don and Gerry were paid a percentage for each delivery. Even if it were only ten per cent between them it would amount to something like £8 million. Could be more, of course.'

Taylor has heard this before when Marcus did a run-through with him earlier in the day, but he is still gobsmacked. For a man who would consider himself well off with a couple of hundred quid in his pocket these are stratospheric numbers.

'No wonder he could afford that mansion house.'

Sarah has started running these figures through in her mind.

'What do you think Gerry's share would have been?'

'Just a guess, obviously. Don would have taken the bigger slice as he set the whole thing up but they were mates and Gerry was the one who kept the network going so he'd need to keep him sweet. Maybe £2 million or so? Like I say, could be more.'

Taylor helps himself to more wine.

'But still not enough for Don.'

'Seems not. Could be he started to divert small amounts of cocaine to sell to someone else. Or it could have been a desk fraud. Some creative accountancy. Whatever it was, it backfired big time.'

He has Sarah's full attention now.

'Shall I continue?'

He gets the nod.

'Don needed to put the money somewhere safe but also somewhere it couldn't be traced back to source.

There's a well-worn path for dirty money. It might not have been exactly like this but I'm presuming he set up some dummy companies. Shells. You can buy dormant companies off the net or just create one yourself. He might even have rented some cheap accommodation to serve as a registered office.

Once you've done that there's a bit of hard slog filling out imaginary accounts for these companies who are allegedly providing services of some sort and receive regular income. The drugs money.'

'Right. I see. And they just drew the money out of the companies as directors.'

Sarah is pleased with herself for catching on so quickly. Marcus gives her a pitying look. Stick to the law, my love, I do the money.

'That would be too easy to trace. No, it's more likely that there are a second set of shell companies registered outside the UK – probably in the more exotic parts of the Commonwealth. Pick the right location and the accounts are confidential.

You transfer money from the companies in the UK to those abroad – allegedly in payment for their services – financial advice or some such crap – and the money disappears from view.

The final step is to make payments to company directors from these offshore companies into their personal, private accounts.'

'In Switzerland.'

'Possibly. Other tax havens are also available. Then, so long as you don't go crazy, you can draw down clean money when you need it, and nobody is any the wiser.'

He closes the laptop down. Tutorial over. Any questions?

Taylor comes in with a final clarification in case Sarah is struggling.

'And these are the accounts they tried to wheedle out of Don and then out of Gerry.'

She stares blankly back at him.

'Thank you, Taylor. I did gather that.'

She leans over and kisses Marcus on the cheek.

'See. All those evenings at night school when you could have been out chasing girls – they were worth it in the end.'

She gets a sickly grin in reply.

'And to cap it all off you're going to tell me how we can trace Gerry's bank account and bail Eileen out.'

'Nice try, but there's a reason that these banks do good business. Unless we get Gerry's or Don's account access details the money will sit there, secure and out of reach.'

'Surely he must have kept a record somewhere. For emergencies. I mean, he sent that letter to Dad. That means he had some plans about what to do if they got found out.'

'Yeah – but maybe he panicked. Took it all with him and then never made it back.'

Back to square one. They need to find Gerry. The three of them sit staring into space. When Sarah watched as the gang was rounded up that night and bundled into the back of a police van it felt like they'd won. But now she's not so sure, and she wonders whether it's even right to think about winning and losing. After all they've done, all the risks they've taken, the net result is hardly spectacular, the only change being that Eileen is no longer under threat from criminals but is now under threat from the police. This does not feel like victory.

Taylor has been racking his brains for films that cover the situation. Ones where the leading characters are in despair, and it seems that all hope is lost; where the night is always darkest before the dawn until a chink of light appears on the horizon and the happy ending is within reach again. Actually, he concludes, that pretty much covers half the black and white pictures ever made, but his heart isn't in it, and he keeps the thought to himself. Instead, the image of a little Yorkshire terrier dangling on a clothesline comes into his head and he is surprised to feel a tear forming in his eye.

'You alright?' Marcus is watching him with concern.

Taylor wipes a sleeve across his face.

'Funny what goes through your mind. For some reason I was thinking about that daft dog, Treacle. What kind of person strangles a pet and hangs it out to dry? I mean, I know it's not like shooting someone but, you know, who would do something like that to a harmless pooch?'

Sarah leans over and pats him on the knee.

'I know. Had a soft spot for him myself. Not like Gerry, though. Eileen reckons he cared more about Treacle than he did for her. You know, the night before he disappeared, he got out of bed and went down to check that the bedding in his basket was alright. With all that he had on his mind. Crazy, isn't it?'

All the sentimental mush sluices clear out of Taylor's mind as he hears this.

'What?'

'Just saying. Men and their dogs. Unbelievable.'

'No, no. You said he got up and went to sort out Treacle's basket.'

'Yeah?'

'And Kelly was saying how Eileen wanted to be sure the dog had his basket with him when you took him to her house. How Gerry was insistent they shouldn't ever be separated.'

No one speaks for a few seconds and then Sarah checks her phone.

'Nearly ten. That's OK. I'll ring her and say we're coming over. One of you call a cab.'

*

Next morning they are standing in a windowless storage room, wearing yellow rubber gloves and sifting through plastic bin liners full of insanitary clothes and bedding.

Kelly had been desperate to make amends when they called to see her the night before but could only offer another string of apologies.

'I'm sorry, Sarah. I didn't think anyone would want the basket after, you know… what happened to Treacle.'

'So you gave it away?'

'Yes, sorry. Does Eileen want it back? How is she by the way? I couldn't believe it when Helen told me…'

'She's fine, but we need to get that basket back.'

'Yes, sorry. I took it to the PDSA shop in town. Thought that would be a nice touch.'

Taylor looks mystified.

'PDSA – what's that? Something to do with veteran soldiers?'

Marcus flicks him on the arm.

'That's PTSD, you numpty.'

'Sick animals,' explains Kelly. 'He was never a well dog.'

Consequently, they were standing outside the PDSA charity shop in Newport Street first thing, waiting for it to open for business. Maureen has been a volunteer at the shop for almost a year, but this was the first time she'd had a queue waiting before she unlocked the door. Taylor and Marcus had scuffled past her and started scouring the shelves while Sarah waited by the till.

'Is there something in particular you were after?'

'A dog basket.'

'Oh right, we have a few in stock. Is the dog in question small or medium?'

'The dog in question is dead.'

Maureen had put on her most serious, concerned face.

'Oh, I'm so sorry. Was it sudden or following a long illness?'

'I think we can say it was unexpected.'

Maureen was getting slightly confused.

'Sorry, if your dog has died why did you want a basket?'

'We're after a particular basket – that belonged to...'

Sarah was struggling to get back on track, but Maureen seemed to be following her drift

'... to the deceased?'

'Err... Yes, that's right. It was donated a few days ago.'

Taylor and Marcus walked over to the till shaking their heads.

'Any luck?'

'Only plastic ones.'

Sarah turned back to Maureen.

'This basket was wicker.'

Maureen brightened.

'Oh yes. I remember now. Very nice lady brought it in. Said it had belonged to a little Yorkie that had passed.'

'That's it. Do you still have it?'

The smile slipped away from Maureen's lips.

'I'm sorry. We threw it out. It was a bit… you know… stained.'

She leaned forward towards Sarah and lowered her voice.

'We wondered… did the little chap die in it?'

Sarah's shoulders slumped.

'I don't suppose you've still got it somewhere?'

'No. It was grey bin day yesterday.'

Sarah turned to Marcus and Taylor.

'That's it then.'

But Taylor gave it one more shot.

'What about the blankets?'

'Oh no, we couldn't do anything with them either. Too far gone. They went to the textile bank.'

She shouted to someone who was clearing shelves at the back of the shop.

'Colin? Did you take the textile stuff to the dump yesterday?'

A bald head popped up above the storage racks.

'Couldn't go. Van's playing up again. I'll get Phil to take 'em for us.'

Maureen stepped back nervously as Taylor made a grab for her shoulders.

'Can we have a look through the bags?'

Maureen sold them three pairs of yellow rubber gloves ('just to be on the safe side') and now they are tipping out the contents of several black bin liners onto two rows of trestle tables. Maureen is standing by for health and safety reasons.

'We're not really insured for this, but I can see it means a lot to you. Be nice to have a keepsake.'

Sarah is holding a heavily soiled sheet at arm's length and screwing up her face in disgust.

Maureen gives her a sympathetic smile.

'People think we take anything. We get a lot of unwashed items, I'm afraid.'

Marcus is looking at a pile of underclothes with a great deal of suspicion. Maureen can see he is reluctant to make a start on them.

'Oh, that lady died. You can leave that. We put all her things in one bag.'

Gratefully, he stuffs the lot back into a bin liner. Taylor has been more fortunate. Frayed shirts, old ties, tattered trousers and the like. He calls out to Sarah.

'Do you remember what Treacle had in his basket?'

Maureen perks up.

'Treacle! What a lovely name.'

Sarah is carefully drooping some old surgical stockings back into a black bag.

'There was like an old tartan blanket with tassels on – you know like you have on a picnic or something. And part of an old blue eiderdown that they used to put over him.'

'What, like a duvet?'

'No, it's like got a bit of pattern on the material and it's stuffed with feathers. Hard to describe.'

'Like this you mean?'

Marcus is holding up a raggedy piece of blue material. Sarah and Taylor hold their breath as he gently runs his finger along the seams, pauses, plunges in his hand and pulls out a cream envelope.

THIRTY-SIX

The seasons are changing. There was a time when September marked a sudden end to summer and the onset of chilly nights and rainy days, but lately the transition is more gradual, the warm weather lingering a little longer. Today feels more like July and as Sarah drives away from her mother's house, she winds the windows down and is glad of the breeze.

She feels as if she is neither here nor there at present. Jim remains on sick leave, so she is running the firm for the moment. The papers for the sale of the business and her father's house are resting in the safe, waiting to be signed. She could do this anytime she likes but there they still sit. For now at least.

Marcus went back to London over two months ago, but she's only made it down for one weekend to see him. That probably means something, but she doesn't like to dwell on it too much. Disturb the silt at the bottom of the pond, she thinks, and you'll end up drowning in muddy water. Helen has a different view. Over dinner last evening she had taken Sarah to task again.

'You can't carry on like this.'

'Like what?'

'Either you love him and want to be with him, or you don't. You can't expect him to hang around indefinitely waiting to see if you come back or not.'

'Mum. It's only been ten weeks. If our relationship can't cope with that then maybe it's better it should end.'

'So you think it's over, do you?'

'I didn't say that!'

'It's not fair on him, that's all I'm saying.'

'It's OK. Marcus understands.'

Helen had given her that look. The one that means – I'm your mother, I know you, so don't try that on with me.

It's only a short drive to her destination in Turton but as she crosses Crow Trees Lane, the sun glinting on the Wayoh Reservoir stretching away on either side, she wonders whether her mother might be right. What does Marcus think is happening? Probably that they would be tighter as a couple after what they'd been through together. After all, she thought, he had been brilliant. Dropping everything to come and be with her despite thinking she was crazy to get involved in the case; probably saving Jim's life that night on the beach; working out how the money laundering must have been done. She couldn't have asked for anything more. Could she?

'Come back with me. Come home,' he'd asked her the night before he left.

'I can't. Not yet.'

'Why not?'

'Unfinished business.'

'It's over. Case closed. You did it. What more do you want?'

She'd let him go, not knowing how to answer that question. And the weeks were flying by without any decision. Should I stay or should I go?

And it was Marcus who had found Gerry's letter with the bank account details on it. When she had phoned Alec Timpson to tell him the good news, he insisted that they did not attempt to access the account unless the police were present. Maybe he didn't trust them or maybe he just wanted to be sure that the police got the credit. In any case, they were politely requested to report to Bolton Police Station the next day and to bring their laptop.

Alec was all smiles when the three of them were ushered into his presence, like a benevolent sovereign glad to entertain his favourite subjects. Another uniformed officer was standing by his side.

'Have to hand it to you, Sarah. Didn't really expect you to come up with the goods.'

'Your confidence in me has always been underwhelming.'

Another beaming smile from Alec. Today is a good day, so no need to squabble.

'Now then, Mr Johnson.'

'Marcus.'

'I understand you're the one with the financial background who pieced all this together.'

'It was a team effort.'

Marcus held his arm out towards Taylor who received the compliment with a shy grin. Alec picked up a file from his desk and flicked it open, spending a few seconds scanning the first page.

'Ah yes. Mr Forrest. We know all about you from your time with the force.'

The smile had frozen on Taylor's face.

'All good, I hope.' A slight tremor in his voice.

Alec skimmed through a few more pages before snapping the file closed.

'Let me put it this way. I shouldn't ask us for a reference if I were you.'

He turned to the officer behind him.

'This is Inspector Blake. He specialises in frauds, scams and digital crime. I've asked him to sit in. Shall we begin?'

Marcus lifted his shoulder bag onto the desk.

'You asked me to bring my laptop?'

'Firewall issues,' said Inspector Blake. 'Easier if you log in from your machine.'

They gathered round behind Marcus. Alec nudged Sarah in what he hoped was a chummy and not a salacious manner.

'Eileen reckons there is upwards of a million in there, does she?'

'So she said.'

Alec had rubbed his hands together enthusiastically.

'Nice little sum for the crime commissioner to spend on good causes.'

It turned out that Gerry Bradshaw, a man who had never been further west than Dublin, had entrusted his nest egg to the Bella Vista International Bank in Belize. As the logo came up on the laptop Alec looked enquiringly at his colleague.

'Central America, sir. Used to be ours – British Honduras. Very popular location for concealing funds. Guaranteed high levels of confidentiality.'

Marcus was flexing his fingers, paused above the keyboard. Alec gave him the nod and he entered the account number, the first password and then the second. Slowly the account came into view, and they all craned forward to get a close view.

Alec became very excited as soon as he saw the figures come up.

'Bloody hell. We've hit the jackpot. The old bastard had more than 3 million in there.'

A discreet cough came from behind.

'Ermm – that will be in Belize dollars, sir. The actual amount will be about...' Inspector Blake inclined his head slightly as he did the sums, '1.2 million in sterling.'

'Oh, I see. Still, not bad. What we were expecting.'

Marcus was continuing to scroll down the screen.

'There's been some activity very recently.'

'What do you mean?' A hint of panic in Alec's voice.

'Takes a few days for international transactions to be cleared. One's going through as we speak.'

They all watched as the data became obscured by a large egg timer on the screen showing miniscule grains of sand dropping away before their eyes. Suddenly the screen went black and started to reboot. The account summary reappeared after a brief stutter showing the new balance.

Nil. This account has now been closed. We look forward to having your custom in the future. If you have time, please fill in the attached satisfaction questionnaire by tapping on the link below. Goodbye.

Shocked silence all round. They stood gazing at the screen for several seconds, willing it to show another message.

Alec shuffled back round to the other side of his desk, lowered himself wearily into his executive chair, rubbed his forehead and looked directly at Sarah.

'I hope you didn't jump the gun and go into that account without us.'

Sarah reared up ready to go on the offensive. Seeing this, Alec raised his hand in apology.

'Sorry. Had to ask. Thought we had a result there.' He paused and looked thoughtful. 'Not good news for your client either.'

Sarah, still thinking through the implications herself, did not respond.

'I dunno. Could be worse for Eileen,' observed Taylor. 'At least she knows Gerry is alive and kicking.'

But when Sarah broke the news to her later that morning, Eileen was less than ecstatic to hear about Gerry's virtual reappearance. She had been allowed home on bail pending confirmation of the charges, but her bank account had been frozen, her car impounded and her passport confiscated. To all intents and purposes, she was still in custody.

'First, he deserts me and now he takes all our money and leaves me to face the music. There's a word for a man like that.'

Sarah struggled to offer some words of sympathy and come up with other ideas for a line of defence but there was nothing to grip hold of and after listening patiently Eileen reached out and patted the back of her hand.

'It's alright, love. You've done your best. It's a pity your father isn't here any more, though. He might have been able to think of something.'

Sarah has thought about this many times since that meeting with Eileen. The look of disappointment and resignation on her face. I came to you for help and now look where I am. The logical part of her brain told her that Eileen had brought this on herself; that she'd never properly confided in Sarah; that she'd conspired to lure Gerry into capture by the gang as well as putting her own safety and Jim's in jeopardy. But that expression and the reproach about her father kept coming back to her and is in her mind now as her car drops down along the road from Entwistle towards Turton Bottoms and she finds a place to park close by St Anne's churchyard. Perhaps it's not too late to find a way through, she thinks, as she locks the car and heads towards an open field.

Tucked behind neat rows of stone terraces and flanked on one side by a small cemetery is the home of Old Sladians F.C., a stalwart member of the Lancashire Amateur League. It's Saturday afternoon and there's a match on but the ground is not exactly buzzing with a horde of eager spectators. There are a few men and, seemingly, even more dogs, idling by the fencing around the perimeter, and a larger gaggle of spectators taking a drink outside the small clubhouse near the halfway line. Sarah can't be certain, but she may be the only woman in sight.

The crowd is usually quite a bit bigger than this, but the first team are not at home today, being engaged in a tricky away fixture against the Failsworth Dynamos. On the pitch is a new addition to the Old Sladian ranks, playing their first competitive game, and this is the team that Sarah has come to watch.

She isn't in the habit of reading the Bolton Evening News, but Helen keeps an eye on local events if only to find out who has died recently. A couple of nights before this they had been sitting together, Sarah flicking through TV channels in the hope of finding a distraction and Helen scanning the local news.

'Something here that might interest you,' she said, folding the paper in half, handing it to Sarah and pointing to an article beneath a photo of a group of undernourished young men in football strips shivering in front of some goalposts.

KICK THE BALL – KICK THE HABIT

The new season can't come quick enough for these budding Ronaldos, who are the latest addition to the ranks of the Old Sladians.

But these lads aren't only aiming to hit the net, they're also hoping to straighten out their lives, because this is a team with a difference. All the members are struggling to overcome addictions – to drugs, alcohol or gambling – and have been referred to the club by health practitioners.

'It's the age-old prescription,' explains Doctor Mark Hopkins, a local GP specialising in tackling addictive behaviour. 'A healthy mind in a healthy body. Exercise produces feelings of wellbeing that can contribute significantly to improved mental health and complement medical treatments to combat addiction.'

The new scheme has been made possible by an anonymous donation of one million pounds to fund a football-based therapeutic service to help young men fighting to overcome their problems and get their lives back on track.

'We're delighted to be a partner in this wonderful initiative,' says Old Sladians' chairman, Keith Freeman, 'and welcome new teammates to our family.'

"The Shakes" as they call themselves will be playing their first match on Saturday when "scoring" will take on a whole new meaning.

As Sarah finished the article she looked up to find Helen smiling at her.

'Extremely generous donation, wasn't it?'

Helen had raised her eyebrows.

'Somebody trying to make amends, maybe?'

Sarah nibbled one of her fingernails as she considered this.

'Looks like a worthwhile cause. I might pop down there and give 'em a bit of support.'

'Why not? It's only about ten minutes from here.'

But now that Sarah has arrived, she isn't sure what to do. Should she join the knot of supporters by the clubhouse who are shouting encouragement – probably friends and family – or wander along the touchline? She opts to find a space against the fence on the far side of the pitch, not too close to any other spectator. In full view.

It's been a long time since she last attended a football match. Marcus claims to be a fair-weather Crystal Palace supporter but as there isn't usually much of that around Selhurst Park he only keeps an eye on things from his sofa. They watch the odd game on the TV but live football, that's something else. She can remember going to Burnden Park with her dad, pushing through the rowdy queues outside the ground, holding tight to his hand in case they got separated, squeezing through the green turnstile cages that clanked around and deposited you safe on the other side. And the smells came back to her as well; fried onions and burgers; the steamy aroma rising from meat and potato pies that were so red hot inside they constituted a health hazard; the sweaty odour of too many men crowded into the same space; the rancid, acidic pong from the urinals drifting across the terraces.

Not that there is too much here to remind her of those raucous fixtures. She scans the ground and reckons there are no more than fifty spectators who've made the trip and they aren't exactly filling the arena with noise. In her memory of games she went to as a child there is a constant thrum and rumble of voices expressing approval or anxiety rising to a roaring crescendo when an incident spikes them – a reckless foul or a penalty shout. Here, she can hear every player as they call to each other for the ball, the rasping cough of a smoker behind one of the goals and even the occasional bird song.

The football is a bit basic as well. Most of the players look like they haven't eaten any solids for some time, and their spindly white legs bear no resemblance to the beefy, perma-tanned thighs of professionals. Less than half an hour into the match and most are puffing badly, pausing after each run to bend double and catch their breath. Finding each other with the ball also seems to be a real challenge with most passes misdirected or simply not having the momentum to reach their man.

'Early days,' observes a voice by her side.

Sarah glances over her shoulder at an elderly man leaning on the fence with his eyes fixed on the game. He has a tweed cap drawn down almost over his eyes, sunglasses beneath and is wearing a raincoat, even though the afternoon is unseasonably warm.

'Won't have had much time to get fit yet. Still be throwing up after training sessions. It'll come when they get stronger.'

Sarah receives this information without comment, and they keep their eyes on the play for a few minutes. She hears him tutting as passes continue to go astray and then chuckling as two of "The Shakes" run into each other trying to get to the ball. He is still following play when he remarks,

'Nice photo of you in the paper outside court. Your dad would have been proud.'

'Thanks. That reminds me. Been meaning to return this.'

She reaches into her bag, pulls out a photograph and passes it to him. He holds it at arm's length and a broad smile breaks over his face.

'Oh aye. Sorrento. Have you been? It's a good one of us. We had a lovely time there. Eileen said she never wanted to leave.'

The smile weakens and disappears, and he places the photo carefully inside his jacket pocket.

'How is she?'

Sarah doesn't look at him but continues staring intently ahead as if the game was all that mattered.

'Bit late to be thinking about that, isn't it?'

'I know what you must think, but I'm not a bad man. I still care for her.'

'You're like a lot of men. Kind and considerate when you want to be. Self-centred bastard when you don't.'

'Your dad never liked bad language.'

'He's dead so he'll have to lump it.'

Gerry shifts his position at the fence and bends over towards the ground.

'I did love her, you know. But it changes over the years. And you think – well, we've lasted this long so we'll have to see it through. But when I heard Don was dead… I knew we couldn't carry on as we were.'

He slips off his sunglasses and rubs his eyes.

'What's going to happen to her?'

'Not sure what the length of sentence will be, but she'll be in an open prison, and she's bound to get some time off for mitigating circumstances.'

'She's tougher than she looks.'

'She is. But you dropped her right in it when you walked out.'

Gerry pushes himself upright, turns to face Sarah and puts his hand on her arm.

'I wanted her to come with me. Leave the house and start a new life somewhere else. But she wouldn't have it. Said we'd worked too hard to get what we had and she weren't about to give it up without a fight.'

'That's not what she told me.'

'When Don got shot, I knew it was only a matter of time before they came for me. And if we didn't give them what they wanted then I'd be next. We had a big row about it. I wanted to offer them most of the money we had saved. Maybe even the house. And in return I'd walk away and that would be the end of it. She told me I were being naïve.'

'So you disappeared and left her to face them on her own? Christ, Gerry, you'd been married sixty years! You didn't even leave a note.'

'It was safer for her that way. The less she knew the better. I knew I couldn't protect her if I stayed but I thought they wouldn't bother her once they realised I'd gone. She couldn't get at the money. Once they worked that out, I reckoned they'd leave her be and come looking for me. But if I was still around, she'd be in danger as well.'

'Well, you were wrong.'

They go back to watching the game again. A young lad with curly dark hair has been brought on as a substitute. He looks like a newly born foal, all gangly legs and awkward movements, but when he gets the ball he skips past a tackle and sprints down the wing, scooping an inviting cross over the penalty spot. No one is there to meet it, but Sarah sees Gerry stand upright and flick his head at an imaginary football.

'That's more like it. Just needed someone to get on the end of that.'

He bends down over the fence again.

'You forget, when you play for a living.'

'Forget what?'

'It's a game. You're supposed to enjoy it.'

The curly haired lad flicks the ball past one defender and chases after it only to be barged over the touchline by the next man. He wheels round and hares after the full back catching up with him near his own penalty area and crashing into him to send the ball out of play. The two of them collapse on the grass and help each other up, laughing as they jog back into position. Gerry gives him an encouraging clap.

'See that? A lot of wingers can't be bothered defending. Makes all the difference when your teammate tracks back to help you out.'

He gives the lad a thumbs up as he trots past them and then turns again to Sarah.

'How did you know I'd be here?'

'I didn't, but with it being their first match…'

'It was that newspaper article, wasn't it? I knew it might attract attention but there was nowt I could do. Club wanted to make a big thing of it.'

'After a bit of redemption, are you?'

'I saw a way of doing something useful with the money, that's all. Summat to give a chance to lads like that.'

'Why this place? Plenty of other charities helping people get off drugs.'

'Don't know your history, do you? Been playing football on this field continuously since the 1840s. Oldest ground in the world. With that money they can carry on. That's got to mean something.'

Does it, thinks Sarah? One hundred and eighty years of chasing an inflated bladder round a field. Does it really matter that much whether it carries on or not? And then she remembers what her dad said after Burnden Park closed – 'Some families have records of their own history. All the rest of us have to mark the time with is football.' Yes, she thinks, Dad would have forgiven him but it's not enough for me.

'Alright… but before you go round asking for an OBE, let's bear in mind you've kept back a couple of hundred thousand pounds for yourself.'

Gerry gives her a half smile.

'I remember when you were a little girl. You were a cheeky little bugger then an' all. Look – I can't claim my pension, can't use my real name, can't stay in one place too long. These people, they never really forget. If I turn up somewhere and get recognised, they'll have me. Just to make a point. So, yeah, I've kept some back for myself. It's not just Eileen. My life's not easy either. I'll never have a proper home again.'

'You expect me to feel sorry for you?'

'Thing is, love, you think you know me. But you don't. Your dad, he would have understood. He knew what had happened to me. How I was treated.'

'And you think that justifies it? Helping drug dealers?'

'I was angry. I didn't realise how much anger I had until Don explained things to me. I wanted to get my own back, but then you realise you've been taking it out on the wrong people.

I wanted to get out – even before Don got killed – but it's not that easy.'

'What about Dad?'

'What about him?'

'Did he know? What you were doing?'

'He was a good friend to me, your dad. But he was also my solicitor. He must have known I was up to something dodgy, but he never asked me about it. It was like he could put what he knew in a box in his mind and then close the lid on it, so that the rest of him never knew it was there.'

Sarah nods.

'Yes. He could do that.'

The half-time whistle goes and the players trudge slowly towards the clubhouse to a background of sporadic applause. Gerry puts his sunglasses on and pushes himself away from the fence.

'I'd better be off. Don't want to risk bumping into anyone else.'

Sarah takes the phone from her bag and waves it at him.

'Give me a reason why I shouldn't call the police and tell them you're here.'

'That's up to you, love. If you're sure you know what the right thing to do is then you should do it. I've learned that much at least.'

He gives Sarah a brief wave and heads off in the direction of the churchyard. She watches until he is lost to sight behind a row of yew trees overhanging the wall, just another old man enjoying a late stroll in the sun.

She decides not to stay for the second half and walks back to her car but sits looking out the window before starting the engine. When she leaves this place then it really will all be over. Case closed. And there won't be any reason not to decide about selling up and returning to London and her old job, about getting back with Marcus and leaving Bolton and her mother behind.

The game ends and she watches the spectators straggle past, some with their arms round exhausted players who exchange sheepish grins with each other, knowing they've done something few people expected of them. And then it's quiet again, only the birds and her, and the sun starts to set over St Anne's Church steeple and the car keys are still on her lap.

Her phone buzzes. A message from Helen. Short and to the point for once.

Are you free to come home now? xx

Good question, Mum.